D1520866

Altered Souls
Witch Avenue Series #2

KARICE BOLTON

ISBN: 1480292966
ISBN-13: 978-1480292963

DEDICATION

To my amazing husband. I love you more each and every moment! It's been an amazing journey so far, and I thank you for always believing in me.

ACKNOWLEDGMENTS

I want to say a simple thank you to Amazon, Barnes & Noble, and all of the other avenues available for the indie publishing world. It allows the art of storytelling to continue to flourish in unexpected ways!

BOOKS BY KARICE BOLTON

THE WITCH AVENUE SERIES

LONELY SOULS

ALTERED SOULS

RELEASED SOULS (Coming Winter 2013)

THE WATCHERS TRILOGY

AWAKENING

LEGIONS

CATACLYSM

TAKEN NOVELLA (A Watchers Prequel)

**TO CONTACT THE AUTHOR PLEASE VISIT
HER WEBSITE AT**

WWW.KARICEBOLTON.COM

http://Blog.Karicebolton.com

OR

EMAIL

INFO@KARICEBOLTON.COM

OR

FOLLOW HER ON FACEBOOK and TWITTER

@KARICEBOLTON

CHAPTER 1

"*Alienam Imagines ex Anima,*" I whispered, as I hovered over the concoction of herbs I was grinding with my wand. One of the many things I couldn't let Logan catch me doing. The fragrance of the crushed marigolds, honeysuckle, and lemon grass was almost intoxicating, but the thought of what this mixture might be able to produce was even more so. Eyeing the large, black spider I had captured in the jar gave me the creeps as it wiggled around trying to climb up the glass before falling back down over and over again. I felt marginally bad about the spider's fate. Who was I kidding? No, I didn't.

After adding the grape seed oil and quickly stirring the mixture, I needed to release and hide everything before Logan came back to the cottage. I didn't think he'd approve of this, but I wasn't looking for his approval, only answers.

Shaking the spider into the herb mixture, I ran down the hall careful to not spill anything as I made my way to the staircase. Yanking on the chain, the ladder released, and I quickly climbed up into the attic. Peeking around the darkened space, it looked as if Trevor was sleeping, which was perfect. I quickly crawled in, and shook out the contents of the container behind one of the wooden rafters.

Taking a deep breath in I whispered once more, "*Alienam Imagines ex Anima,*" and headed quickly back down the steps trying my hardest to push the staircase back up into the ceiling. *Curse my shortness!* Propping myself onto the closet shelves, I was able to give the attic steps one more push and then it locked.

Having just closed the closet door, I heard the click of the front door as Logan stepped inside with the latest bundle of wood for the fire. My heart skipped a beat at the sight of him. I was finally allowing myself to truly think of a future with him, and I enjoyed what I envisioned, especially when he wore those particular jeans.

"What have you been up to?" Logan asked, eyeing me playfully. His hair was flopped to the side from the storm that was brewing outside. Knowing what I was hiding from him caused me to freeze as the guilt ran through me.

"I've got lasagna in the oven," I replied, kicking myself for lying to him, but it wasn't really lying just omitting a few things.

"And?" he asked grinning, "did you go check on—"

"What are we going to do with *him*? We can't keep him in the attic forever," I asked Logan, trying to stifle my giggle and avoid what I had just done. "Or can we?"

Logan's laughter filled the air as he tended to the flames in the fireplace. It was still hard for me to swallow that not only did one my friends from high school try to kidnap me, but my father was the one who sent him. My father was one of the few in the world who would have been able to send anyone through the protection spell that Logan had cast around our property. It did little to comfort me that my father would go to so much trouble to try to steal me away like my mother. I couldn't fathom his sudden interest in me, considering he had abandoned both my mom and me over eighteen years ago.

I sat on the couch, grabbing our family's spell book to keep my mind occupied. Flipping page after page, my mind kept wandering to how everything turned upside down in my world. Maybe I would let Logan in on my little secret.

"Are you okay over there?" Logan asked, turning from the flames to face me. His brilliant blue eyes were completely void of darkness, and it was difficult to resist the urges running through me.

I nodded as my eyes landed back on the spell that seemed too perfect to ignore. The one I had just perfected in the kitchen. Should I share it with Logan?

"This might be something we could try," I spoke softly, tapping the page with my finger and gesturing for Logan to come sit next to me. I knew Trevor couldn't hear anything up in the attic, but I felt more comfortable discussing his fate in a hushed voice.

"Did you know there were things out there like this?" I asked, as Logan sat down next to me.

Placing the book on his lap, I watched him carefully, hoping to gauge his reaction, and of course he didn't give me one as he stared at the picture of a spider feeding on someone's flesh.

"I think we should give it a shot," I tried again, hoping to let him in on my little secret.

Logan's lips barely began moving. They looked deliciously soft, but I couldn't get caught up in that right now, especially with our captive only one floor above our heads. It would be wrong on so many levels.

"Triss," he began, while closing the spell book and turning to face me. "That's not exactly what I'd call white magic."

Looking into his eyes, I saw mischief stirring behind them. I grabbed the book from him and placed it on the couch. Climbing onto his lap, I watched the smile spread across his lips as he wrapped his arms around my waist. It felt so good being in his embrace.

"I wouldn't *exactly* call it black magic, either," I replied wryly, "under the circumstances."

"So you were hesitant about the snake spell, but you're willing to jump on a spider spell?" he asked, his voice low.

"It's getting chilly, isn't it?" I asked innocently, squirming my way deeper into his hold.

His lips were inches from mine and they parted slowly, but not for the reason I hoped.

"It's really distracting being this close to you," he whispered, his jaw tightening.

"It is, huh?" I smiled, trying to take control of the situation. "I think this could be a really good spell for me to take a stab at."

I let my fingers slowly glide through his dark hair, making my way down his neck landing on his shoulders. I couldn't help but smile, seeing the effect I had on him.

"I know your plan, Miss Spires, and I'm not going to be swayed based on what you're trying to do to me," he smiled coyly.

"I'm not trying to do anything to you," I whispered in his ear.

Propping myself back up I tried again, "I was just thinking since Trevor tried to kill you, it's only fair. Not to mention his failed kidnap attempt on me. I mean we've got to do something with him, and I'd like to get him off our property as quickly as possible. This would get us the answers, and then we could be done with him."

He was silent.

I plunged ahead. "I think under the circumstances, it wouldn't be considered black magic. Have you ever used anything like this?"

He shook his head. "No. I haven't. And Triss, don't fool yourself. You're very much on the edge with this spell." His stare was intense, ensuring I fully understood what he was telling me.

"I know, but I think when people's lives are in danger it changes things a little bit," I countered.

"Our lives *were* in danger. They aren't any more." Logan's voice was strained. He was rubbing his eyes, and my guilt was multiplying by the second.

I knew he was right, but this spell was so easy. It was so perfect. No detail, no memory would be missed. It would only take one tiny spider bite, and we'd have so many answers.

"Besides," Logan continued, "I think Trevor's coming around naturally. The longer he's out of your father's grasp, the more his senses are coming back."

The fact that Logan was saying these things when only days earlier he wanted to pulverize Trevor made me take notice. Then the panic started to spread. What had I done by releasing the spider up in the attic?

"You know," Logan squinted his eyes at me, "we could just ask him. I think he's starting to feel more like himself and guilty for what he tried to do to you."

I jumped off Logan's lap, almost falling over the coffee table as I ran to the hallway.

"Where are you going?" Logan hollered after me.

"I already let the spider loose up there. I've got to catch it before it's too late," I yelled back. My insides were tightening at the thought of the spider reaching Trevor. I never intended to invite black magic into my world so easily. What was I doing? Was this how so many fell into it?

Logan was right behind me, reaching up for the attic stairs, and I refused to look in his eyes. I was so disappointed in myself, and I didn't want to see it reflected in his as well.

"Where'd you release it?" Logan's voice was completely calm.

"Right behind the beam to the right," I whispered. "Here's the jar."

"Listen, he might let us use this on him. You never know. If he gives us permission all is not lost," he said, touching my chin. "It's okay. I know you were only trying to help get answers."

Watching Logan climb into the attic began to put things in perspective. I needed to get control of my emotions. If Logan could keep his darkness in check, the least I could do was not unleash mine.

The attic seemed as unfriendly as it did when I was a child. It was like the wonderful memories that Logan and I had shared up here only weeks before had been completely erased. The darkness didn't lend itself well to trying to find a black spider in the shadows either. The air was cold and musty, which made me feel slightly guilty for keeping Trevor up here — that was until the memories of him attempting to kill Logan reemerged.

"Got it," Logan whispered, while he attempted to push the spider back into the jar.

"That's too bad," I murmured only half joking.

"Got what?" Trevor's voice startled me.

"Nothing." I snapped, not wanting to discuss anything with him. "Let's get downstairs."

Moving back towards the steps, Logan nodded and followed me carrying the jar of hope that was quickly diminishing. Putting my foot on the first step, I stopped.

"Trevor, I'll bring dinner up a little later," I said.

"Yeah, no problem," Trevor's voice was completely defeated, and I tried not to let it get to me as I made my way back down the stairs.

Waiting down the hall for Logan to close up the attic door, I paced back and forth with all sorts of thoughts racing through my mind. I wanted Trevor out of here, but I needed to get the answers first. I didn't want to waste any more time.

"I think when I bring dinner to him tonight I should ask him to let us perform the spell," I said, crashing on the couch.

Logan nodded, "I agree."

"It's so hard to trust him. It seems like he's out of the grasp of my father, but who knows." I sighed. "I never would have imagined that he was capable of the things he accomplished."

"It wasn't Trevor's doing," Logan replied, sitting down next to me. "That entire evening had your father written all over it. Trevor was just a pawn."

"Well, he certainly performed well and that's what scares me. I feel like he's so weak-minded that the longer he's around us, the greater the chance that my father will reappear in some way." As I spoke the words, I began trembling. I had to get Trevor out of our cottage. Logan pulled me close, wrapping his arms around my shoulders.

"It's gonna be okay," he whispered, pressing his lips against my hair.

"Will you take him to the bus station right after the bite? Just get him out of here?" I asked.

"I don't want to leave you alone while you go through the process," Logan said softly.

"I'll be fine. I don't want him around when I go through it, and we only have a small window where I can complete the spell. I think it would just be better with him out of here. You'll probably get back here before it's even finished," I insisted.

"I guarantee I'll be back here before it's finished," Logan whispered, shaking his head, while the tip of his finger traveled up my arm. "I can't believe what I let myself get talked into with you. But don't forget we haven't even asked him yet. He might not agree."

"On *that*, I think the lasagna's done. I'll go check it, and maybe we should bring him down to eat. Something tells me that he won't be trying to escape. Maybe he'll be more helpful if we treat him a little less like an animal," I said, turning my head quickly away as Logan stood up to stretch. I couldn't afford to be distracted. Closing my eyes, I tried to corral my thoughts.

I felt the warmth of the flames reach my bones while I let my mind wander to the possibilities that this opportunity could bring. Finding out what Trevor knew about my father and mother was quickly becoming an obsession. Glancing up at Logan, he stood directly in front of me, grinning with his arms crossed.

"Do you know how enticing you look in that shirt?" I blurted.

"Do I?" Logan's lips spread into a huge smile.

"Yes you do, and we really need to get him out of the cottage tonight," I muttered, unable to stop myself from looking at how deliciously low his jeans hung.

"And why's that, Triss?" his lips turned up slightly in amusement.

Looping my finger into his jean pocket, I pulled him closer and looked up into his eyes. He raised his eyebrow with anticipation, and I couldn't help the smile that was spreading across my lips.

"Just because," I whispered, quickly releasing my finger from his pocket.

Standing up next to him, I quickly pecked him on the cheek before I headed to the kitchen, hoping I had left him wanting so much more.

I needed to get out of the cottage.

Opening up the oven, I peeked under the tinfoil at the rubbery mess, which seemed all too fitting considering my life at the moment. I took the foil off so the cheese would brown and shut the oven door with a thud. Here I was, once more, trying to internally debate the rights and wrongs of our actions and the consequences that they held.

"Hmm. Not quite there yet. Probably another fifteen minutes or so," I sighed, looking out the kitchen window.

"It'll have to be quick with what the weather seems to have in store for us." Logan said, placing the jar on the end table.

"How'd you know what I was thinking?" I asked.

"I can just tell," Logan said, letting his fingers glide into his front pocket. "Seriously though, it looks like it will be pretty nasty soon, but we can go outside for a few minutes. At least until the lasagna is done."

Stepping outside onto our stone porch, I took a deep breath in and felt the freshness of the mountain air run through my system. Rain was definitely on the way, but I didn't mind. There was nothing better than being in the cottage during a rainstorm. Well, that wasn't quite true. Having Trevor tied up in the attic kind of complicated things, which was why I just wanted to get answers from him and get rid of him. Grabbing a basket and flower clippers, I looked back at Logan as he secured the door.

"Ready?" I asked.

"I'll follow your lead," he said grinning coyly. "Looks like you've got some collecting you'd like to do... And here I thought this might lead to something else."

He shoved his hand deeper into his pocket and wore an absolutely adorable smile that stole my heart.

"Maybe I'll follow *your* plan," I said, shrugging and tossing my basket back down on the porch.

"Works for me." He grinned, quickly moving toward me.

I backed my legs up against the porch banister to brace myself, the cold of the stone alerting my senses even more. My heart screamed with delight as he reached around me and wrapped his arms around my waist, creating a perfect circle. His stare was intense with the same feelings of desire I felt.

"I think I like your plan better," I whispered.

He reached up and tucked a piece of hair behind my ear sending such a shudder through my body that I was certain he felt it.

I gripped his arm as he lowered it back to my waist. Closing the gap between us, I craved his touch.

"You are so beautiful," he murmured, as he gently cupped my face, allowing his finger to trace its way back down my neck to my collarbone. "Do you have any idea how hard it is to be so close to you every night?"

"I think I can imagine." I tried to stifle a nervous giggle.

Leaning down, his lips met mine as all of my muscles tingled from head to heel. I could feel the softness of his lips mold to mine as I slid my arm around his waist. Feeling the firmness of his entire body pressed against mine created an unstoppable force between us. Wrapping his shirt around my knuckles I brought him closer to me, but I felt him pull away slightly. Opening my eyes, I saw where I had pulled on his shirt. My tug of his clothing had revealed something dark on his skin that caught my eye, but he pulled his shirt collar back up quickly.

"You have a tattoo?" I asked, not wanting our session to be over.

"Kind of. Listen we should get back inside," Logan's words hit me like the thunder out in the distance. I wasn't sure what I had done or why a tattoo would be a big deal, but it seemed to be.

"I didn't think we were done?" I smiled, hopeful that whatever might have made him back away would quickly be forgotten, but it wasn't.

"To your point earlier, let's get this over with and boot him out," Logan said, trying to change the subject. "So we can start where we left off."

"I don't understand what just happened, but you can bet I'm going to figure it out and who's to say I don't think a little ink is sexy?" I joked, only to have Logan looking a little more horrified than before.

CHAPTER 2

"It's more than just brainwashing," Trevor said, looking uncomfortable. He had barely picked at the lasagna.

"How so?" I asked, thinking that brainwashing was bad enough.

"Your father is fond of altering souls. It goes beyond the basic spells. He tweaks memories and all sorts of things. He calls it his little army of Altered Souls," Trevor replied flatly. "He's very proud of his accomplishments. Your father can even tweak someone's desires, hopes, and dreams. It's very dangerous."

Looking over at Logan, I saw his eyes carrying a burden as he listened to Trevor intently. He didn't touch his dinner either. Instead, he stood the entire time watching Trevor's every move. I wanted to know what Logan was thinking, but I couldn't find out right now. We couldn't afford to discuss anything that Trevor might be able to relay to my father.

"So he's used that on my mom?" I asked Trevor. A lump formed in the back of my throat. I wanted to find out as much as I could, but I wasn't sure I really wanted to know the answers.

Trevor nodded. "And on me."

Logan's eyes locked on mine. Now was the time to ask Trevor.

"I'm so sorry, Triss," Trevor continued. The pain in his voice was evident, but I couldn't let myself fall for it. I wasn't sure how much of what Trevor was saying or feeling was authentic. We had to do this spell to get the real answers. I only hoped Trevor would agree.

"Trev, would you be willing to do something for us?" I asked, touching his hand, while Logan stepped forward making Trevor recoil. "It involves telling us everything you know, of sorts."

"Of course. I'd do anything to make it up to you. What do you want to know?" he asked.

"Well, unfortunately it sounds like there might be some problems with differentiating between what memories are real or tampered with. There's a spell that can cut through all of that. I've already prepared it, if you're willing," I said.

Trevor's eyes were full of worry as Logan's presence continually towered over him.

"What needs to be done?" he asked, his voice beginning to tremble. I vowed I would not let myself feel sorry for him. This could still all be a ploy.

"This spider would need to bite you, and then

we'd be able to find out everything that has really gone on between you and my father," I said, pointing at the jar. "We would be able to witness what you saw, heard, experienced. It's the only way, considering everything you've been through." I paused, waiting for a response.

Logan stood behind me, placing his hand on my shoulder. I had a feeling he was just glaring at Trevor.

"I think it's the best thing to do for all involved, Trevor." Logan's words seemed to have quite an effect on Trevor since he began nodding quickly.

"Whatever I can do, I'll do it. I want to make things up to you. I'm just so sorry."

"Well, I'd like to get things started right away and if everything goes as planned, Logan can give you a ride into town, and you can hop a bus back to Seattle tonight."

"You're going to let me go?" Trevor asked puzzled.

"This time," Logan replied flatly. "You won't be so lucky if there's a next time."

I nodded in agreement catching Logan's glance.

"I was hoping I could help you guys," Trevor replied. "Try to repay you in some way."

"Not a chance," I scoffed.

"Not happening, man." The anger in Logan's voice started to rise.

"If you don't want any more dinner, I think we should get started before the spell wears off," I said, looking at Trevor.

"Will you not tell Jenny or Angela about any of this?" Trevor asked.

"I can't promise anything, Trevor," I said, shaking my head. "You really took away your right to ask for much of anything after you tried to attack us. You should've thought about these things before you so eagerly joined the ranks of my father."

"I thought it would bring me closer to you," Trevor said, glancing sideways at Logan as if he was worried he'd get decked again

"Let's just get this over with," I mumbled, glaring at Trevor.

Logan grabbed the jar with the spider, and a shiver ran through my spine. It wasn't going to hurt Trevor at all, except for the bite. I was the one who was going to feel all of the pain. According to the explanation in the spell book, the one experiencing the implant of the memories would feel the majority of the discomfort.

"Things happen for a reason, Trev. I'd like to think that your weakness can be used to our benefit. If you hadn't attempted what you did, we wouldn't be getting handed such amazing information so easily," I said, pointing at the chair by the fire. "How about you just sit over there?"

Trevor nodded and Logan followed behind him with the jar. As Trevor sat down, the fear in his eyes probably would have made most people try to save him from this situation. Instead, I wanted to be the one who initiated the process and quite possibly scare him a little myself.

Taking the jar from Logan, I unscrewed the lid and began tapping the spider out of the jar onto Trevor's shoulder. This one small act started to give me a little satisfaction.

"Thanks for allowing us to do this, Trevor," I said curtly, feeling the anger beginning to surface again at the thought of *me* thanking *him*.

"*Alienam Imagines ex Anima,*" I recited, as I stepped back careful not to run into the table behind me.

Trevor only nodded as the spider began crawling along his shoulder up his neck. Little beads of sweat began forming on Trevor's forehead. He wasn't as calm as he'd like us to believe. I reached for Logan's hand as we both watched the process unfold in front of us.

The spider was moving slowly as if it was looking for the perfect place to bite into flesh, Trevor's flesh. Imagining the spider's fangs pierce Trevor's skin pumped a sense of euphoria through me. I knew I shouldn't be feeling this delighted over Trevor's pain, but I was. Promising myself that the emotions were only because of the information this process was going to provide, I squeezed Logan's hand for support.

Quickly glancing at me, Logan's expression changed to alarm as he recognized what I was feeling inside. He saw the look in my eyes. I couldn't hide it from him.

Shaking my head, I let go of Logan's hand, feeling ashamed and confused. If I couldn't fool myself over what I was feeling how could I expect to fool Logan? He's been through this.

The spider slowed its journey, and I watched as it began to feed on Trevor, right behind his ear just like the diagram showed.

As every second ticked by, I felt more consumed by the power that this experience was bringing me. This was exactly what I needed to avoid, this feeling right here. Slowly letting the breath escape from the deepest pockets in my lungs, Logan wrapped his arms around me.

"It's okay. I know what you're going through," Logan whispered in my ear. "We'll get through this. I won't let you fall."

Trevor continued staring at the floor, refusing to look at either of us as we watched the spider finish what it was handpicked to do. Trevor's hands were squeezing the chair, the skin on his knuckles stretching white. His part of the process wasn't supposed to cause pain, so I was perplexed at what was going on.

I squeezed Logan and pointed to Trevor's hands that were now shaking. Something was wrong. The spider wasn't stopping.

"Triss, grab the spell book. Trevor, look at me," Logan was trying to get Trevor's attention by smacking his leg, but Trevor wasn't moving. He was like a statue – completely catatonic.

Logan grabbed the spell book from me and flipped to where I bookmarked it. I darted to Trevor unsure of what to do next. Kneeling in front of him, I wiped away the liquid that was beginning to dribble from his mouth. This was getting worse by the second. I tried to get his attention, but he wouldn't budge. His stare was cold and unresponsive. My heart was pounding with the fear that he was on the way out of this world. I didn't know what went wrong, but something did. What could I have done incorrectly? I had followed the steps perfectly.

"Logan, what does it say?" I screamed. "Is he dying? What's wrong with him? What did I do to him?"

I glanced at the wall of herbs, wondering if something could help him — if anything could help him. No matter how much hatred I had built up for him, I didn't actually want him to die.

"A catatonic state occurs when the participant isn't pure of heart or is cursed," Logan said coming over to us. "There's nothing we can do until it wears off. This isn't your fault. You wouldn't have known. Plus, it was in Latin."

The spider slowly began to crawl away from the insertion point. Maybe things were looking up.

"So it will wear off? Do you think he was cursed by my father?" I asked, looking at Logan for reassurance. I didn't want to believe that Trevor might just be this way – *this evil*.

"Probably." Logan's eyes dropped to the floor. He was hiding something.

"The spider still holds the answers you're hoping for. The process sounds like it completed. I think we need to proceed before the spell wears off, and you *can't* get the answers, Triss." Logan's words were somber, as he watched me walk to the kitchen. "What are you doing?"

I was searching the cupboards for some of the vials that my aunt had given me before we had left for the cottage. I thought her selection was odd until now. My hands were shaking as I moved the tiny brown bottles out of the way, knocking a few over as I tried to get to the blue bottles in the back. Uneasiness began spreading through me, and it wasn't only about Trevor.

"What's going on? We've got to get the process started on you or everything will be in vain," Logan tried again, his voice pleading with me.

"Don't you find it odd that everything my aunt managed to pick up at the apothecary store for us is coming in handy?" I turned to face Logan, trying to hold in my anger.

Having found the vial I was looking for, I tossed it to Logan. He read the label and looked up at me. His eyes flashed with the same realization that I had.

"You don't think —" Logan stopped.

"I don't even know, but figure out how to get Trevor to ingest two drops of that solution. It will calm the tremors and give him some peace while he's out of it," I said, walking over to Trevor to grab the spider.

"I hope I'm wrong about my aunt," I sighed.

"Me too."

I plunked the spider back into the jar and watched it crawl much slower along the base of the glass. Logan was right. Time was running out.

"Off I go," I said, walking toward the bedroom.

I looked at Logan one last time and his eyes

were filled with the same sense of dread that I was feeling. Glancing at Trevor I reminded myself how quickly a spell can go wrong.

"Triss, wait."

Logan placed the vial meant to help Trevor on the coffee table and glided over to me. His eyes said it all as he picked me up. I wrapped my arms around his neck, while still holding onto the jar. The strength from his embrace gave me the last amount of courage I needed to get this process over with. I needed this support. I wasn't used to it completely, but I did enjoy it.

"I love you, Triss," he whispered, nuzzling my neck.

"I love you too," I said, as he released me back to the floor.

"You're not going to turn out like what's-his-face over there," Logan's lip curled slightly. "You have a pure heart."

"I don't know about that, but thanks," I said.

Shoving him playfully, I tried to distract myself from the fear that was beginning to take over.

I reached up to the dried flowers I had hung on the wall and traced the crispness of the leaves feeling how fragile they had become. Lifting a tied bunch of lavender off the wall, I crushed it in my hand as I started back down the hall. I would take any sort of calming attributes that I could get.

"I'll be in as soon as I take care of our patient."

"Thanks," I replied, hoping the smile I plastered on my lips would make me feel less nervous, but it didn't.

I walked into the bedroom. The sun was setting and only a few rays of daylight were making their way into the room, but I didn't want the light on. I wasn't sure I wanted Logan to see the process unfold that clearly because I certainly didn't. The idea of a spider crawling on me in this set of circumstances was really creepy. It's one thing if a spider lands on me. It's quite another to think that I've stirred up a recipe to have this spider sink its teeth into me.

Besides, I wanted to think that the process would finish before the evening made its full appearance. Shaking the jar lightly to ensure that the spider was still with me, I took a deep breath and spread myself out on the bed. My hand landed on the pillow with a gentle thud as I stared at the ceiling. I began letting my eyes trace the tiny cracks in the exposed cedar. Unfortunately the ceiling wasn't that riveting, and I switched my focus to the task at hand. The images of Trevor drooling in temporary paralysis made their way into my mind, attempting to hijack any calmness I'd started to experience.

Squeezing my eyes closed and quickly releasing my lids back open, I knew the time had come. Letting out a deep breath, I shook the contents of the jar onto my chest and recited softly, *"Adducam Imagines Velle Captivum Animum."* Then I waited.

Feeling nothing from the spider at first, I fought the need to fidget, and I attempted to maneuver my eyes to see the spider on my chest without moving my body. I hoped I wasn't too late – that the spider could do what it was cast to do. Just as I thought I couldn't stand it anymore, I felt the crawling sensation on my neck. With each leg movement, a tickle from the arachnid's many legs caused a sense of panic. My heart was pounding and the flush of fear started spreading through me. Trying to steady my breathing, I thought about Logan, hoping that that the images of him would distract me. Instead, it made me more anxious worrying about him out there with Trevor, which was completely irrational because Trevor was completely out of it.

The hall light flashed on alerting me to Logan's presence just as the spider sunk its fangs into my flesh. Rising up from the bed, I released a howl carrying the pain of the poisoned memories that were being transmitted through my system. Logan rushed to my side, but there was nothing he could do. My body fell limp against the mattress, and the room began spinning. The burning was centralized at first, but the sensation quickly changed to a web of pain in every extremity, darting back and forth. I was immediately freezing — shaking uncontrollably. I grabbed for the blue chenille blanket but had to let go as the pain paralyzed my fingers.

Logan grabbed my right hand as scream after scream echoed off the walls in the bedroom. There were no images flooding my mind; no comments from my father to Trevor; no information on why mom left me. Was I going through all of this for nothing?

My body squirmed and contorted into positions I didn't think possible despite my best efforts at controlling it. Logan's fingers combed through my hair. I tried keeping my eyes on him as my body writhed in agony. He was my center, but now even he was getting blurry. It was like I was in the state between dreaming and waking up. Nothing was clear, but everything was vivid. The feelings and emotions were all at surface level waiting to escape, but none of them came together to create anything tangible.

The sun had made its complete finale for the day making the light from the hallway hurt my eyes. I wanted to tell Logan, but I was afraid I might need my strength for something else. The temperature in the room turned quickly from ice-cold to overly hot. The already small room was closing in on me from all sides, and my mind was getting too tired to fight the pain much longer.

"You're gonna be okay, baby," Logan said, wiping away the sweat that began forming at my hairline.

My entire body was burning up and my mouth was so dry I thought my tongue was twice its normal size.

"Help me," I whimpered, looking into Logan's eyes.

"The worst is almost over," Logan brought his lips down to mine and softly kissed me. "We'll get through this. I'm not leaving your side."

One last shot of pain ran down my spine as the world I called my own turned to darkness.

CHAPTER 3

"There isn't anything we can do until she wakes up, Trevor. You need to leave her alone," Logan said.

I'm up! I'm up. I can hear you. I just can't move, but I'm here.

"I promised her you wouldn't be here when she woke up, and you managed to make me break that promise," Logan snarled. "And now I can't get you out of here because I know she's about to wake up. You did this on purpose."

"You wanna blame me for that?" Trevor asked. "Do you think I enjoyed the state I was in?"

"Get out of her room," Logan said, seething with anger. "I'm warning you."

Footsteps were coming closer to the bed, but I didn't know whose they were. Oh no! It's starting again. I don't want to sleep again. I've got to stay up.

"Or what?" Trevor asked.

A hand landed on my arm. I wanted to pull away, but I couldn't. It wasn't Logan. I wanted Logan.

"You know, don't you?" Logan asked accusingly.

Know what? What was Logan talking about?

"Oh, you mean about that little caveat on the spell you two performed on me? Yeah, I know about it," Trevor replied coyly. "Doesn't Triss?"

"Get out of here!" Logan yelled before a tumble of two bodies hit the floor.

Someone slammed against the dresser and fell to the floor. Was it Trevor or Logan? Another crash sounded behind me and then there was silence.

I've got to open my eyes. I've got to open my eyes.

I barely heard the shoes struggling along the floor when I realized someone was being dragged out of my room, and I didn't know which of the somebodies it was.

My spirit was heavy. It was happening again. Sleep was calling, but I couldn't afford it. Not now. I had already learned enough. I didn't want to see any more, but it was too late.

My father was holding my mother in his arms, as she sat so content on his lap. They were all seated around a large dining table that could easily seat twenty. There were strangers in every direction I looked. The cherry wood paneling was covering all four walls from floor to ceiling. The chandelier in this one room wouldn't fit in the entire first floor of our Seattle home.

Everything I saw seemed far too grand compared to what I was used to. It was actually quite ridiculous. Looking out the window behind my father, the surface of the lake glistened with a brilliance that rivaled Puget Sound.

The joyful laughter coming from my mother did nothing but cause me confusion. That wasn't her…or was it? How could she so easily forget me and so easily fall back in the arms of a betrayer?

"Well, Trevor," my father's voice boomed, "you could have this, too, with Triss."

My father squeezed my mother tighter, and she nestled his neck.

"Yes, sir," Trevor replied delighted.

"It's in your blood, isn't it? The draw you have to my daughter?" my father continued.

"It is, sir. I couldn't imagine life without her," Trevor said.

"No need to call me sir any longer." My father wore a brilliant smile. "Nicholas is just fine. You're almost family now, after all."

"We're getting close. I need my family back together, and my daughter needs someone to love just as her mother loves me." My father's smile was wicked. Trevor didn't have a chance.

I wanted to escape from this surreal world that I had borrowed from Trevor, but I couldn't. Not yet anyway.

"My daughter's got some pretty important talents that need to be developed. As she's grown older, they've become more apparent. I think with the right training, she could help change the face of witchcraft for everyone.

Make it more..." he paused, "...acceptable."

A murmur grew from the crowd of strangers sitting around the table. An excitement filled the air that I couldn't understand.

"Absolutely, master," one of the men spoke up. I looked at the male who spoke and saw a vacancy in his spirit. I didn't know what it was exactly, but as I scanned from one person to the next, they all seemed to carry that same expression.

My eyes darted back to my father. He certainly had a charisma surrounding him, but there was more to it than that. He seemed to be the only one who carried any sort of vitality. It was as if he was feeding off these people.

"Don't be frightened, Trevor. This isn't mind control in the normal sense," my father said, as if he could sniff out Trevor's possible apprehension. "You have complete control over what you actually do. There's no such thing as brainwashing. That's a myth. What I can do for you is give you the tools to tap into my arsenal of experience. The only thing I ask in return is for you to trust me."

The room was silenced with my father's statement. They were all waiting for Trevor's reply.

"I'll get your daughter for you, Nicholas. But I've got some terms of my own."

"You do?" My father seemed pleased at Trevor's feeble attempt at negotiating. I'm sure my father had no intention of actually granting Trevor anything, but I don't think Trevor was smart enough to figure that out.

"I want your permission to destroy Logan," Trevor replied.

My mother bolted upright. She recognized on some level what Trevor's statement meant, *who* he was referring to — her best friend's son. But I wasn't sure she was strong enough to debate it.

"Nicholas, I won't allow it," my mother found her voice. "There's no need for that."

She began removing herself from my father's lap in protest, but my father was too calculating to allow that to happen.

"Absolutely not, Trevor. Logan's not to be touched."

Relief started flooding through me. My father didn't give a directive on Logan.

"I apologize, but I think that it would make it much easier for your grand scheme if I eliminated him," Trevor said. I could detect a slight tremble in his voice, but that was only because I knew what he used to sound like in school when he got worked up.

The room filled with whispers and judging by my father's expression, he wasn't used to being spoken to in the manner that Trevor was attempting.

"You trained him, Nicholas. You know what he's capable of," Trevor continued.

My mother craned her neck and glared at Trevor for a few moments before speaking.

"You will not touch him," my mother's voice was as cold as ice. "His mother is supposed to come up to our camp at the lake." She turned back to my father. "You promised. If something happens to her son, she won't come."

That's it? That's why my mother's concerned? I couldn't believe what I was seeing. This was not the woman who raised me. My mother was pouting because her potential playmate might not want to come to the lake retreat if her son was killed. She's not fighting for Logan's life, but rather so hers would be more fun.

"You heard my wife, Trevor. I'm sorry," my father replied, winking at Trevor.

"That I did," Trevor said nodding.

I wanted to run away, but I'm the one who put myself in this position to see and hear everything.

My head was pounding and my eyes felt bruised, but I had to open them. I had to force them open to begin my real life again. I physically couldn't stomach any more visions from Trevor. Between what I had learned from earlier and this, I knew enough to know we were all in trouble. I wanted no more. I wanted to escape.

My body was rocking back and forth. It felt like I was on one of the roughest seas imaginable with no land in sight. I wanted out of this spell. I could no longer allow myself to be trapped in Trevor's mind.

"Hun, you're okay."

My eyes flashed open to reveal Trevor staring back at me.

CHAPTER 4

The room was completely dark except for the light from the hall that trickled in. The covers were mashed at the bottom of the bed, presumably from my nightmares.

"Where's Logan?" I asked, backing myself away from Trevor. "Where is he?"

"It's okay, hun."

"It's not okay and don't call me hun," I snapped. "Where is Logan?"

I wasn't sure I felt strong enough to get up and stay up, but the fear of being alone with Trevor would surely push me through whatever weakness my body might present.

"He's a little out of sorts at the moment," Trevor said sardonically.

"What did you do to him?" I demanded, starting to sit up.

"Nothing. I didn't do a thing to him. I swear."

"You're lying. He'd be here if you hadn't done

something to him."

Trevor put his hands up and shrugged his shoulders.

"Believe me or not."

Scooting down to the end of the bed as far from Trevor as I could get, I let my feet fall down the side of the bed. I needed to find Logan. Standing up slowly, it felt as if a tidal wave was attempting to hijack my stability. The room started spinning and Trevor only smiled, knowing full well what I was feeling.

"Stay away from me," I ordered. I didn't care if I collapsed on my way to find Logan. I wanted nothing to do with Trevor, especially after seeing what he told my father.

"Not a problem, doll," he replied. "I'll give you all the time you need."

Apparently my father's tentacles were in far too deep to worry about whether Trevor had any good qualities worth saving, but why would he let us do the spell?

Focusing on the light outside of the bedroom, I lifted one leg and felt its weight plop in front of me as I managed to repeat the steps several times before I had to lean against the wall. I still couldn't see into the family room, and with the heaviness of my extremities, I knew it would be a challenge to even make it there, but I had to find Logan. I had to press forward.

Looking behind me, light filtered onto Trevor's features highlighting a swollen lip and red cheek. His smugness shined as he watched me struggle with every step. At least with whatever scuffle I heard earlier he didn't remain unscathed. I hoped with every ounce of strength that Logan was okay, but if he was all right wouldn't he be here for me?

"Logan?" I called but only silence was returned.

"I doubt he'll be able to hear you."

Turning back toward Trevor, I couldn't hide my rage.

"Why is that?" My head started spinning as the words tumbled out.

Realizing Trevor had no intention of telling me much of anything, I turned my attention back to the hallway. Gliding my hand across the wall for support, I scanned the space in front of me — empty.

The two vials that Logan had used on Trevor were still on the coffee table. And to think that I actually tried to make his discomfort go away seemed unbelievable.

Feeling like I had conquered a climb on Mount Kilimanjaro, I rested my body against the couch. There was no sign of Logan anywhere. No sign of a struggle. In fact, the kitchen had a couple of plates with sandwich crumbs. Nothing I awoke to was making sense. The thought of being stuck alone with Trevor at the cottage made the situation feel even more dire. If I could get out the front door and to some fresh air, maybe some of my strength would return and hopefully some of my senses.

Scuffling to the wooden door, I began to hear voices outside and stopped to listen.

"I don't know what I'll do if she goes to him," Logan said. The sadness in every syllable radiated through the thick wooden door.

"Is that why you left her alone in there?" a woman's voice asked. "To save yourself from your own emotional anguish?"

"I guess," he paused. "Yeah, I guess it is. I'd rather it just happen right away so I'd know what to expect going forward. The thought of them being together makes me sick."

What was Logan talking about? Why would I suddenly go to Trevor? And who else was at our cottage? I wished I wasn't so foggy.

I continued squashing my ear to the wooden door hoping for some clarity and partially using the structure as a support.

"Did she know of the possible side effects?" the woman asked.

It's Aunt Vieta! What was she doing here?

"No. It was in Latin, and I knew she'd do the spell no matter what. I kinda thought I'd better my chances if she didn't know of the possibility. I didn't want to place anything in her mind right before she went under."

"And you're worried that at some point she had feelings for Trevor?" Aunt Vieta asked.

My eyes landed on a bouquet of daisies that were by the sink. I wondered if Logan had intended those for me. Why wouldn't he have brought them to me? Why wasn't he sitting there with me?

There was silence for what seemed like an eternity before Logan started speaking again.

"If she even had a mild interest in him at some point, after this process, they'd be connected for life, and I don't know if she ever did. She said she never liked him, but who knows. If it was for a fleeting second even, there's no turning back. This spell would capture that, and there's nothing I could do. I'd never be able to have her. I'd never be able to save her from him. You can't trade memories without consequences it seems."

My aunt sighed and footsteps came closer to the door, but it didn't sound like the conversation was ending.

"You can't leave her hanging in there. Is Trevor still unconscious?" My aunt asked.

"I clocked him pretty hard, so I'd imagine," Logan murmured.

"Well, I say you get yourself back in there before she wakes up with the bunch of daisies you gathered for her and quit worrying about the spell's downfalls. We can only face the repercussions once they present themselves. Until then, I'll get Trevor out of here and drive him to the train. I think if we can get him out of here before she sees him that would be the best."

"Won't that only prolong the inevitable? I'd rather just know if they are connected."

I couldn't take it any longer. I sprung the door open to see Aunt Vieta and Logan on the porch staring at me in disbelief. The porch light sprayed down on Logan showing no visible marks from the scuffle so maybe he was the one who did the attacking. I hoped so.

"You're up!" Logan said surprised, as he

reached for me while I attempted to steady myself.

"Yeah and so is your buddy," I said wryly.

Even though my surroundings still spun around me, I was astute enough to see Logan freeze in his tracks as he caught Aunt Vieta's gaze. Why were things so complicated right now? The pile of velvet-cushioned pillows stacked in the corner in the great room called to me, and I had to fight not to plop myself down and start the night over. Maybe that's all I needed. Start everything over.

"You saw him?" Logan asked tentatively. His deep blue eyes canvasing me for something I didn't understand.

"Not much to look at, but I saw him," I nodded. "You did a number on him."

I grinned, reaching for Logan's hand. His lips did a slight curl upward but fell almost immediately.

My aunt came toward me and my body recoiled at the thought of her touch. Too many unknowns were going on right now and apparently my subconscious was on high alert.

"Sweetie, what's the matter?" my aunt asked, obviously hurt by my reaction.

"I'm sorry. I—" stopping myself, I looked over at Logan.

Why was she here? What had he told her? I thought we were on the same page about her right now.

"Maybe you could go get Trevor out of here like you guys were discussing?" I asked her.

"You heard that?" Logan's voice was strained.

"Parts," I nodded.

My aunt scooted by me, and I stiffened as she patted my shoulder, "I'll let Logan fill you in before I return. I'll get Trevor out of here. If he'll go."

"He's got no choice," I replied coldly. "I want nothing to do with him. The images the spider bestowed on me were enough to let me in on Trevor's true character, regardless of what I was hoping for him as a person. I don't want him anywhere near me. And *you* —" I said pointing at Logan. "Letting me wake up to see that monster staring back at me first thing? I need an explanation and an apology. Do you know how frightened I was?"

The stress began trickling out of Logan's eyes the more I ranted.

"I didn't expect him to regain consciousness so soon," Logan replied grimly.

"He really thinks he's got me in the bag. Is there a reason he's so sure of himself?" I questioned Logan. "I heard something about a side effect of the spell?"

Logan shifted uncomfortably and closed the front door behind him. The dizziness began again, and I walked toward the kitchen table with Logan's help.

"I've gotta sit down," I said, rubbing my forehead. "This is brutal."

Logan glided the chair out for me, and I felt the weight of my body slump into the wooden seat. I seemed to be functioning on autopilot at this point. Every part of my body was bent on reminding me of what I just went through.

"I never meant for you to wake up without me there," Logan apologized, grabbing the daisies from the counter, he placed them on the table in front of me. He pulled a chair out next to me and sat down, propping his elbows on his knees as he ran his fingers through his dark hair. I wasn't going to let him off the hook. I needed answers because right now everything seemed like a jumbled mess.

"It really sucked. Not to mention I had Trevor too close for comfort when I finally opened my eyes. I don't understand. You *promised* you wouldn't leave my side. The daisies were a nice gesture, but —"

My aunt's voice was getting louder as she unsuccessfully pleaded with Trevor who apparently had no intentions of leaving the cottage. My agitation level was soaring. I had so many things to tell Logan not to mention find out from him, and Trevor was being quite a nuisance.

"Why's he making things so difficult. He certainly makes it easy to want to perform black magic on him," I paused, throwing a smile at Logan hoping it would make him relax a little. "Where's my snake?"

"It's good to see you're as spirited as before," Logan teased.

"I could use some more target practice," I said only half-joking. "Seriously though. He's bad news. Whatever grain of goodness we thought we saw in him before the spell was all a mirage.

Guaranteed."

Logan furrowed his brows. "It can't be that bad."

"It's worse. For starters, he wants you dead." Certain my last point would hit home, I sat back in the chair, crossing my arms in front of me waiting for his reaction.

"That's nothing new."

"He asked my father for permission," I countered.

"First, your father wouldn't give it to him. Second, if someone has to ask permission to kill someone they don't really have it in them to do the act. They wouldn't ask, they'd just do it. Plus, he's pretty incapable."

"Glad you can be so sure of that."

"We've got other things to worry about that are far more important." Logan rubbed my arms.

"Trevor, she's not interested in you. She wants you to leave," Aunt Vieta's words tumbled down the hallway followed by a couple sets of footsteps.

Oh, no. Why does this have to be so difficult?

"What is going on?" I asked Logan. "Why is he so entitled feeling?"

Logan let out a sigh. "It's part of the spell. If you ever had feelings for him— even subconsciously— you'll desire him, be connected to him for life. He's banking that you have had some sort of thought about that, even if fleeting."

Horror didn't even begin to describe the emotion running through my veins. I never thought of Trevor in that way. Not even for a second. Or did I? What about the first time I saw him? No. No way. He was attractive and the girls loved him at school, but I wasn't one of them.

"You're worried about it, aren't you?" Logan searched my eyes for any sort of affirmation.

"She should be," Trevor's voice startled me.

My finger traced the wood's grain in the table over and over again while I tried to contain my anger. I wanted to hurt him so badly. His arrogance was infuriating.

"So you knew the entire time?" My words finally found a voice.

"Why else would I have agreed to go through that spell?" He shrugged his shoulders.

"I don't know, Trevor. Maybe to be a kind and decent human being, but that seems to be asking too much," I snarled.

Trevor's eyes narrowed at Logan. "So what's the plan?"

"Plan?" I interjected. "The plan is for you to get out of here."

I stood up quickly, knocking over my chair and feeling extremely woozy at the same time. Logan was immediately by my side, wrapping his arm around me as I tried to ground myself. I needed peace and quiet. Not this.

Aunt Vieta walked quickly around Trevor. "Triss, you've been through so much. Let me get you something."

"Just get him out of here and that will do plenty for me."

"Why are you avoiding the inevitable?" Trevor walked toward me, and Logan held on tighter.

"The inevitable?" I squinted at him. "There's nothing inevitable about us. I don't care what you think that spell's capable of."

Trevor reached for my hand, but not before Logan released me and grabbed Trevor throwing him to the floor. Logan had him completely subdued with his knee digging into Trevor's chest. Catching Trevor's glance, my heart twisted in knots, and I didn't understand my reaction. I hated Trevor and Logan was completely in control. Oh no. Please let this not be happening. There's nothing to be conflicted over. I'm not feeling bad for Trevor. This was impossible.

"You heard Triss. She wants you to leave. Let her aunt take you to the station, and we'll pretend none of this ever happened," Logan growled. His knuckles were turning white with anticipation. He wanted to annihilate Trevor and a few seconds ago, I wanted that too. Now I was confused and wasn't sure.

"I'm guessing he doesn't know about the kiss?" Trevor shouted, trying to dislodge from Logan's strength.

"Kiss?" Logan's pain cut through to my heart. My eyes locked with Logan's but no words would come. This was a complete misunderstanding. I had forgotten that Trevor had tried to kiss me once. He kind of managed it, but it was many years ago and inconsequential. That couldn't count for anything. Could it? Why wouldn't words come?

My head continued throbbing, and I reached behind me for the table to lean against. Logan's eyes were filled with such agony, and my aunt's hands were raised to her mouth in complete shock. All I could do was keep shaking my head no, unable to speak.

Logan stood up, and released Trevor by throwing him against the wall. What's he doing?

"It didn't mean anything, Logan," I whispered.

"Maybe not in your head, but all we can do is wait to see what your heart says," he replied. "And I don't know that I can be around to watch." Grabbing his jacket, he spun around and went outside leaving me in my own personal hell.

Trevor started toward me, and I raised my hand to stop him.

"Don't."

"We are meant to be together," Trevor's voice had new warmth to it.

"Quit saying that," I cried, running after Logan.

CHAPTER 5

The porch light did little to illuminate the forest beyond the porch, but it didn't matter. I had to find Logan. I had to explain. The darkness brought with it silence, except for the occasional flutter of leaves or bats circling above searching for their late night snack. My body felt as if it was glued to the forest floor beneath me. Every movement I made was delayed with the heaviness of what life might have in store for me. None of which I wanted.

"Logan?" I called out to the night doubtful I'd hear anything returned.

A cracked twig off in the distance gave me hope, and I started toward the anonymous sound. The slight rustle of leaves ahead of me signaled that I was getting closer, but with every step it seemed the noise moved that much farther ahead of me. My stomach was in knots, and I wasn't sure what I would say. There was no way I would have purposefully traded my future with Logan for Trevor. I only prayed my subconscious hadn't betrayed me at some point in my life.

I was getting closer to the pasture that, only a week ago, held a magnificent carpet of blue bells. It was where Logan told me he was holding off college to help find my mom. He had done so much for me since he returned. Made me the priority. There was no way Trevor was going to get in the way of that regardless of the spell's outcome.

Finally making my way to the clearing, the moonlight sprinkled its goodness onto the pasture leading the way. The blue bells had finished their bloom, leaving only the mounds of foliage behind for me to walk on. As far as my eyes could see, there was no Logan. Anger quickly displaced the worry and sadness that had been running through my system. How could he give up on me so easily?

Across the pasture, where the woods began again, a shadow danced at the slightest movement giving away Logan's location. He was leaning up against one of the pine trees. His head extended as if he was looking to the sky for answers.

Despite my weakened state, I sprinted towards him. Surely he'd seen me coming as I barreled across the field. Upon approach, each step was heavier than the last, and I was completely breathless and fully agitated at him for making me come after him out in the woods.

KARICE BOLTON

"Hey, you," I called to him.

I was trying to catch my breath, which seemed impossible. This was why I never attempted the mile-long runs in gym class.

The blood was pounding in my ears, and it was safe to say I'd done too much too soon after the spell. I reached for the nearest tree, but my complete inability to gauge distance caused me to miss the trunk as I fell to the ground.

"Whoa. I gotcha," Logan said, grabbing me before I hit the bed of pine needles. His voice was as gentle as his touch, making it nearly impossible to be as angry with him as I felt.

Bringing me to his body, he wrapped his arms tightly around me.

"You can't do this to me," I whispered, placing my arms around his waist. "You can't give up on me before you've even gotten me."

I looked up to meet his eyes, which held a bit of the darkness we had done so well at eliminating.

"You've already started putting your walls back up," I said.

"And you haven't?"

"No. Because I know I've never had feelings for him."

"What about the kiss?" Logan growled.

"I wouldn't call it a kiss where both parties participated. He came in for it, and I was completely taken off guard. It made me cringe at the time, and the memory still makes me ill."

"I wish it was that simple," Logan replied, his embrace loosened some.

"Are you serious?" The fury was starting to build again. "Why don't you take my word for it? Why doesn't that count?"

"It's not that I don't believe you. I just —"

He looked away, and I caught a glimpse of moistness edge the blue of his eyes.

"I wanted to kill him." Logan looked into my eyes, gauging my reaction. "And I would have. This is when I know how close to dark magic I still am."

"I have a confession too," I whispered. "That thought crossed my mind as well. See? It has nothing to do with dark magic. It has to do with being human. Ridding the world of evil."

A grin spread across his face.

"Is that so?" his voice low.

I nodded as he embraced me tighter.

"I don't want you to see that side of life," he replied, his words strained. "I want to shelter you from all of that."

"Too late." I paused, wondering what to say next. "We've got to face everything head on, Logan. Together. We'll be stronger as a team. No more ditching me. From now on, take me with you."

"I didn't mean to leave you in there like that, but shocked doesn't even begin to describe the emotions that came over me when I heard about that kiss. I spent all night telling myself there was no chance you had feelings for him. And even in my darkest nightmares, I never thought there was a *kiss* involved. He was so smug, and I just needed to get out of there."

"Still, you can't take off like that. I don't care what was going through your mind. I'd rather have you hit him again than be left with him. You abandoned me."

"I'm sorry. Figuring that I'd lost you to him was more than I could handle. I didn't want to see it unfold in front of me."

He pulled me closer, and I rested my head against his chest.

"You still think you could lose me to him?" I murmured.

"Only time will tell."

"How's that? Wouldn't I already be showing signs?" I asked.

"Possibly. I'm not really sure how it works."

I let out a sigh, trying to find a balance between anger, sadness, and fear. I didn't want any emotion to outweigh the other and tip me toward something I didn't want to be a part of.

"You don't feel anything for him. Do you?" Logan whispered, gazing down to the woodland floor. At night, it wasn't that interesting so his avoidance technique killed me.

I shuddered at the thought of Trevor, but then worry crept in as I thought back to the fear I felt about Logan *hurting* him. Could that be a sign? No. It couldn't be. My mind was all clouded from everything — that's all.

"I hate him more now than ever." It was true.

I needed to get far away from Trevor. I completely understood Logan's desire to distance himself from the situation, and maybe it was better if I did as well. I didn't want to know the outcome, and if I didn't see him I wouldn't have to worry about it.

"Let's get out of here," I whispered, looking up into Logan's eyes. "Right now. Let's just go."

"Where would we go?" Logan's eyes lit up slightly.

"I found out so much about my father and mother tonight that I think the sooner we make our way back east, the better. I'm still unclear about a motive behind my father's actions, but I think that it will come out in time. I think there's still hope that I can bring her home. And I don't want to get caught up in the Trevor drama. It's not worth it. We're here now together and that's what matters... So are you game?"

Logan brought his hands up from my waist, cupping my chin as he brought his lips slowly down to mine. I wanted to taste his mouth, his lips, everything about him. He was who I wanted, not Trevor. No matter what the spell tried to hijack from me, my feelings wouldn't change for Logan.

As our lips met, the search for our security began. Neither of us wanted to believe that we could lose this. Running my fingers through his hair, I gripped his neck with my other hand. I didn't want this closeness to end. The firmness of his body stretched along mine as he lifted me into his arms. I wrapped my legs around his waist, not wanting to detach from his kisses as they led away from my mouth down my neck. Feeling his breath dance across my skin as he kissed my collarbone brought a shivery delight to my senses. The softness of his lips was such a contrast to the firmness of his grasp as he guided his hands down my back.

He spun around, pinning me up against the tree with his weight, as I let my mind wander to what might be waiting for me next. My breathing got faster with each second of anticipation. He slowly brought my chin up and his lips began exploring mine once more. With every kiss, his mouth pressed harder along mine, and my heart exploded with curiosity. I let my hands find their way back to his neck up to his hair, twisting and pulling him closer to me with all of my strength.

He pulled away slightly, and I opened my eyes to see him searching my expression for something. For what, I wasn't sure.

"I don't ever want to lose you, Triss." Logan shook his head. "I couldn't—"

"Shh." I placed my index finger to his lips. "You won't."

My hand trailed down his chest to the first button that I attempted to unfasten. His eyes closed briefly as he took a deep breath in, and I enjoyed the reaction I evoked. Working my way down his shirt, I never let my gaze leave his. The blue of his eyes began to cast a desperate stare as I reached the last button.

Opening his shirt, my hand slid along his warm skin and his lips began to curl into the familiar grin that I loved.

"Enjoying this?" I asked, hiding my smile.

The moonlight was bouncing off of his gloriously smooth skin as my fingers began discovering the dips and peaks of his stomach. I had no idea it was so defined.

"You seem a little distracted, Miss. Spires," he whispered, catching my eyes gazing at the definition where his shirt once was.

Unable to hide my smile any longer, my finger glided down toward the first button of his jeans. The warmth of his skin beckoned me to explore every inch of his body.

Logan grabbed my hand, disrupting my next course of action, and he swiftly pinned it above my head. My other hand glided along his back and he captured that one too, securing it above me. I was at his mercy and loving every second of it. I struggled a little bit, just for fun, and he tightened his grasp on me. Managing to wriggle one hand free, I let it slide along his skin until it hit an ice-cold patch. My breath hitched in surprise, and I glanced at him before attempting to see what my hand came across.

"Triss, don't," he muttered.

The tattoo he shielded me from earlier was freezing. His entire body was laced with warmth, except for this symbol — a symbol that I didn't recognize. His hand enclosed mine, bringing it away from the chill of his flesh.

"What is that? Why is it so cold?" I said, attempting to make out the shape of the black ink against the glow of his skin.

"It's nothing," he whispered, bringing my hand up to his mouth where his lips began placing gentle kisses along each finger.

"Tell me. Share with me," I pleaded.

Doing his best to distract me, his stare was intense and burning with the same desire I experienced in his presence. His eyes traced my lips creating a thirst for something more. He placed my hand above my head once more, leaning in to meet my lips, promising to quench my yearning. His kiss deepened with every passing moment, allowing me to forget the situation, time, and place where I stood suspended. I quietly begged for my hands to be freed so that I could let my fingertips grace his skin, but he wouldn't allow it, only deepening the stir within.

A rustle of leaves destroyed our private sanctuary, and Logan stiffened as he dropped my hands from above my head. It had to be Trevor. He'd found us. My heartbeat quickened and I brought Logan's ear close to mine.

"Let me deal with him. Follow my lead," I whispered.

Unwrapping my legs from Logan's waist, I centered myself on the ground again while Logan quickly slid his shirt on, buttoning it up as fast as he could.

Trevor was in earshot now and a situation like this might not present itself again. He was coming up from behind me, and it sounded like he was alone. My aunt must have stayed back in the cottage.

"Logan, I'm sorry," I started, locking eyes with him, and winking. "I didn't expect it to end this way. I never imagined this could happen."

The words themselves created a sickness

within me even though they were completely false. Looking into Logan's eyes, I could tell they were producing the same feeling inside him too.

"I don't understand, Triss," Logan attempted to play along. "I thought you never felt anything for him."

Logan's voice was full of anger. Even in the most spurious of situations, it was impossible not to let the absurdity of my actions taint his words.

"I never knew I did. I'm so sorry," I whispered, moving toward him.

A hand from behind me rested on my shoulder, and I did my best not to cringe even though that was my natural inclination.

"Triss, you came around," Trevor said. "I knew you would."

Bringing me closer to him, I stepped back quickly into his arms so I didn't lose my footing. The pain in Logan's eyes was no act as Trevor brought me into his fold. Doing my best to play along, I caught Logan's eyes and apologized with every second of our connected gaze as I wrapped my arm around Trevor's waist.

"Logan wants to take off tonight. I thought I'd drive him to the station," I replied coldly.

"Oh, that's too bad. He's the one getting dropped off now, huh? What a pity." Trevor's arrogance rolled off his tongue with ease.

"Can you blame him? Cut him some slack, Trev," my voice was sickly sweet, but Trevor believed me and that's all that counted. "This has to be torture for him. You're the better black sorcerer *and* you get the girl?"

A laughter that was not my own echoed out of my gut, and I had to look away from Logan.

"That's how it's meant to be, I suppose." Trevor loved every minute of it, and his own ego would never allow him to see the absurdity of his actions or the situation.

"Promise me one thing, Trevor," Logan started.

"What's that?" Trevor replied, squeezing me harder.

"That you'll take good care of her," he replied flatly.

"The best," Trevor replied.

I gave my best performance yet and placed my head on Trevor's shoulder. Logan quickly looked away, and I knew my act must've been far too believable.

"If we leave now, you might be able to catch the next train," I said, feeling Trevor's grasp relax around me a little.

"I'll help you get packed, and we'll get you there as quickly as possible," Trevor echoed.

Panic started to set in when I realized that Trevor assumed he was coming with us. Standing in a frozen state, I realized I needed a backup plan. And as if on cue, a friendly reminder of what I was capable of began to slither around my ankle.

The dark forest was closing in on me from all directions. I didn't want to be in the woods any longer. There was too much at stake and not enough places to escape to.

"Let's get back to the cottage. I'm sure Aunt Vieta's about to have a coronary," I said.

One way or the other, Logan and I were going to leave the cottage alone, and I felt confident that I would be able to do whatever it took to make that happen. I let Trevor grab my hand as we started back to the cottage, with Logan following behind us.

I had no idea what was about to take place, but it would change our future. That I was sure of.

CHAPTER 6

The blaze was dying out in the fireplace, causing a bit of smoke to pool in place of the flames. My aunt sat at the dining table with an expression that I was unable to read. Her eyes wore a blank stare. So much uncertainty had found its way into my psyche about everyone I loved. I really hoped my suspicions about her were wrong.

"Hey, Aunt Vieta. We're going to take Logan to the station." Her surprise gave me a little hope that my suspicions were wrong.

"I'm gonna go pack my bags," Logan replied solemnly. He was doing quite well at this charade.

"Trev, I hate to ask this but can you go get the firewood to keep the fire going? That's *your* job now," I flashed a huge grin at him, trying to imply so much more than I ever wanted. "It looks like

56

it's about out. When we get back from dropping Logan off, I don't want it to be an icebox in here."

"Uh, sure." Trevor looked uncertain as he glanced at me and then at Logan. He smoothed his blond hair back with his hands, seeming particularly uncomfortable.

"I'll help him pack. Not to worry." I assured him. "I know he wants to get out of here too."

Not wanting to lose the momentum we had created, I planted a quick peck on Trevor's cheek before ushering him out the door. I caught Aunt Vieta's stare as she was gauging my every move.

"What are you two up to?" My aunt stood up from the table, her smile wide.

"Nothing," I replied, not wanting to look at her.

"Just accepting the inevitable," Logan replied, before taking off to the bedroom. I could feel his smile hit me even though he was facing the other direction.

"Doubtful," My aunt smiled. "I'll help however I can."

Wanting with all of my heart to trust her, I shook my head and followed Logan down the hall without saying a word.

The front door clicked, and I turned to see my aunt no longer in the kitchen. I wasn't sure what she was up to but hoped her words could be trusted.

"Do you think I was overreacting about my aunt?" I whispered to Logan.

"I don't know. I honestly can't figure it out. Part of me thinks we're so paranoid that we're reading too much into things. The other half thinks, we'd be foolish if we welcomed her into our plans with open arms." Logan's lips tightened into a thin straight line once he finished, and I knew he felt the same turmoil as I did. What might that say about his mother?

"With everything I saw from Trevor, I feel like there is nobody that I can trust, aside from you," I replied, quickly stuffing my own items in the suitcases first. I needed to tell him about his mother but now wasn't the time. We needed to get out of here.

Logan opened up the chest of drawers tossing everything on top of mine in the bags.

"We don't need to worry about grabbing any of the herbs or oils. The quicker we get out of here the better. We can hit the apothecary shop in Seattle to grab whatever we might need," I said, feeling the beat of my heart begin to escalate.

"Sounds good." Logan finished emptying the last drawer and scanned the room quickly. "I think that's everything."

I nodded and he reached out for my hand.

"If not, oh well," I said, smiling.

"It's going to be fine. Things will get better," Logan murmured under his breath. "Now let's get out of here before he comes back in."

I strapped the two small bags on me while Logan grabbed the larger ones. I looked around the room one last time, wishing I wasn't leaving it in this manner. We had everything that we needed, but I felt like we were leaving so much behind.

"The spell book," I whispered. "It's in the cupboard."

I ran into the hall with the small bags banging into me with every movement. I made it to the kitchen in record time, which was where I had crammed the book in between the recipe books. I thought it was a good hiding place until I tried pulling it out, and it wouldn't budge.

"Logan, I can't get it out. Gaawd," I said in a hushed tone. My fingers kept slipping off the spine, and I couldn't finagle it out. Trevor would be back to the house any second. It didn't take that long to get to the woodpile. Granted, he had to split it, but it still wasn't that long of a task.

Logan dropped his bags and reached for the book, his fingers replacing mine.

"He's going to be here any second," I said completely panicked.

"I've got it." He slid his fingers in between the books that anchored the spell book in place, and he gave it one last pull. Out it came, along with all the other recipe books, papers falling in every direction, but I didn't care. It was out.

"Do you hear that?" Logan asked.

Freezing in place, I listened carefully but didn't hear a thing.

I shook my head.

"Come on," he said, grabbing my hand and pulling me to the front door.

"Oh, no," I replied. "Now I hear it. He's coming up along the side of the house."

Logan nodded, his eyes filling with anger.

"I've got my weapon at the ready," I whispered, not feeling the least bit guilty.

"We aren't going to need that." Logan squeezed my hand gently. "When I open the door, run to the car."

Logan gave me the keys, and all I could do was nod.

"As soon as you get in the passenger side, start the car. I'll be right behind you."

Logan flipped off the outside lights and opened the door, allowing me to slip by him into complete darkness.

My feet hit the porch running. Unable to see anything, I had my hands outreached feeling for anything that resembled a post so I wouldn't tumble down the stairs. I heard crunching alongside the house as Trevor's footsteps quickened. Trevor was almost to the front of the house. What was Logan waiting for? Why wasn't he behind me?

I unlocked the car remotely while in a full sprint, praying I would make it without interruption. Aunt Vieta's car was parked behind ours, but it looked like we'd be able to make it around when the time came.

"Triss," Trevor hollered. His voice sounded closer than I expected.

Opening the passenger front door, I collapsed into the seat, tossing my bags behind me while trying to catch a glimpse of what was happening outside. Logan was running toward the car, but it was difficult to make out much beyond that with no lights. I turned on the car and the headlights completely blinded Trevor, who was still holding the stack of wood. My aunt stood in front of him, blocking him from moving.

Once Trevor realized what was happening, he dropped the wood and shoved my aunt to the ground. The fury in his eyes was like nothing I'd seen from him. He ran as fast as he could toward Logan, and I let out a scream.

The snake around my ankle tightened a little, reminding me of that option. I wanted to take Trevor out so badly.

My fingers touched the cold plastic of the door handle as Logan neared the car. Trevor was only feet away. Now was my chance. I pushed the door open, allowing Logan to dive in.

"*Scalpere de Carne, SUPPURO Vulnerum,*" Trevor's voice boomed.

My knee inadvertently hit the window open button as I grabbed the bags from Logan, propelling them into the back seat. Logan slammed on the accelerator as he closed the door. The dust swirled from the tires only partially blocking the view as my aunt, back on her feet, pointed her wand at Trevor.

"She thinks she can run from me, but I'm her future. She's only delaying fate, not controlling it," Trevor yelled after us.

"Trevor, enough," my aunt commanded, as Trevor crumpled to the ground.

"Can you roll up the windows?" Logan asked, as our car bounced along the gravel driveway leading us away from the cottage. "I think your aunt has it handled, and the dust is awful."

The windows rolled up with a flick of the switch, and I flipped down the makeup mirror so I could get one last glimpse of what was occurring behind us.

"Trevor's still on the ground, and my aunt is doing some sort of chant," I replied in amazement. "Maybe I shouldn't have been so skeptical about her. Do you think she'll be okay?"

"She'll be fine," Logan replied, grimacing slightly. His voice was different somehow.

Flipping the mirror up, I glanced over at Logan's hand bracing himself on the console.

"What's wrong?" I asked. At the same time my eyes met a red stain growing on his white shirt. "Oh my god. What's going on? Where'd that come from?"

"It's the chant he threw on me. It's going to complicate things a little," Logan muttered, slowly letting air escape his lungs.

"What do you mean? Pull over!"

Logan shook his head. "No need. I know what's going on. We need to keep driving. We should be able to reverse it, but not until we get to Seattle."

"Should be? Reverse what *exactly*?" I was in full panic mode at this point.

"In so many words the spell translates to *Slice of Flesh, Fester of Wounds.*"

"Oh no. You've been cut? Pull over. I can help," I yelled completely aggravated at his lack of urgency for the situation.

"It's not like that," he paused. "It's not a normal wound. It'll keep growing until we can reverse it."

"No, no, no. Please pull over. We aren't going to make it in time. Seattle is hours away. Please, I know I can help." I cried.

My eyes were glued to his side where the crimson puddle on his shirt grew larger by the minute. Taking a deep breath in, I tried to control my emotions. This wasn't part of the plan. Logan's breathing was labored. His fist gripped the wheel in pain.

"You can't help. Not yet. Please just trust me on this." It was a struggle for him to get the words.

"You should have done it back to him," I said after several minutes of quiet. The anger inside of me was growing as I thought about all of the chances I'd given Trevor. I could have taken him out, and this would never have happened.

Logan released his right hand from the steering wheel and placed it on mine. It still maintained the strength that he always possessed, even under this amount of pain.

"I'm fighting every moment not to resort to black magic," Logan murmured. "They're targeting everyone I love, knowing that it will tempt me to go there. I might have to, but not over something like this." His eyes focused on the winding road ahead of us, with only the headlights from our car guiding the way. This was not a place anyone would want to have a car breakdown. There were no streetlights, only tall pine trees towering over the two-lane road.

"Pull over at the next pullout. I need to take it

from here," I said, pointing up ahead. "I think we're far enough away."

He nodded, and we sat in silence. I had so much I needed to tell him but now was not the time. I couldn't tell him about his mother. Not now. Not yet. The color of his skin grew paler with every passing second. His lips followed, turning to a shade of blue. He was losing a lot of blood and supposedly there was nothing I could do about it. I didn't buy it. I had to be able to help somehow.

The car bobbed over the large pieces of gravel and shale that had accumulated on the side of the road until he found a wide enough place to stop. I could only imagine how much going over the bumps hurt him.

He left the car running and got out. He couldn't stand up straight while he walked so he used the car to gain his bearings. My heart ached with every grimace and shallow breath that he took.

Meeting him around the back of the car, I slid my arm through his, helping to brace him as we made it to the passenger side.

"I thought I'd play the sympathy card so you'd stay with me," Logan joked, as he climbed in.

"Well, it's working." I smiled. "Can I see the wound so I know what I'm dealing with when we get there?"

Logan shook his head. "There's no point. A couple hours from now it will resemble nothing like it does now."

"This is not how I planned on showing off my

healing skills," I replied flatly.

Never a fan of racing down the mountain roads, hearing those words changed everything. I quickly closed the door and ran to the driver's seat, buckling myself in and peeling back onto the road. I couldn't let anything happen to Logan. Not now. Not ever.

The speedometer climbed to seventy miles per hour on a forty-five miles per hour road. With every turn, the gravitational pull anchored us to our seats, and I said many little prayers to any deity who would listen.

"Whoa, Triss. It's okay. I'm going to be fine," Logan said after suffering through thirty minutes of my newfound driving technique. "I don't want to die getting there."

We were about a quarter of the way off the mountain and the surroundings were getting a little more populous. Every now and then a small lit-up cabin would pop up amongst the trees or an old-fashioned gas station from another decade would appear. Seeing these little signs of civilization made me feel a little safer.

I knew Logan was trying to make the best of the situation, but I also knew, deep inside, whatever spell Trevor had cast at him could have grave consequences. I didn't ask. I didn't want to know. It was my task to get him off the mountain and to try my best to save him before it was too late.

Logan coughed, interrupting my stirrings. I glanced over and saw the dullness spread through his blue eyes. I slipped my hand off the wheel and slid it onto his, which was ice-cold.

"You're freezing," I whispered, trying to choke back the fear.

"One of the many side effects of a wound like this," he teased, but the effort made him cough again.

"I'm not going to let anything happen to you. I promise," I said, squeezing his hand.

"Don't make promises you might not be able to keep."

His words shocked me into another world. A silent one where I refused to argue or believe what he was trying to tell me. I didn't have the strength to offer a rebuttal, and he certainly didn't either.

I slid my now sticky hand from his so that I could up my speed even more and feel slightly safer doing it. His blood began drying on my fingers and palm, tightening my skin like someone had slathered egg whites on them.

We'd managed to cover another hour of ground in thirty minutes, and we were so close to Seattle now — so close to life. The entire bottom half of his shirt was red. I didn't want to think what that could mean, but I prayed my suspicions were wrong about his wound.

Unable to hold in my fear any longer I blurted, "Hold on. Please, hold on."

Logan was silent. Only his breathing signaled that he was still alive. My mind started going through all the different healing herbs and spells that might work in this situation. If he became unable to tell me what I would need to do to reverse this then I'd have to figure something out on my own. Soon I'd have to hop off the freeway and begin battling the Seattle streetlights and intersections. Thankfully it was the middle of the night so traffic should be pretty sparse.

"We're almost there, baby," I whispered. "Almost there."

"You can't trust your aunt," he mumbled, startling me. "My mom might be suspect too. Jenny and Angela might be helpful or at least a good place to hide in Colorado."

"Stop it," I replied.

"Your father will stop at nothing until he gets what he wants. You've got to figure out what that is. It's not just you he covets."

"Knock it off, Logan. You aren't going anywhere. Quit acting like you've got to tell me everything now. Save your energy. If anything, tell me what to do to reverse this," I replied.

"I love you, Triss. Always have and always will," Logan replied softly as he moved his hand to my leg.

His breathing quieted. My eyes filled with tears as I turned the car onto the Seattle exit. I would not let it end this way.

CHAPTER 7

I slid the car up to the curb in front of my aunt's apothecary shop with a hard stop. Logan's breath was almost inaudible as I jumped out of the car. I ran to the shop door, unlocked it quickly and propped it open while trying to figure out how I would get Logan inside. I couldn't drag him, but I couldn't lift him either.

Sliding my arm under his back, I resisted the urge to raise his shirt to peek at the injury. That would only delay getting him inside. I would see it soon enough.

A strength I didn't know I possessed ran through my veins as I attempted to lift him from the car. Wrapping his arm around my neck, I heaved him partially onto my back as we moved toward the shop. His breathing was shallow, but it was still there. I felt one step closer to getting him back. I only wished he would open his eyes — his beautiful eyes. Forcing back my tears and doubts, I held onto his arm as we made our way to the concrete sidewalk.

We were only about ten feet from inside the store yet every step felt like a struggle with this amount of weight perched on me. Logan's legs would sometimes take a step and other times only drag, but we would make it. We had no choice.

Making it to the doorway, I scanned where to place him on the floor when it hit me. Several large workbenches, where my aunt, mom, and I often mixed tinctures and oils, seemed like the perfect option. Instead of every step feeling like a struggle, it felt like a victory.

"Almost there," I whispered not sure if he would even hear me.

The overwhelming smell of whatever my aunt was working on last filled the air. It was an odd mixture of sweetness. It wasn't a combination I was familiar with.

Finally landing on the last table, I turned my body to gently wriggle out from under Logan. Trying to work as fast as I could without causing further pain, I climbed on the tabletop, and began hauling him onto the planked surface.

"Come on, baby. We've got this."

His eyes were closed, skin pale, and shirt completely saturated with a deep crimson as I struggled to pull him into place.

"Now about that reversal spell…" I said quietly, not expecting an answer, but praying for a miracle.

I wasn't sure if I should start trying to heal the

slice on his skin or the possible infection that the spell referred to, but I knew I wouldn't be able to figure anything out until I raised his shirt to assess the injury. I had no idea what to expect, but I was usually pretty capable around people's injuries. At least that's what I told myself.

I ran behind the counter and grabbed a whole bunch of towels. Folding up one, I placed it under his head to act as a pillow and threw the others next to me. I wanted Logan to know everything I was doing, whether or not he could hear me.

"Okay," I whispered, "I'm going to start unbuttoning your shirt. I'm starting from the top and will work my way down."

He remained lifeless until my finger gently glided along his collarbone. A slight twitch of his mouth signaled life.

Please let that be a sign.

Not able to remain calm any longer, I ripped his shirt open, horrified at what I saw. It was alive — active. The room started spinning, and I braced myself. My legs began to buckle slightly, so I looked away trying to refocus my attention. I couldn't associate the laceration with Logan. I needed to focus on healing the wounds, not the person. The injury could be on anyone. I had to separate the two; otherwise I'd never make it through.

The strength returned to both my body and mind. I looked down at his injury to gauge what might be happening. Figure out how it was forming.

From the look of the slice, the initial insertion

point was where the infection began so the older the cut, the more likely the infection's core.

The positive side of that observation, if there could be one, was that the bleeding tended to stop wherever the infection had started. Infection points were signaled by tiny red veins darting under the surface of the skin, allowing me to figure out how the cut was spreading. As far as I could tell, the flesh wound broke off into two more directions and that was where the blood continued to escape. I couldn't believe this was Logan I was staring at.

"We're going to get through this," I replied.

I tried not to look at Logan's face. "First we're going to purify your blood. I'm going to grab some sarsaparilla bark, senna leaves, and grape root. I'll boil it quickly and apply it to the oldest part of your wound."

Talking to him helped me feel not so alone.

"Once we get you conscious again, I'll feed you lots of hoppy beer. See how crazy I can get you while I continue to purify your blood," I hoped my fake sense of reality would help bring him calmness. Who was I kidding? I needed it to bring me calmness. "Hops actually have a lot of good attributes. When you get better we've got to find time for you to learn."

My stomach started twisting in knots at the thought of never getting to teach him healing or —I couldn't go there. I needed to stay on task.

Going to the far shelves, I realized whatever my aunt had cooked up last involved the main ingredients I needed, hence the sweet smell of root beer and grapes. The tincture was already on the shelf. How could that be? Not that I would have faith in her version— I needed to cook up my own batch— but why would she have brewed that particular tincture? Remembering Logan's words about not trusting my aunt, I quickly grabbed the raw ingredients and headed to the stove, pouring everything into the pot.

While the mixture heated, I continued onto the next compress for the other part of his wound. This wasn't reversing the spell, but at least it might make his body begin to fight the infection so he'd regain consciousness, and we could go from there.

"I've got what I need now," I hollered back to Logan. As I grabbed the compresses and white pine and tea tree oils, I headed back to my patient. The mixture on the stove was beginning to boil, releasing more of the familiar scent of root beer and grape. I couldn't worry about my aunt's overwhelming ability to provide the right ingredients at the right times just yet.

"This is going to sting a bit," I told Logan, sprinkling the white pine oil on the freshest part of his cut.

He gave no reaction — not even a grimace.

"You can't tell me that doesn't hurt," I teased him. "You don't have to act this tough."

Instead of crying like I wanted to, I grabbed the compress and began dabbing away the dried blood and replacing it with tea tree oil. The pungent smell started to arouse a little movement from Logan. His brows furrowed slightly and excitement filled me. I wiped quicker and placed the open container of the liquid by his head, hoping it would add the extra oomph he needed.

"Your blood and mind will be so pure after this episode, I won't know what to do with you," I whispered, but my voice caught, and I pushed down the tears that threatened to make an appearance.

Grabbing the salve made from Red Oak bark, I began smearing it on his wound. Not that I was trying to hurt him, but I wanted some sort of sign as I applied the pressure that he was still with me. I wasn't getting one. The fear that the infection was too rampant, and the blood loss too severe, frightened me to an almost paralyzed state. I couldn't allow myself the luxury of a meltdown.

My work stopped the infection, at least temporarily, from creeping up to the newly produced openings, which only created a small amount of gratification. I needed him to wake up. We needed to purge this spell. That's the only thing that would completely stop it.

The mixture on the stove was ready to use. The entire shop smelled like a sickening root beer float. I placed the pot on the next table over and shoved the gauze compresses into the pot. Watching the steam rise worried me a little, but I wanted to shock him. Using tongs, I grabbed the long pieces of white material out of the liquid and placed them on top of Logan's abdomen. His back arched up, and his eyes flashed open in agony as the heat dove and swirled deep into his abdomen.

"Please tell me how to be brave like you, Logan," I whispered.

He hollered in agony, but at least he hollered. He grabbed my hand and wouldn't release it.

"I love you, Logan. Please stay with me. Tell me how to reverse the spell," I begged. "I don't know how much time we have left."

Holding onto his fingers tightly with one hand, I tried comforting him with my other. Surprised by how much dried blood managed to cover my hand and arm, I quickly hid it from him to not cause more alarm.

His breathing was erratic, but no longer shallow. There was a subtle strength stirring inside him. A moan escaped deep from within as his body began to slowly relax back down to the table.

"Do you think you might be able to drink a sip of water? Valerian might help with some of the pain," I said.

He shook his head. The muscles in his neck completely strained.

Letting go of my hand, he turned toward me and placed his palm on the tattoo that was almost completely hidden by the mess his wound created.

"Is this part of it?" I asked. "The spell?"

He nodded while attempting to sit up.

"Whoa, let me help."

"I got it," he replied as he inched his way up slowly.

Words! He spoke! Hearing his voice sent a shock wave through my system as it hit me that only minutes before there was part of me that wasn't sure I would ever hear his beautiful voice again.

"I was so worried—."

"We aren't in the clear yet," he mumbled, his voice almost hoarse.

"You don't want anything for the pain?" I asked.

"I need a clear head for this. We need to stop him. Make him unconscious."

Even though it felt like I just resurrected the dead, I was quickly reminded of how dire our situation was by watching Logan's somber expression. We clearly weren't out of the woods.

"This right here," he said pointing at the artwork permanently embedded on his skin, "links me to your father. His organization. And as you know, Trevor's part of that organization."

He avoided looking at me and continued.

"It's also what enabled Trevor to throw this kind of spell on me so quickly. I was hopeful he wasn't capable, but I guessed wrong." His words were filled with exhaustion and pain.

I nodded waiting for him to proceed.

"I can't get rid of it, and I really don't want to. It has some very helpful attributes…"

"Logan, I love you. I do, but can we just get to how to reverse this? I don't know how much time we've bought." I placed my hand on his, searching his eyes for the sparkle I was so used to seeing, but only dullness was returned.

"Do you have a small knife of some sort?"

Nodding, I ran to the drawer where we kept all of our knives for preparing the herbs. Grabbing the smallest one, I poured a vinegar disinfectant over the blade while trying not to worry about what Logan wanted me to do with it. I had an idea, but hoped I was wrong.

"Okay. Got it," I said, standing in front of him.

"When I recite the spell, there should be a part of the tattoo that glows. When that happens, I need you to insert the tip of the knife into that portion. Not deep, just into the flesh."

A lump formed in the back of my throat. I wanted to swallow but couldn't. I was horrified at the thought of having to dig into his skin and couldn't begin to understand why this would help. Maybe I should've let him continue explaining.

"What will this do?" I asked, hoping he would look at me.

"It should stop the person who cursed me."

"Trevor," I stated.

He nodded, "We are all bound together whether I want to be or not."

I wanted to learn more but didn't have the luxury of time to find out.

"I'm ready when you are," I whispered. "You're sure it will glow?"

"Hundred percent," he replied, attempting to smile. "You've got this."

I'm glad he had faith in this process because I sure didn't. I took a deep breath and stared at the circle of darkness that swirled from quadrant to quadrant with one symbol after the other that I didn't recognize while I waited for his words to deliver the spell.

Quietness filled our space. The air was heavy with anticipation. I was about to look up when his words began.

"*Nota Liberaret Ancillam Inveniret, qui Prodit Mendacium ante Omnes.*"

Fixating on his tattoo, I began to get nervous when nothing happened. Afraid I might miss something, my eyes stayed glued to his abdomen.

After a few moments of seeing only bare skin, a faint light began to radiate from a tiny portion of his tattoo. The area was no bigger than a pinhead, but it was large enough for me to complete the instructed task.

I placed the blade against his abdomen, barely allowing the tip to enter into the ray of light that was guiding me. He'd been through so much agony in the last few hours. I didn't want to make things worse, but I kept promising myself that this would end it all. The tip went in a little deeper and the light began to spread. Not knowing what to expect, I looked up at Logan who nodded his head, and he began again.

"*Partum a Somnis Tantum Possum Perturbare.*"

The apothecary shop filled with a brilliant light that poured out of Logan's wound. He tipped his head back causing the light to disperse in all directions. Mesmerized by the beautiful glow that was canvasing the entire shop, I accidentally let go of the knife. Watching it tumble to the floor, I began to hyperventilate as worry rushed through me that I might have interrupted the process. How could I be so careless?

"It's okay. The process is in full swing now," Logan whispered. Recognizing my panic, he softly touched my hand that was frozen mid-air. Moments earlier he was near death, and now he was taking care of me. Unbelievable.

The muscles along his jaw were completely strained, but his expression no longer seemed filled with agony. He tipped his head back, took a deep breath in, and a smile spread along his lips as the light was sucked back into wherever it had come from. The tension inside me began to quickly dissipate as I realized that he was beating the curse. He was really going to be okay.

Logan let out a groan that stopped my internal victory dance. I thought the worst was over. He squeezed my hand, slowly pulling me to him, but I was afraid I'd hurt him. He leaned forward and smiled, touching my chin with his thumb sending a current of happiness through me. His reaction wasn't for the reason I feared.

Unable to hide my smile, I looked into blue eyes that were full of the life I'd come to expect from him, and as mischievous as always.

"Oh, my god," I whispered, sliding my arms around his waist. "It's a miracle."

"No, it's magic," he replied coyly, bringing me into his embrace.

"Are you going to be okay?" I asked, resting my head on his chest.

"Thanks to you," he replied. "But I think it's time I quit underestimating Trevor."

"You think?" I laughed, feeling Logan's energy returning to its normal state.

"We should probably grab what we need and get out of here," he replied, his arms not letting go even though his words said something else.

I nodded and felt the tears beginning again.

"I thought you'd slipped away," I whispered. "And there's so much I've wanted to tell you."

"Well, I think we've got plenty of time for that now. It's a long trip to New York."

"We need to stop in Illinois first," I said.

"Why's that?" His embrace loosened slightly.

"I'm worried about your mom. I think she's in danger."

CHAPTER 8

He turned the car down a narrow street where rows of trees created a canopy over the road. We had finally made it to Illinois.

"Are we close?" I asked, in awe of the sprawling homes that lined the street.

"Yeah...a little farther." His voice was tense.

We had driven over two thousand miles and the entire time we were unable to reach his mom. Between the images that Trevor's mind spilled into mine, and my mom's own disappearance, neither of us ran on much hope.

"Maybe she didn't charge her phone," I offered, attempting to believe my own words.

"Thanks for trying," Logan replied, placing his hand on my knee. The familiar tingle ran through me, and I scolded myself.

"We'll find out soon enough," he replied.

The homes began to decrease in size but only

slightly. Our home in Seattle was amazing — awesome really, but I think four of them would fit in one of these.

"That street sign we passed didn't say Logan Loop, did it?"

Looking somewhat embarrassed, he gripped the steering wheel a little tighter.

"I'm guessing we're in your neighborhood now," I continued.

"My mom couldn't resist moving to this street for obvious reasons."

"You left this to come out to Seattle for college?" I turned in the seat to look at him, giving him my best skeptical expression.

"I left this to come out to Seattle for *you.*" He shrugged and wore a crooked smile. "I kinda thought we'd established that." He raised his right eyebrow, and a full smile spread across his lips.

"Well, I didn't think you'd be leaving *this* behind." I smiled, waving my hand at everything I was seeing through the windows.

"That's a little superficial." His laughter filled the car. It was the first time since we left Seattle that his wonderful melody reached my soul. It was nice to hear it again.

"I'm only human," I replied, trying to hide my smile. "And this is pretty impressive."

Who was I kidding? This actually frightened me a little. First, cleaning it would be horrible. Second, I wouldn't want to be home alone in it. It's too big. Third, well I guess that was it. I'd probably adapt pretty quickly.

Unaware of the smile that had planted itself on my lips, Logan touched my chin softly to interrupt my daydreaming episode.

"Too bad I'm not the one who owns it." He slowed the car down as we approached a beautiful stone home.

"Is that a guest house?" I asked, spotting a miniature replica of the grey house we were now parked in front of.

"Yeah. That's actually where I stayed the last year or so of high school," he said, turning off the car.

Wow, that's some freedom to have in high school.

It's funny. I knew Logan's father sold his business right before he passed away, but I never thought it was a business that would provide something like this.

"It's not looking promising," Logan replied, snapping me back to the task at hand. "She rarely uses the garage unless she's away, and her SUV's not in the drive."

He got out of the car and walked to the mammoth wooden door that looked more like it belonged on a castle than a house in a Chicago suburb. Well, maybe *house* was an understatement.

Not sure whether I should give him space or not, I slowly followed behind hoping the situation would direct me. I freed the snake from the box in the backseat and let out a sigh as I prepared for the inevitable. My heart already knew the answer as he unlocked the door and pushed it open. Peeking from behind, I saw the same thing as he did — nothing.

"Hey, mom?" Logan's voice bounced off the entry's slate floor.

I followed behind him as we entered the home, and I shut the front door. We both knew she wasn't here. It didn't need to be said.

"I'm so sorry," I whispered, sliding my arms around his waist. He pulled me into him, and I rested my head against his shoulder.

"It never occurred to me that she could be a target."

"My father seems to have an uncanny ability to persuade people to do what he wants though," I stopped myself from continuing. Logan didn't need to hear anything else. We were both well aware of my father's abilities. I was finally starting to understand what we were dealing with, not who. Pure evil.

"So your mom wanted my mom to come visit or live?" he asked, dissecting everything I had told him from Trevor's images. I wished I had more answers for him.

"It was strange. It's like he's got this compound where people are coming and hanging out. I don't get it. But from what I could tell from Trevor's memories, my mom wanted her there for a while. It's really creepy what's going on at his compound. He had all of these people, who seemed to be completely void of personality, pouncing on every word my father uttered."

"Like a cult?" Logan's eyes narrowed, as he

ushered me through the gigantic foyer.

I nodded my head.

"Yeah, like that," I sighed, walking down the endless hallway wondering where I was actually heading. My thought that this house was smaller than the others on the street was seriously mistaken.

Logan's touch gently steered me to the right as the hallway came to an end, but I didn't move forward. I couldn't. The view was too breathtaking. In front of me was a wall of windows overlooking a shimmering carpet of water. Lake Michigan was this home's masterpiece. The room framing this view was no less sensational. It was the size of our cottage, and this was only one room in the house.

There were beautiful sea-blue drapes falling in between each of the floor-to-ceiling windows. The walls were canvased in a velvety ivory with nautical sconces hung every few feet. There were several sets of overstuffed chenille couches placed in their own seating arrangements. It was quite astounding. I didn't want to act impressed, but it was hard not to be.

"So what was your family's business again?" I asked, turning to face Logan. "I thought it was fabric or something."

"Textiles," he replied, placing his hands on my shoulders.

I squinted at him as I tried gauge what to say or do. This wasn't what I expected — not that it changed anything. But I was surprised I didn't know.

"Huh. So that's why you have such nice décor." I wrinkled my nose at him as I thought about this new development.

"Oh, Triss. One of the many reasons I love you," he replied, gently tapping the end of my nose, reminding me to relax.

"Let me give you a quick tour, and we can figure out what we want to do next. Since they're both together in Saranac Lake maybe it'll make it easier."

I glanced quickly at the room that I'd become quite fond of as he led me to the next space over, which was just as lovely and also offered a grand view of the lake.

"Every room outdoes the last, I see," I replied, admiring the walls covered in cherry wood.

"This is where I hung out most," Logan said, gesturing at the large flat screen tucked in between bookshelves. The weathered leather couches fit the space. It did seem more masculine than the other room. I could see Logan hanging out here.

As I followed Logan from room to room, all seemingly more spectacular than the last, I started to get restless. It felt like the house was never ending. I was following him down the stairs when the doorbell rang, startling me out of my euphoria of getting to see where Logan called home.

"Do you get visitors often?" I asked.

"Nope." Logan slipped by me on the stairs, and I followed closely behind. It was probably a harmless salesman or something. Following him for what seemed like forever, we finally made it to the foyer.

"They've probably already left, whoever they were. That was a hike," I replied, only half joking.

He swung the door open to have a girl, about my age, standing with her hands on her hips looking very aggravated. She didn't seem to notice me at first. Her eyes were locked on Logan's, and a smile started to appear. Her light brown hair was pulled up in a sleek ponytail, and she was dressed in a tight fitting pale lavender dress. It seemed pretty over the top but maybe that's how people our age dressed in neighborhoods like this, as opposed to my jeans and a hoodie.

She held out both arms readying for an embrace when Logan stepped back from her and grabbed me instead.

"Did you need something, Caitlin? My mom's not home right now," Logan's tone was harsh and dismissive. I was secretly thrilled.

"So you're the one who stole Logan's heart," Caitlin said. She was now standing with her arms crossed, glaring at me on the front porch.

"Guess so." I nodded, glancing at Logan who was beaming.

"She's the one," Logan said, wrapping his arm around me tighter, infuriating Caitlin even more.

Unable to resist the territorial urges that were whipping through me, I stood on my toes and kissed Logan's cheek.

"No line of girls, huh?" I whispered into his ear.

Logan's laughter irritated the girl, and I enjoyed every second of it.

"Did you drop by to say hi or what's up?" Logan asked.

Caitlin's glare was etching a place in my mind while I tried to figure out who she was... what her place was. She certainly wasn't part of the welcoming committee. Her eyes held something familiar in them.

I gripped Logan tighter.

"I dropped by to deliver a message, but it seems that you might be too busy. I'll catch you later," Caitlin said, spinning around to leave.

"Don't be your dramatic self. Just spit it out," Logan snapped. I'd never seen him this annoyed before. There had to be some sort of history between these two.

She turned back toward us with a wicked grin and reached into her bag, searching around for something. Logan stepped in front of me like he was trying to shield me from some imaginary force.

"Where do you know Caitlin from?" I asked, while she still fumbled around in her purse.

"The coven and school." His voice was only moderately softer because he was talking to me.

"Huh."

"Here it is," Caitlin said, handing me a small envelope.

"Whoa," Logan said. "I've got that."

Caitlin took it back and shook her head.

"Nope. I was told I had to give it to the girl you were so fond of, Logan." She pretended like she was stuffing it back in her bag.

"From who?" I asked, feeling something familiar about her.

"Your father," she replied, slipping the envelope into my hand. Her eyes held the same vacant stare that I had seen from my father's followers.

"You know my father?"

"Some of us have been following him for quite a while," she said, winking at Logan.

I felt sick. How did I manage to stay in such a wonderful bubble through the years?

"Thanks, Caitlin," Logan said, not waiting for a response as he slammed the gigantic wooden door.

Shoving my insecurities aside, I stared at the blank envelope unsure I wanted to open it.

"Do you really think it's from my father?" I asked, my heart beating too quickly for its own good.

"Want me to open it?" he asked.

I shook my head and started tearing into it. A note was sprawled on the white cardstock inside, and I realized it was an invitation – one that I never wanted.

My dearest Triss:

You've grown into a beautiful young woman. I'm very proud of you. With your mom by my side, it would be wonderful to be a complete family again. I've got ambitious plans that include you. Your talents can't be ignored any longer, and your mother and I would love to help you explore your gifts.

Your father,

Nicholas

"I can't believe this," I whispered, shoving the note at Logan. "Does he really think this note will make things all better?"

"I don't think so," Logan said. "He's taunting you. He knows this won't do anything."

Logan set the note on the table, bringing me into his arms.

"You don't have to hold the anger in," Logan whispered.

"I'm really sorry you got dragged into this mess. I'm so sorry about your mom." The anger turned to tears. The steady stream of wetness began its parade, and I didn't even try to stop it.

"This isn't your fault. I got myself involved years ago. Don't put this on your shoulders," Logan assured me. "We'll get our families back."

"I want to do more than that. I want to destroy my father and whatever he thinks he's creating."

One of the reasons I loved Logan was that he knew exactly what to do in this situation, which was nothing. I just needed to be held.

"I thought I knew my place in the world. Everything seemed so easy and obvious. Spend a few months carefree before starting college, get a degree in herbal science or something from Bastyr, and continue working at my families' businesses. So simple and harmless." I took a deep breath.

"I never expected this either." Logan shook his head.

"When you were injured, you mentioned that I

KARICE BOLTON

shouldn't trust my aunt. Was that your delirium speaking or did you figure something out?" I stepped back from Logan, rubbing the dampness from my eyes. I couldn't let the weakness take over.

"Nothing concrete. Probably the same observations as you," he replied, pulling me toward the back of the house.

The couches beckoned me, and I slumped onto the nearest one. Logan sat next to me. It was nice — normal almost. It was too bad it couldn't really be like this. There was nothing carefree about what we were facing.

The evening had settled in, replacing the beautiful lake with an eerie darkness. Not the atmosphere I really wanted at the moment.

"I find it odd that my father took my mom and your mother, but not my aunt. My mom and aunt were so close," I began.

"Like he already had her? Almost like your father let her remain on the outside working for him," Logan offered. He leaned forward on the couch, resting his forehead in his palms.

I nodded. The quietness of our surroundings allowed me to think about my aunt. Truly analyze her actions.

"She was so quick to trust the coven when my mom disappeared. She could have stopped the memorial, but she accepted its speed. If my aunt was in contact with my father, following his plans, that would make the most sense. It's not that my father was all-knowing, it's that he's got an informant." The anger was mounting inside.

"It does make more sense. From the very beginning, actually," Logan said.

I closed my eyes, letting my mind wander back to everything that had happened to us since my mom's disappearance. Whenever I was going to be somewhere, she knew. *The beach, the florist shop, the cottage — how could I be so naïve?*

"How could she do this to her own sister?" I asked letting the realization settle over me. "And for how long? Was everything one big charade?"

"It all fits though, doesn't it?" Logan's voice was low, hiding the anger that I too felt.

"It does," I paused. "She was the only one who knew I went to the florist shop after the memorial. She never answered —"

"You think she sent the spirit after you too?" he interrupted, his eyes scanning mine with a mixture of relief and worry.

"Possibly. The library incident even! I bet she alerted them that we were there," I replied.

"That's a logical reason for Trevor finding the cottage." Logan grabbed my hand.

"And since she hadn't heard from Trevor since his attempted attack, she probably came to check on everything at the cottage." I looked at Logan and saw the same emotion I felt — relief. My father wasn't *that* capable. He had help.

"Well, since everyone knows we're here, I guess we need to be extra careful," I said, turning my attention to the darkness outside. "Right now, we are on stage for the world to see. Let's close up the curtains. It'll make me feel better at least."

Logan hopped up and rather than move toward the curtains, he went behind us and flipped a switch.

"Nice," I said, watching the drapes close automatically. "I should have known."

Logan's lip turned up slightly. He looked good — really good. My gaze dropped to the floor not wanting to tempt myself any more. Oh, how I wanted to be a normal eighteen year old with nothing to worry about except a college exam and what to wear on a date. Instead, I was plagued with bringing home a mother who didn't want to be found and the prospect of a father willing to unleash dark sorcery on his own daughter. Welcome to adulthood, Triss.

"Seems like you're getting wrapped up in your Triss world again," Logan said softly.

I blinked up at him in confusion. How did he always know when I went to that other part of my mind? He was one of the few people who could get me out of the place of worry I trapped myself in.

"You know, I never did show you the guest house." He held out his hand.

"You mean guest house turned Logan house," I said, allowing him to pull me to my feet. "Is it safe to go out there at night? I'm not sure I actually want to go outside. Between being paranoid about family members and unwanted visitors..."

"My father had an underground hallway built beneath the driveway. He didn't want guests to have to go outside to get there."

"Of course he did," I replied. "Lead the way."

"Very few people have actually seen this place." His eyes mischievous, lifting the gravity of the situation.

"I'd hope that's the case," I scolded him.

Hopefully Caitlin wasn't one of the people who set foot in his home away from home. The idea of her perfectly-coifed self wandering around here irritated me beyond belief. I squinted my eyes at Logan, trying to determine how she actually did play out in his life. Did I want to know? Why was I being so childish? It's not like he didn't have a life out here.

"I can't get over my aunt. My mom trusted her with everything she had to give. It's hard to wrap my mind around it. I hope we're wrong."

"It does explain a lot of things." He tugged on my hand directing me down the hall. And then it spilled out before I could stop it. So much for being mature.

"So how well did you know Caitlin?"

Catching him off guard, I saw a flash of remorse in his eyes before he turned away.

That was not the reaction I expected.

CHAPTER 9

Following Logan through the hallway, it was easy to forget that it was underground. It wasn't, however, easy to forget that Caitlin might have been on this *same* walk with him. I was trying desperately to be an adult here, but it was difficult. As ridiculous as it may seem, I wanted to believe that I was his first love. I liked the little story I had created in my head about him and his feelings for me. Granted, he'd placed it there, but I believed it.

"You're certainly quiet." Logan stopped and turned around to look at me. "It's probably not what you're thinking."

I looked up at him wondering what he thought I was thinking because I wasn't even sure myself.

"Let's keep moving. It kind of creeps me out to stop in the middle here." I lied.

"Okay," he nodded. Looking pained in his

expression, he pressed forward but then came to an abrupt halt resulting in me almost crashing into him.

The door was only a few feet away, and I was anxious to see where Logan called home before coming out to Seattle. I would shove all of these ridiculous thoughts about Caitlin out of my mind. It didn't matter. He was here with me now.

"You know what?" Logan startled me. His was voice gruff. "I'm not gonna move until you tell me what's up. Remember the whole communication thing we promised each other?"

I began fidgeting and shoved my hands in my pockets to stop myself from feeling so ridiculous. I could see the frustration playing out on Logan's face. I better say something. Oh my God, the embarrassment my paranoia was going to land me in was going to be brutal. This was the least of our problems, and I was bringing it to the forefront.

"Triss?" he asked softly.

Here it goes. *Nothing like acting like the jealous type.*

"There seemed to be something between you and Caitlin, and I can't truly expect you to have waited for me. It sounded nice when you implied that, and I liked the idea of it and all, but I know it's not realistic." I smiled at him. "I can't believe I'm even letting it bother me, but... it is. I'd rather know. I'm nosy like that." I gave my best effort at trying to downplay what I was feeling inside, which was a tormented jealousy that I was completely bewildered with.

Bracing myself for an answer I probably didn't want to hear, I impatiently waited for his response. The anticipation continued to build inside of me, but he gave no sign of which way his words were going to lead. He stood there watching me, looking completely bemused. Reluctantly, I glanced at one of the paintings hanging on the wall to avoid looking into Logan's eyes any longer.

Still not saying a word, Logan turned back toward the door and unlocked it, opening it wide for us to enter.

"After you," he finally replied, escorting me through.

The staircase looked quite steep, and I wasn't exactly thrilled about going up it first, but it seemed like he wasn't going to answer me until we got inside. I started up the stairs, but he closed the door behind us and locked it, making the small area pitch black. There was no way I was going to continue going up the steps. I'd certainly trip over my own feet.

"Lights, please?" I squeaked out.

I knew he was near. He had to be. This area was so confined he was only an arm's reach in any direction.

"Nope," he said softly from behind me.

"Seriously, Logan. This isn't funny." My heart started racing, but not because I was afraid. "I'm not that coordinated."

I knew he moved closer. I could feel the heat of his body and the breeze from his movements gracing my skin. The continued silence was bristling a different type of activity, preparing for something larger. Something I really wanted.

He slid his finger along the waistband of my jeans, and I pulled away slightly in protest for extra effect.

"Everything I've told you is the truth," Logan whispered. "Remember, I'm the one who left this big house for you." I could hear the smile in his voice.

"There was something there when she was talking. I could tell that—"

He moved up on the stairs to meet me. I could only see his shadow.

"You're right. There was something there," he interrupted. His lips were so close to mine. "That *something* can only be summed up as hate now."

I wasn't going to allow him to distract me from getting the answers I wanted.

"Hate now... but what about before?" I asked frustrated at his cryptic technique.

"Before the deceit and betrayal?" his words were icy.

"That's a little melodramatic," I said, letting his hands trace around my waist. There were some emotions impossible to turn off.

"Not really for what she did," he dropped his hands. "Seriously want to know huh?"

I nodded hoping my desire to learn every detail wouldn't ruin what I hoped could be our future.

We only shared silence for a few moments, not words. My eyes attempted to adjust to the darkness. I wanted to see what his eyes would tell me. He bit his lip as he deliberated — thinking but not speaking.

The silence was excruciating. I prepared myself for him to tell me all sorts of crushing things. That they had been together, and that he had loved her. That she had broken his heart, or she had chased him out of Illinois to Seattle. I readied myself for anything but what he was about to tell me.

"She's the one who introduced me to your father's practices," he sighed, "in a roundabout way."

"I thought you found him on your own," I replied, feeling faint and really wishing the lights were on for this discussion. I needed to find the wall to support myself. Instead, I found Logan to lean on.

"I don't know what to think any longer. I kind of did. She became my support system after my father's death," he started.

My fault. Completely my fault. His words hit my heart like a jackhammer. My insides churned and the hate toward her began multiplying, but not before the insurmountable guilt came crashing down on me. I hadn't been there for him. What did I expect? He had to find support somewhere.

"I'm so sorry, Logan," I whispered.

"There's nothing for you to apologize about," he continued. "It's my own fault. In hindsight, I can see it all was a setup. She probably didn't even completely realize it. But it has your father written all over it. Especially seeing things unfold now."

"Don't stick up for her," I replied, surprised at my own reaction.

"Believe me, I'm not. I can't stand her. I just —
"

"I get it. It's like the Trevor thing." I rolled my eyes for only the darkness to see.

"If I had been there for you this never would have happened," I whispered.

"We were both so young. Don't even go there." His finger slid along my cheek. "She only confirmed how wonderful you are."

"Yeah, I'm sure that's what was going on," I laughed.

He shrugged. "You can accept that this is the truth or not."

"So she was there for you and I wasn't, yet you have feelings for me and not her? I look like the real prize here. It's hard for me to think that you never had feelings for her. I mean, I don't blame you if you did. I would understand."

"Nothing happened between us, Triss. I'm not going to continue pleading my innocence to you. But there never was anything. She tried, but I never went there. Ever. There's not going to be any surprises that you find out about either. No spells to dig anything up."

The last words dug deeper than they were probably intended.

"I'm sorry. That wasn't nice," he replied, trying to hide his laughter. "Guess I'm not quite over it either."

"Well. Good. Then we can both just stand here

miserable and jealous of things that never happened."

"I've got a better idea," Logan said, flipping the light on at long last.

The comfort his words brought infused my heart, and I could no longer let myself worry about a past that I wasn't included in purely by my own doing.

He grabbed my hand and slid by me on the stairs, pulling me up to the top. I let myself enjoy what he was insinuating regardless of what was in store. We both were carrying a heavy burden, but it was as if neither of us could bear to think about it any longer.

He unlocked the door to his makeshift apartment, and I pushed the door open amazed at what I saw.

"Really roughing it out here," I giggled, taking in the beautiful slate floor that was encircling me. "You had your own kitchen?"

"I didn't use it much."

"Huh. I had no idea that Ellsy would let you get away with this," I said, narrowing my eyes at him. "Seems suspicious."

"I think she was happy that I was out of the house, to be honest. She sensed a change in me."

"When you were studying the dark arts?"

He nodded. "After my dad died, I really didn't see eye to eye with most of what my mom was studying. She was trying to find answers in the goodness of our beliefs, and I refused to see the positives. I tried to hide my views, and I think I did a pretty good job of it, but anyway this seemed like the best option to avoid any potential conflict."

"I can't believe my mom didn't tell me," I replied.

"I doubt my mom told her. She wasn't proud of it. I think she felt like a failure." His words were riddled with guilt..

"My mom would never think that about your mom."

"All your mom ever did was brag about you, so I'm sure there wasn't really a moment where my mom would want to divulge that info."

"So that's where you got all of your misinformation about me. I'll have to thank my mom for that."

Promise flickered in Logan's eyes as his arms wrapped around me.

"She did a pretty good job of convincing me of your perfection," he teased. "Now let's move on to the rest of the place."

"I have to be honest. I think I'd rather stay here than the main house. That other is so big."

I stretched to place a kiss on his cheek, before the rest of the tour began, and I caught a bit of the sparkle in his eyes. I hoped someday soon we would both be able to enjoy the simplicity of normalcy.

He flipped on the lights exposing the rest of the main floor. The kitchen opened up to a large great room that housed an overstuffed chair and couch, along with a desk that had been used quite a bit, judging by the wear marks on the wood. There was a set of double doors that were open to what looked like a solarium.

"Is that what I think it is?" I asked.

He nodded and led me through the great room to a beautiful glass space that was full of foliage every direction I looked.

"An indoor greenhouse?"

"Of sorts," he replied coyly.

"Did you take care of these?" I asked, letting my hand glide along the glossy leaves, wondering what other surprises Logan might have in store for me.

"I always wanted to have something like this," I mumbled, walking into the magical space.

"You've got herbs too?" I asked, seeing one of the corners taken over by a table of hard to come by varieties.

"I knew you were interested in that, and I thought it would be a good idea if I sharpened up my skills a little. When I left, my mom had to hire a gardener to help keep them going though. I guess they've done a pretty good job of it so far."

"I'd say so," I was giddy with excitement. "Let's finish up with the tour so I can come back here and stare."

"There's not much more to it. Upstairs is the bedroom and another bath." He went back through the kitchen to where the front door was, not the door leading to the other house, and turned the corner. Must have been where the stairs were hiding.

My heart started racing, and I scolded myself for being so ridiculous. But I was thoroughly flustered at the thought of seeing Logan's room. I didn't know what I thought would happen in there, but I was thoroughly intrigued.

"I'll sleep downstairs, and you can take my room," Logan hollered.

I rounded the corner to see him waiting for my reaction with his brilliant smile and a twinkle in his eyes.

"Nice try. I'm no less scared here than I was at the cottage. I'm not sleeping alone." I swatted him but missed as he climbed the stairs two at a time.

"We'll see about that," he replied. "I might want some space to stretch out."

"Oh, yeah?" I asked. "Fine. I'll sleep in your room all by myself."

He waited at the top of the stairs with his arms crossed in front of him and the grin that melted my heart every time I saw it. So nice to see it surface again and remain for longer than a minute. Maybe we could pretend things were all right for now.

The entire upstairs was a loft. One wall was covered in floor to ceiling bookshelves that led to a window overlooking the lake. In front of the window was a king size bed, begging to be used.

"Wow. This is pretty spectacular — again," I teased, pointing at the surroundings.

"It seems more so with you here." His lip turned up ever so slightly. "You still want to sleep alone?"

"How do you always manage to turn things around?" I put my hands on my hips, scowling at him.

"That's what I thought. I'll go grab our bags out of the car and bring them in. I can lock everything up over there too. Turn on the alarm and stuff."

For some reason this revelation of him leaving made me freeze. I hadn't really been alone since one of the spirits was conjured at the cottage, and since then, some pretty creepy things happened. Never being the type of girl who was frightened easily, I was kind of irritated with my helpless reaction. Nope. I'm not going to play that card. I've got the fear thing handled.

"I'll come out with you and grab some of the bags to make it easier and then you can lock up," I offered. "I can't be afraid of going outside. I'm not going to let *him* or anyone start having that kind of control over me. That's not my style."

"Agreed," Logan said smirking. "I don't think your father has a clue what he's up against."

"I couldn't agree more," I said smiling.

"I caught that," Logan laughed.

Mortified, I realized I had been gazing at the bed without realizing it.

"I'm just exhausted. We've had a long trip."

"Uh-huh, I'm sure that's it."

"Whatever," I shot back at him grinning. "Let's get on with it."

With my newfound bravery, I decided being cautious was still a must.

Scanning out the downstairs window, I saw nothing and gave Logan the go ahead for us to go out to our car. The evening was quite chilly since we were on the lake, and it made me hustle as I gathered everything I could.

"One trip?" I asked surprised.

"I think so," he replied.

Heading back to the guesthouse, I saw a car driving down the street slow down. It was only in my head. People were allowed to drive slowly in a neighborhood.

Logan locked the car doors and we were back inside and my paranoia dissipated.

We dumped everything off in the great room, and I sprawled on to the couch while Logan locked the deadbolts.

"I'm gonna go get the rest of the house locked up. I'll leave the door in between the two open if you want." He bent over and kissed my cheek, but I pulled him into me letting my lips wander to his.

"Don't be long," I whispered, letting go of his shirt.

"With a sendoff like that, you have nothing to worry about." He gave me a quick kiss and headed back to the main house.

I looked around the space and was happy to be staying on this side of the property. The other was gorgeous but it was huge, and with my nerves on edge this place fit my imagination much better.

On the long car ride to Illinois, I spent a lot of time studying the spell books from my side of the family. I had no idea what was going to be waiting for us in Saranac Lake, but I didn't want to put us at any more of a disadvantage with my skill level compared to Logan's.

I grabbed the spell book from my bag that I was in the middle of studying and sat back down. I started skimming the pages, hoping Logan would get back soon. I didn't really feel like studying. My mind flipped back to Aunt Vieta. Could she really be responsible for some of these things? I couldn't even begin to guess what would have happened to her to make that choice. I hoped I was wrong. Forcing myself to push those thoughts aside, I focused on something useful.

I had tagged some spells that had to do with brainwashing and started staring at the different descriptions. Maybe that's what happened to my aunt too. More tired than I realized, I had to fight to keep my eyes open and finally sleep won.

Shoot. I wanted to be alert for Logan's return.

Leaving the in between stage and landing in a place where my mind took over, I felt content. Relaxed. I enjoyed every second of the peace — until I became trapped. My body was hot with worry. What was I seeing? This couldn't be real. I wanted to wake up.

"How could you have done that?" Ellsy screamed. Her back was up against a stone wall. It looked like something from the middle ages. I couldn't see who she was talking to. "He was my everything, my world. Logan's world."

Oh no. Please let this not be…

"Besides his son, he was the only real threat I had," my father responded. "I couldn't allow that type of opposition."

"Did Veronica know?" Ellsy choked on the

words.

Silence was returned.

"Did Veronica know?" Ellsy screamed at my father, charging at him, but something held her back. The sound of clanking bounced off the walls. Her feet were shackled to the floor. What was this place?

"No. Of course not. She wouldn't have approved in her prior state."

"Her prior state? What's that supposed to mean?"

"You'll see soon enough, my dear," my father said.

"You better not touch my son, Nicholas."

"Come on, Trevor. We should let her rest," My father replied.

Ellsy's screams were all I could hear. They were all that echoed through my mind.

I didn't want to be stuck in this nightmare. Please let me out. The uncontrolled sensation of falling ran through me, visceral and terrifying. Why wouldn't my eyes open? There's nothing more to see. I want to be done.

A light tapping began and its persistence allowed my mind to slowly break free. My forehead was damp and my body behaved as if I'd been out for hours, but I'm sure it was only minutes. Staring up at the ceiling, I tried shaking off my foggy frame of mind. There was nothing worse than finally getting some sleep only to have it stolen by nightmares. The tapping continued and it was kind of aggravating in my current state.

"Well, that was fast," I hollered to Logan, hoping that would make him stop.

He didn't respond.

"Logan?"

I texted Logan, but his phone buzzed from one of the bags we brought in. That has got to be a new rule we implement. No more leaving phones. He must still be at the other house. I've got to calm down. The noise was probably an animal or something.

The tapping became more aggressive, and it wasn't coming from the stairwell. Light scratching replaced the tapping, and it was coming from the front door. Fear outweighed my curiosity. Maybe I was still asleep. It was the only hope I had, false as it was.

CHAPTER 10

Their unearthly cries were filled with fury and disappointment. The message was clear and the sender even more so. With every hiss and howl, the walls felt like glass ready to be shattered, and the safety and security of the double bolted door felt like a distant memory. The rattle of the lock echoed into the air as the creatures continued their entry attempt. A quiet beat of metal began next, overtaking the fear that had buried its way into my psyche from the screams. The constant rhythm was a reminder of how close they were to entering. This noise was far worse than their hollers.

Keep focused. Keep focused. My eyes scanned one of my family's spell books — the one that stayed out of the coven's library. Flipping page after page, I desperately searched for the spell that I had come across only days earlier. I needed to send these spirits back to where they came from and this time with a message of my own.

Scanning the pages, my heart was pounding so fast until I found the spell I needed. Then it was like my world stopped. As I tried to memorize every part of the spell, their screams began replacing the pounding. They seemed to be getting frustrated at their inability to break down the door.

I couldn't allow myself to get distracted. There were three different chants listed on the page, depending on the type of spirit. I had to find out what kind I was dealing with.

Not allowing the terror to debilitate me, I stood up from the couch, clutching the spell book, as I made my way to the window next to the door. This was how I would defeat my father— head on. Even though every breath I inhaled was shaky with fear, I knew I could do this. I needed to see what I was faced with. Pulling the drapes to the side, I immediately recognized the beasts from the drawings in the book. I had hoped they were Lonely Souls, but they weren't.

Two of the creatures noticed the curtains move and immediately turned to face me through the glass. They let out nefarious shrieks into the dark sky as if signaling the world that a fight was about to take place. There was a large group of them. I had no idea how many my father sent, but I was ready, and I wanted to do this alone. I took a deep and steady breath, analyzing what set these creatures apart.

Instead of staring into eyes that were recognizable, I was looking into cavernous holes that led to the creatures' withering souls. There was no doubt that these malformed beings staring back at me had been called from the underworld. They were pieced together from dark sorcery. They were manmade. I could defeat them.

Their clay-like flesh clung to a human silhouette without joints. Opening their gaping mouths in unison, I braced myself for the shrill round of wailing they wanted to shower on me. Their mouths, dark at first, revealed a fiery tunnel of destruction. I needed to end them before they unleashed what they were sent here for. My gut told me it wasn't me who they were told to destroy.

Sliding the spell book on the floor away from me, I was ready to send these messengers back. These weren't Lonely Souls. They were one step beyond. There was no saving them.

Taking a deep breath in, I looked directly into the horde knowing what I needed to do before they got to Logan. I yanked the curtain closed and stood back from the door. I needed to invite them in.

"Aperto Ostio," I hollered.

The door flung open with such force a gust of wind pushed me back. The spell worked!

Instead of the creatures rushing toward me like I had prepared, they turned toward the hallway. They *were* here for Logan. I had to stop them.

"Unguibus Pugionibus," I recited quickly.

The mob of creatures froze and turned to stare at me.

My fingertips burned as claws replaced my nails. This had to work. If they were a form of Golem, I could do this. I could end them.

Unsure of their thinking capabilities, or attention span, I wiggled my finger at them, hoping I could distract them from their initial goal.

"Tsk, tsk," I uttered. "Your master would be disappointed."

One of the creatures quirked its head to the side and opened its mouth.

"How sharp are your teeth?" I asked.

A gurgling response was evoked from the being. It started moving toward me with lightning quick speed. I held up both hands amazed at what I saw. Each one of my fingertips carried a shimmering razor-sharp claw. Perfect for shredding these creatures to bits.

"Recipio Vestris Malis Interserit. Pelle Conditori Fallaciis et Conminuito in Eius Excitate," I hissed. *"Ego Praecipio tibi ut Dimittas."*

As long the spell worked, these beings would deliver my message.

The first creature ran right into my claws. The flesh turned to dust, collapsing into a pile in front of me. It was a Golem. I lunged toward the group, thrilled to reach the next victim. They opened up their stance, inviting me into their circle. My excitement turned to fear.

I slowly pivoted to greet every single creature

whose gaping mouths did little to alleviate my worry. Some of them moved slower than others, but they all had a robotic quality. Driven by a task. They walked around me slowly, squawking, pointing. Facing the uncertainty of what these creatures wanted, my courage began to fade. The circle of beasts moved counter-clockwise in slow, deliberate steps. It was almost hypnotic.

"Recipio Vestris Malis Interserit. Pelle Conditori Fallaciis et Conminuito in Eius Excitate," I repeated. *"Ego Praecipio tibi ut Dimittas."*

I needed to do anything to keep my mind and body active. One of the creatures tugged on my hair from behind, which allowed an opening for one of the larger Golem to throw itself at me. I dove out of the way only to be left attached to the creature gripping my hair.

My heart raced and there was no denying I might have bit off more than I should have. If only these creatures would get in arms reach, I might be able to get my claws in them. Unfortunately, I made a lesson for the one I took down and they were staying away out of my reach.

The creature tightened its grip on my hair and threw me down to the ground. Motivated by desperation, I kicked my feet and tried to escape, but with each movement, the hair on my scalp pulled and tugged without freeing.

One of the Golem staring over me reached out giving me an opportunity to grab its wrist and pull it toward me. The creature tumbled on top of me, and I dug my claws deep into its flesh. The pile of dust fell on me. The others took a step back, except for one.

In a gesture of defiance, he stared at me with pitted eyes, opening the slit where his mouth should've been. Flames began spitting toward me. My claws were digging into the wooden floor as I braced myself for whatever might be coming.

"*Corvorum Mundi Venire et Providere Auxilium ad me,*" I whispered, hoping my connection with nature wouldn't fail me now.

My neck muscles were getting tired from the force of the Golem holding me down and my own body fighting against possible fate. The heat from the Golem's mouth burned my flesh, but I stayed focused.

"*Corvorum Mundi Venire et Providere Auxilium ad me,*" I repeated.

Wind began swirling through the room. The chill was coming from the front door. Arching my back, I attempted to see what was causing the change in the air, but the Golem had me pinned. I couldn't move.

I closed my eyes and heard a faint sound of swooshing and flapping of wings. They were on their way. My call for help worked. I had very little time now. I needed to tell the Golem my message.

"Please tell my father we're coming for my mother. We will bring her home no matter her condition. I'm not afraid and neither is Logan. We will bring our mothers home, and we won't be stopped by such a cowardly man or his followers."

The high-pitched calls bounced off the walls as the bats swooped into the home. The tiny brown mammals dove from every direction, making it impossible to see much of anything. But I heard what I needed to. The Golem had been taken by surprise, and their squeals and screams were nothing compared to the beautiful winged creatures I had roused to my defense. Their sounds were magnificently haunting, and those were only the sounds I wanted to hear.

The flesh of the monsters was picked and scratched to pieces as my winged friends came to my rescue. One Golem after the next dropped.

"Don't forget my message," I hollered to the few that remained.

"Triss," Logan yelled.

"Logan, stay back." Turning my neck quickly, I strained to see through the tiny mammals hovering in the air.

The strands of my hair began loosening as the last Golem released his grip, and I raised my head toward Logan's voice. The small brown bats began to exit as quickly as they arrived, but I was still unable to spot Logan.

"Are you okay?" Logan's voice was closer. He had no intention of listening to my instruction.

Even though the Golem were no longer surrounding me, my body didn't respond to any request. I attempted to prop myself up on my elbows, and they wouldn't even budge. This wasn't a spell, a curse, or any such thing. It was my body allowing the exhaustion of the last several days to sweep through me, and I didn't mind. The room was cleared. I had managed to pull it off.

"Golem were sent," I replied, lying on the floor. "Lots of them."

Logan stood over me now. His eyes filled with rage.

"And you survived," Logan murmured.

"Don't look so happy about it," I said completely perplexed.

He sat down next to me on the floor, running his finger along my collarbone. I watched the rage turn to concern as he thought about what to say.

"I was so worried about you. That you would come in while I was trying to destroy them."

He raised his eyebrows in confusion. "Worried about me?"

I slowly sat up.

"Yeah. They rushed by me on their way to you. It wasn't until I taunted them that they stopped to play." I couldn't help but feel proud with my accomplishment.

His mouth twisted as he pondered what I told him, and I began wondering why he wasn't more thrilled with my abilities to wipe out an entire Golem set. This could mean great things once we get to Saranac Lake.

"This was a test," Logan finally spoke, interrupting my delusional fit.

"A test? How so?" I asked, eyeing him carefully. I wasn't about to let my achievement get blown to smithereens.

"If the Golem wanted you, they would've

taken you. They couldn't touch you."

"I'm not following you." I moved so I was sitting directly in front of him with my arms crossed. "They had plenty of opportunity, but I fought them off with the help of some spells."

A grin covered my face at the last thought. For once, my ability to commune with nature had paid off.

"You're protected." Logan's eyes darkened.

"Protected. Protected from what?"

Logan avoided looking into my eyes.

"If a sorcerer conjures a soul or commands a spirit against someone," he began, "and that person is righteous, they can't be touched."

If it weren't for the look in Logan's eyes, I would've started laughing, but I could tell he was completely serious.

"I'm far from righteous, Logan. Thanks, though."

"You're a pure soul," he whispered.

I shook my head, thinking back to the horrible things I had acted on, even just recently.

"Logan, you of all people know what I've done." I started getting sick at the thoughts running through me. I didn't know if I'd ever be able to forget the image of the black sorcerer falling to the ground after my arrow etched a place in his chest.

"The thoughts that have gone through my head about hurt—"

"Those are just thoughts. You haven't acted on them," he interrupted. "I'm not making this up."

"I think that's a fantastical

misrepresentation," I protested. "I've *killed* people. I've wanted people dead. You can't tell me there's anything righteous about that."

"That was self defense."

The chill from the open door had become impossible to ignore. I couldn't stop shivering and gestured toward the opening. Logan closed it and helped me over to the couch.

"I'm so proud of you. I really am," Logan said, while he tried unsuccessfully to warm me up. "You were so brave and the spells were flawless, but it wasn't enough."

"I threw so much at the Golem. How can you be so sure that it wasn't my spells that did it?"

I looked down and saw that one claw still remained in the place of a finger.

"See?" I said waving it in front of him.

Logan pulled me into him, pressing his lips on my head. The pace of his breathing shifted.

"I'm not that innocent," I mumbled.

"You're pure. This proved it. I'm telling you they could've taken you or destroyed you if they were allowed. Even the underworld has rules, and the righteous and pure of heart can't be touched. That's why you survived this. That's why you've survived everything. The meeting in the floral shop, the one at the cottage..."

The wetness spilled down my cheek.

"It was a test," he said softly. "The others I made excuses for, but this one I can't ignore. Those creatures were too powerful."

"Why would my father do this?"

"Think about all of the pawns he's collecting

to do who knows what," he paused, taking in a breath. "Imagine if he had one who was untouchable."

Logan's words spread through me with a harshness I didn't want to believe. I couldn't shake the power behind his words. I snuggled into him as his embrace tightened around me.

"Whatever he's planning is big, isn't it?" I asked, letting the uncertainty about both of our mothers' fates slowly settle in.

"I doubt it only resides in the confines of our world," he replied, anger bouncing off each syllable.

"Before the Golem came, I had a nightmare."

"What was it about?" he asked softly.

I took a deep breath in and was unable to let it out.

"Your mom."

He stiffened.

"It was a horrible dream. A short dream, maybe ten seconds, but I still can't shake it."

He let out his breath slowly before he asked.

"What was the dream?"

"My father had your mom shackled. They spoke about your father's death. It was horrifying."

"What was said about my father's death?" Logan asked in a low voice.

"That my father killed him," I felt my throat begin constricting as the words escaped. "Your mom begged for your life."

My body began trembling as the silence filled the air. It was only a dream, but speaking the words created a sickness deep within my soul. The more minutes of silence that passed between us told me something I didn't want to believe.

"You want something to eat?" I asked, jumping off the couch and out of Logan's arms.

This couldn't be happening. There was no way.

"What you saw was real," Logan started.

"Nope. Impossible," I shot back, busying myself as I looked in all the kitchen cabinets for an escape.

"Babe, it's not impossible. It's what can happen with that spell you two shared," his words were filled with a pain that I didn't want to acknowledge.

"It can't be," I said, turning around to face him, holding an unopened box of crackers.

"You're still sharing memories with him, only in real-time now," he continued. "It can only happen if—"

"Don't say it," I yelled. "I hate him. Truly hate him. How's that for pure?"

I threw the box of crackers against the wall letting my body slide down the cupboard.

Logan was by my side instantly, scooping me into his arms.

"It can't be." The tears wouldn't stop and neither would the nausea. "I'm not connected to him. I'm not."

"This can work to our advantage," Logan replied, once I'd managed to calm myself down. "If we can figure out what triggers these images, we might be able to know what to expect along the way."

I scowled at him and moved back against the wall.

"I know I've never had feelings for him."

I looked into Logan's eyes, which darkened about ten shades as he acknowledged what this connection might mean for our future together.

"We'll deal with things as they come," Logan replied flatly.

"You believe me, don't you?" My voice broke before I could finish.

Logan reached for my arm, avoiding my gaze, and pulled me closer to him.

"Listen," he said softly. "I've waited a long time for you. I'm not letting go that easily."

His gaze finally met mine, and I saw love mixed with the desperation of our circumstance. I would not let him down. I would fight for our love no matter what I had to do.

CHAPTER 11

"I thought you said this was a cottage?" I asked, attempting to see the house in the dark. The air was different here, warm and moist, with a hint of woodsy goodness.

"I had to get what I could," he said, taking my hand and leading me up the stairs. His eyes were full of mischief.

Logan opened the screen door, allowing me in first. I knew he was excited to show me where in the Adirondacks we'd be calling home. Rather than bunk at a hotel, like I had suggested, he had quickly come up with this weekly rental. He said it was cheaper this way, but after driving up to this place, I doubted it.

"Thought we should stay in Lake Placid. It's far enough away from where your father seems to be, but close enough for us to get the job done. Whatever that might be."

I nodded in agreement.

"I didn't think we'd want to run the risk of bumping into him."

"No doubt," I said, dumping my bag off in the foyer.

He flipped on the lights, and I stopped in my tracks to take in our new surroundings. The antler chandelier dangling in the entry hall was the size of a kitchen table, and there were two staircases leading out of the foyer.

Logan eyed me closely.

"This is beautiful," I whispered, "but I don't think I can afford this, splitting it or not."

"Ooh, hmm. I guess I can tell the rental agency we won't be needing the place then."

Logan smiled and raised his eyebrows at me.

"Well..." I said unable to hide my grin. "Maybe just for a few nights."

"Since I've got an uphill battle against a spell, I thought I'd better pull out all the stops."

I smacked him harder than I intended, but his words held far too much weight.

"Not funny," I replied quietly.

"Let's check out the place and go to town. Maybe pretend that our world's not caving in on us." His words shook me to the core, knowing what seemed to be on both of our minds no matter how hard we tried to push it away.

"That would be a nice change," I said, wandering into the great room.

A stone fireplace was the centerpiece, with overstuffed, green cushions on the floor, and a beautiful bouquet of daisies placed on the coffee table.

I spun around to see Logan facing me, smiling, His eyes danced as he looked at me with wonder. And love. I wasn't going to let anything or anyone take that away.

"Daisies?"

He nodded.

'This is a pretty special place," I said, motioning around the room. "But do you know what I love the most?"

Not saying anything at all, he came closer to me, and I held out my hand.

"You," I whispered, taking his hand as I forced all of the fear and sadness out of my mind. "I wouldn't care if we were staying in a tent, I just want to be with you."

"That might be next. You better be careful," he murmured, bringing me close to him.

"Really? That could be kind of fun," I giggled, leaning my head on his chest.

"Wanna go grab some food?" he asked.

"Probably should before everything closes up."

Going to town felt like the most normal thing we'd done in months; like something most couples took for granted. For so long, everything had been about dealing with the grief from my mom or mentally trying to reconcile what my mom's disappearance meant to us all. I was getting used to the feeling of expectations being blown to pieces when it came to the thought of my mother. Now having Logan's mom dragged into everything, and the possibility of Trevor being more involved in my life than I'd like, I needed just one night to play along as if everything was going to be all right. Something told me that this could be the last moment of reprieve for quite some time.

We were only minutes from town and my stomach was calling. We parked our car at the end of town. I looked forward to spending a little time walking around.

"Do you think there'll ever be a future when we can be normal *all* of the time?" I asked, squeezing his hand.

It was a balmy night and the heart of the small Adirondack town was beautifully nestled along Mirror Lake, offering many places for couples to stop and admire the view.

"Normal isn't all it's cracked up to be," Logan said with a half-smile. "But it would be nice to have the option."

The warm glow from the many shops lining the street bounced onto the sidewalk, but one in particular stood out.

"Oooh, there's a chocolate shop," I said pointing. "We've got to check there first."

The window display was filled with glorious mounds of dark chocolate blocks, peanut brittle, and caramel apples. As soon as Logan opened the door, the wave of deliciousness hit me.

"I think I've entered heaven," I whispered, as I walked under Logan's arm while he held the door open for me. What a gentlemen.

The sweetness in the air reminded me of a more innocent time. I scolded myself for letting anything slip into my mind to disrupt the happiness spreading through me.

"Chocolate covered strawberries!" I pointed at the back counter. "Must get those."

Logan stood back beaming, with his arms folded. This is what it could be like— our future— wandering through shops, indulging on chocolate *and* each other.

Someday.

I spotted marshmallow bars, and my heart instantly plummeted. Those were one of my mom's specialties. Would I ever get to have her back in my life or was it over, truly over?

Logan came behind me and wrapped his arms around my waist, guiding me to an area of the store I had missed. It's like he knew where my brain went.

"I'm going to do my best to keep your mind occupied," he whispered.

I let my hands rest on his as I felt his body direct me.

"How about some of that?" I followed his finger to see buckets of homemade ice cream hiding behind the glass calling to me.

"I'm going to gain like ten pounds in one night. I'm sure of it."

The bells dangling on the door, jingled as a wave of new customers entered.

"I better get a move on it," I whispered.

Going up to the counter, I ordered about half as much as I wanted, which was still triple what I could probably manage to consume. The shop was getting packed as the confectioner handed me bag after bag of my order.

"A movie must've let out," Logan said, nodding toward the theater across the street. "Do you realize we've never even gone to a movie together?"

"I'm telling you this normal thing might not be so bad," I said grinning, holding my bags of candy up.

We walked back outside, and the warmth from being out of the air-conditioned store was nice. I reached in for the caramel apple with walnuts, and Logan took the rest of the bags from me to hold as we walked along the sidewalk.

"Do you think my mom's too far gone?" I asked, surprised at myself when it popped out.

"All we can do is run on hope. I don't think she ever intended to have this happen. I know she loves you," Logan said, pulling me into him.

"I don't know what I'll do if she's not able to return to her old self."

"Don't think of the worst. Enjoy your caramel apple and let's try our hardest to make this evening as ordinary as possible," he said and quickly kissed the top of my head, sending warm sensations through me.

"You know what I'm really impressed with?" I asked.

"What's that?"

"That we made it across the entire country on a road trip without killing one another." I smiled. "And we still want to hang out. I think this thing might actually work between us."

Logan's laughter echoed through the evening air, inviting me to think of the *afters* of life; the fairytale endings that I'd been shutting out of my mind since that fateful summer evening when my mother was stolen from me. He allowed me to imagine the possibilities that life had to offer, and I wanted them all to involve him.

He followed my gaze and pulled me to the crosswalk.

The view of the lake was incredible, and there was no one around this lookout point in the park. Logan climbed onto a large boulder and pulled me up, wrapping his arm around me.

"This is nice," I whispered.

I looked at the barely rippling water in front of us, but I could feel Logan's eyes on me, and I started to fidget. Scanning the small boats that were bobbing along, I began feeling flushed and avoided his gaze at all costs.

"Okay, just wanted to make sure I *still* had that effect on you," Logan said, bringing me closer.

"I don't know what you're talking about," I shot back smiling. I turned my attention to him.

"Oh, I think you do," he grinned.

Doing my best to ignore him, I closed my eyes and stared out at the lake once more. The smile that was threatening to give me away felt nice, natural. I could sense he enjoyed every minute of it.

Out of the corner of my eye, I saw that he began looking toward the lake too, so I turned to look at him. It was my turn.

"Two can play that game you know, and I'll

win," I chided, feeling like my old self again.

He looked at me in a penetrating gaze filled with roguish desire. How could any one guy be allowed to exude that much power with one glance? Totally not fair.

"But would you want to?" His voice was low.

I quivered, and I was sure he felt it as his smile turned into a full-blown grin. This was what things were supposed to be like — innocent flirting turning into not so innocent thoughts — brought on by a spectacular smile or quiet glance. This is what I wanted my life to be one day very soon.

His dark hair was looking especially disheveled, and his grin was unbearably wonderful. Oh, how I wanted this to last.

"That caramel apple kind of filled me up," I teased. "Maybe wc should just go back to the house?"

"Hmm." He pressed his lips together.

A noise behind us caught my attention, and I carefully turned to see a woman standing on top of a Land Rover with her friends gathered around cheering her on. Her arms were splayed out like she was gesturing for a flight somewhere.

Logan followed my gaze. "That's weird."

"Hope that's her own car she's denting up," I replied. "She's definitely had one too many."

Logan squinted his eyes as he took in the scene. His body tensed slightly and his jaw tightened as he leaned in to take a closer look. I quickly turned my attention back to the woman on top of the car, when she jumped. She attempted to land on her feet, but unfortunately she fell to her knees. The group gathered around her praising her flying ability before they all took off flapping their arms down the sidewalk.

"Creepy." I smiled at Logan who turned his attention back to me. His eyes were soft, but they held concern.

"What's up?" I asked.

"Something seemed off," he replied.

"Drunk people generally are," I giggled.

My phone buzzed, and I pulled it out of my pocket without thinking.

"Oh no." I showed the phone to Logan. "I can't believe this."

"What's wrong?" he asked, grabbing the phone.

"It's from Jenny in Colorado."

"Oh, Triss," his voice was heavy.

"People are talking about a movement my father's leading. He's everywhere, isn't he?"

He stared at me not saying a word.

"I've got to text her back."

"What are you even going to say?"

"Under no circumstance let anyone know we're friends." I let out a sigh. "I just don't know what to make of this. All I want is to get my mom back — your mom back too. Now it seems like there's so much more to learn. I've got to keep her safe."

He jumped off the rock and grabbed my hand helping me down. Here I was in a strange place, wearing a mask of happiness, pretending that I could escape the inexcusable acts my father had committed.

"I'm so pissed. I want this all to be over with so that —" I huffed and scowled at Logan before turning away.

"I love you so much, Logan," I tried again, avoiding his stare. "But no matter how much I want you — us — to be alright, I feel like to move forward we should concentrate on getting our mothers back, nothing else."

The street was bustling now, but everything devolved into slow motion. The only thing I could hear was the beat of my own heart pounding. Logan pulled his hand away. He was staring directly at me, maybe through me.

"Don't play these games, Triss." He couldn't hide his anger or his surprise.

"I'm not trying to play games," I started, but the fear almost choked out my words. "I am so lost and everything seems insurmountable and —"

Logan narrowed his eyes at me and was quiet for several minutes and then took off. I shifted uncomfortably wishing I could take my words back.

Should I follow him?

"You coming?" he asked turning toward me, his eyes completely darkened by whatever thought occurred to him.

I skipped a step and ran over to him.

He slid his arm around my waist as we hurriedly left the hillside. I stole a glance at him, and his face was completely devoid of expression.

"Logan, I never meant…" I began.

"Come with me," he interrupted, his voice kinder.

We were walking quickly down the sidewalk and before I realized it, he pulled me to a secluded area up a grassy hill on the other side of the street.

"What is this place?" I asked. We were standing in front of a small wooden building with stonework covering the front. It looked beyond old and superbly spooky.

"I don't know some church or something," he said, glancing at the church sign. "I just needed you to myself."

I looked at him puzzled, searching his eyes for any clue he might give. His hands gently cupped my face, bringing it up to his. The softness of his touch did wonders for my spirit.

Why had I acted like I could turn off these feelings?

"Listen," he said softly, stepping closer to me. "This isn't your fault. I know you didn't mean what you said. Maybe it's the spell. Maybe Trevor has gotten into you more than we realized."

I shook my head violently, unwilling to accept that possibility. I would *never* love Trevor.

The intensity of his stare melted me in place. I wanted to prove to him how much I loved him. I would do anything for this type of love.

"I don't understand how that slipped out. I'm not feeling like that at all. I mean I'm confused, but I don't want to put anything on hold between us. I love you. I love you more each day."

"I know, baby. I feel the same way," he said, his voice gruffer and lips hovering so close to mine I didn't think I could take it much more.

His fingertips lightly ran over my shoulder, tracing his way down my arm, igniting a flurry of emotions deep inside. His eyes were burning into my soul, bringing intensity to the night that I desperately needed. I wanted to forget what had spilled out of my mouth. I wanted him to forget it.

"Things might be a little difficult for awhile," he whispered, "and I need to get used to it."

He wrapped his arms around me, bringing his mouth down to mine. The heat of our skin together built a fiery anticipation of the unknown. This kiss was deeper, hotter than any we'd shared before. My body began trembling against his as I felt his embrace tighten. Running his finger up my spine, a wave of chills ran through me as I felt his lips break free.

"I've promised you before, and I'll promise it again," he whispered, "I'll never give up on us."

CHAPTER 12

The panic my earlier words carried finally subsided, but I didn't feel any more settled.

"This might be a stretch, but what if we did the spider spell again? I know the feelings I have for you are far stronger than anything that stupid spell might have captured between Trevor and me. Maybe a new spell would overpower the old one or something," I offered.

We were sprawled out on the floor in front of the fire on a pile of cushions and blankets. This seemed to be the perfect spot to discuss possibilities privately.

"Mmm," he replied, twisting his lips as he thought about my idea.

Logan was stretched out next to me, and even with the seriousness of everything, he was difficult not to admire. His hands were behind his head, which only did worse things for my imagination due to the fact that his shirt was raised far too high for my own good.

I reached over and tugged on his shirt, but he

wrestled me into his arms instead.

"You're too distracting," I complained, burying my head into his shoulder.

"Am I?" he quipped. "I'll have to keep it up and layer it on even more."

"Whatever works," I whispered, snuggling into him. "Try to wear those jeans as often as possible as well." If teasing about the Trevor thing will help him get through it so be it. "Seriously though, do you think that might work with the spell?"

"It's an interesting idea. But my major concern is that it would somehow connect me to Trevor."

"But he can't see my images, right? I was just allowed to see his."

He nodded, "But who knows once it's done twice with the same person."

"I say we try it."

"I don't know about that. You seeing my deepest, darkest secrets and all?" His lip curled up slightly and the overwhelming desire to kiss him came over me.

"It's getting hot in front of the fire," I teased, scooting away slowly.

"Right here is perfection," he said, letting out a sigh bringing me back to him.

"It is," I agreed, closing my eyes.

The crackle of the fire kept me hypnotized as my mind wandered back to the possibilities of avoiding Trevor or thwarting the spell entirely.

"One thing we're going to learn through all of this is to never give up," I mused. Logan's embrace tightened.

"That's for sure," he whispered.

"Now for my father and motive," I started again.

"Don't you ever stop?" His laughter lingered.

"I thought that's one of the things you loved about me? My stubbornness." I opened my eyes and rolled on top of him, staring straight into his gaze.

"One of many things."

"If my father's got a network in some states, or worse yet, all states, he's planning something big."

"Right."

I rolled off Logan. It was far too difficult to be that close to him without my heart's desires taking over.

"I saw something about my father's side of the family being around during the Salem witch trials," I paused, "but they weren't listed as suspected of practicing or any such thing. Kind of odd."

"Where'd you find that?" he asked, propping his head on his elbow.

"In one of the books from the Witch Avenue Coven's library. It's on the table over there. I'm surprised I caught it all. It was only touched on lightly in one of the passages, but it got me wondering."

"Yeah, that is strange."

My phone buzzed, and I grabbed it off the table. It was close to one o'clock in the morning in Lake Placid, but a couple hours earlier in Colorado.

"It's got to be Jenny." I touched the screen and sure enough, Jenny's smiling face appeared next to her name.

"What's she got?" Logan asked, sitting up now.

"It looks like there are several people in the coven who are considering creating an offshoot for something called The Praedivinus Order. Praedivinus? What does that even mean?"

I began typing it in my phone's dictionary, but Logan already knew the answer.

"It's like prophetic, an oracular being or idea." His eyes darkened as he stared at the flames.

"My father thinks he's a prophet?"

"Someone connected to the Gods," his voice trailed off.

"Or?"

"The underworld." He shook his head.

"This might be a stretch, but what—" I stopped.

There's no way. Now I was just being paranoid. I sat up and leaned against the stone of the fireplace, allowing the heat to penetrate the back of my head. Maybe I'd fry the crazy out. Trying to find excuses for my father's abhorrent actions was not going to help anything. I can't just say it's in his genes and be okay with it. Besides that would imply it was in my genes too.

"What? Might as well throw it out there," he suggested.

I texted to Jenny again, hoping I'd divert Logan's attention.

How did she find out about this? I couldn't afford to lose any more people I cared about. I hoped she followed my request to stay away from those members and leave well enough alone.

"So what's your thought?" he tried again.

"What if this wasn't my father's initial plan, but something passed down through the generations. Maybe going back to —"

"1692?"

I bit my lip and nodded at him.

"Crazy?" I asked.

He shook his head, "Not at all."

"I mean I'm not trying to make excuses for him, but if we could trace something back through the years there might be a method to stop it."

"I don't know how we're going to figure this out, but we've definitely gotta give it a shot." He looked concerned, like he was contemplating something.

"You always make me feel less crazy."

His eyebrows furrowed, and he shook his head. "How so?"

"Ever since you came back into my life, you've been this grounding force. Always willing to believe or try out my harebrained ideas, hear me out, whatever it is... You're there, and I thank you for it."

He was in the kitchen, grabbing a glass of water, when my phone buzzed again.

"So far your ideas have been pretty close to reality. I don't think they're as crazy as you think. Intuition is an important part of our world and very few people listen to it. I'd say I'm simply the lucky one who's in love with someone who's dialed in pretty good to the universe." He was coming back with his water and a bowl of chips. "Your mom's side of the family has always been tapped in to the energies of the world, and it's even stronger in you. Hopefully it will work in our favor at some point." He smiled.

A flash of silver caught my eye out the window.

"Logan," I hissed. "Did you see that?"

He turned toward the window I was facing and looked out. It was gone.

"I don't see anything."

"I don't know. It must've been a reflection. It's fun to be this jumpy." I laughed nervously while he continued to look out the window.

"I saw it," he announced. "A flash or something."

"Yeah. That's what I saw," I said, looking at him.

He was already at the window, staring out when I reached his side.

"I don't see anything out there," he said, shaking his head. "But I saw what you were talking about."

We continued staring out the window for several minutes when I finally decided I had enough.

"Let's just close the curtains," I said, sliding the fabric shut. He closed the wooden blinds I couldn't reach, and I felt immensely better.

"You know if that stuff from my mom can come down the family line, why wouldn't the other be able to?"

Even though I was next to the fire, I began to get chilled as I let my worries vocalize again.

"The black magic?" he asked.

"What if the darkness is inside of me waiting to be roused, and there's nothing I can do about it? All of this time, I've been worried about you leaving me for the dark side and what if it's me who's called to it?"

"Is that what you want?" he asked, setting the bowl on the table.

"Of course not."

"Well, then get it out of your head. We need to recognize that these forces exist out there, but we can't let the idea rule our lives. Life is about choices. I would've thought the one I made would've had more of an impact." His brow rose.

A smile spread across my face, knowing that he was right on so many levels. He did choose me over black magic. So why was I teetering on the edge of madness worrying about things that I couldn't control when there were ones that I could solve?

"Kind of like that spell with Trevor," I said, staring at Logan. "I don't care what the spell's trying to create for my future. It's not going to happen. I won't let it."

"That's a little different," Logan said softly.

"It's not," I insisted. "I'm not going to play the victim on this one. I'm going to find a way to make it stop."

"Triss," he began again, but I interrupted him.

"I've got some ideas, and we're going to try

them all until one of them works." I folded my arms in front of me. "Like it or not."

"It's not that simple."

"It's not that complicated. I remember you telling me how much you admired that I wasn't like the other girls who always agreed with you. Told you what you wanted to hear and all that." I got up from the floor and sat on Logan's lap, and he couldn't hide his happiness.

Logan took a deep breath in and slowly let it out as he let my words settle over him.

"So I take it we'll be starting with the spider bite?"

I nodded and grabbed my phone, glancing at a new message from Jenny.

"She asked if I'd heard from Trevor lately?" I waited for Logan's reaction.

"Huh, that's a tricky one." His smile did a pretty good job of hiding the pain.

"I guess we'd need to get our story straight. You still think we can trust her, right?" I asked.

"For the most part. Don't you? I think more than anything she might not believe us before she actually turned on us."

"I haven't told her anything about my mom, us being back here...nothing."

"Maybe now's the time," he suggested. "Just not in text."

My stomach began feeling sick at the thought. Where would I even begin? What good would it do? Would she think I'm crazy? She told me not to hide anything from her or Angela.

Logan sat on the couch and nodded at me for

encouragement.

"I can leave if you want, if it would make it easier."

"No way," I said, dialing Jenny's number. "Maybe I could build a network like my father, only for the good of Witches everywhere instead of the destruction," I told Logan as the phone rang and rang.

***

"Think we should scout out the town of Saranac Lake?" I asked, thankful for a good night's sleep.

He nodded, finishing his cereal quickly.

"Let's get a Starbucks on the way out of town. Try another attempt at normalcy maybe?" I joked.

I don't know what it was about the evening, but come daylight I felt tremendously better from whatever might have plagued me the night before.

"I'm tellin' ya, the whole normal thing isn't for everyone." He winked at me and placed his cereal bowl in the sink. "Now let's get a move on it."

"Still get to go to Starbucks, right?"

He smiled and out the door we went. I hadn't seen the property in the daylight, but it was absolutely delightful. The landscape was mostly natural, but there were benches and garden paths in many directions.

"This place is pretty lovely," I said, plopping into the passenger seat.

"I'm glad you like it."

Logan turned onto the road leading into town. The main drag was already pretty busy with cars and people, but we managed to find a spot to park right beside Starbucks.

"I hope to make this outing as uneventful as possible," I smiled, feeling a little sheepish for the previous night's outburst.

He tossed a couple coins in the parking meter and into Starbucks we went. Logan lined up at the counter to order our drinks, and I wandered off to the community board, noticing all of the fun festivals, paddle boarding lessons, and local plays that were posted. Then my eyes landed on the flyer.

My heart began racing. I knew it was him. It was my father staring at me. Did he place this for me to see? Does he know we're here? The flyer was bright yellow with the words 'The Praedivinus Order' above tiny fringes allowing people to tear off the phone number. And many were already missing.

Logan came up behind me with our drinks, but I was frozen. He followed my gaze to the invitation.

"He knows," Logan whispered.

I turned to face him and saw disgust in his eyes — a darkness like never before.

"I don't care that he's my father. I want to destroy him."

"He's trying to plant hatred in you and it's working. Don't let it."

I took the cup from Logan, and we walked out

of the coffee shop in a daze.

"Why would he want me to hate him though? Think we should still go to Saranac Lake?"

He nodded and pointed to one of the empty benches where we both took a seat.

"Hate is hate. It's a powerful tool. It doesn't matter what you initially hate because in time it will grow to include other things," Logan was staring across the street. He became silent, stirring with something that worried me. The darkness seemed to be slowly reappearing. I wondered if it had to do with his own father's death.

"What's going on?" I asked, unable to wait any longer. I needed to know what had suddenly changed inside of him.

"Last night, I thought about what you said and looked some stuff up. You're right about your father's family being in Salem and playing a part in the hysteria." Something was really bothering him, and it was more than that flyer.

I reached for his hand, and sat closer.

"And?" I asked.

"I think they started it, actually."

I looked at him puzzled.

"In Salem?"

"Even before. When I started tracing your father's ancestors, the coincidences were far too great to ignore. Looking at all of those pages you managed to scan from the library allowed me to see things we'd usually ignore."

"Like?"

"There seemed to be a glaring coincidence

over the years...everywhere his family was, Witch Hunts soon followed, possibly as far back as 1581 in Europe."

"If they're witches why would they want to start problems for their own community?"

"Possibly to distract from what they were really up to? Or maybe it was a way of eliminating the competition?" He shook his head. "I have no idea."

"I remember seeing maps and dates going back that far, but it never occurred to me to look for that connection."

"There's no way either of us would have guessed it by just looking at the books. I'm not sure what drove me to find the pattern, but —"

"Maybe we do have help after all," I suggested.

"Yeah, maybe so."

"Well, we've got two options. Your mom or my aunt, and I'm guessing it's not the latter."

"Probably a good assumption."

"If it is your mom, that means they haven't turned her yet," I replied. "She's still herself."

"All we can do is hope." He dropped his gaze to the sidewalk. "If your father's trying to incite something we need to be careful."

"I haven't stopped being careful. I feel as if my entire life is built around me looking behind my back. I'm beginning to pride myself on my different levels of paranoia, real and otherwise." I smiled, craning my neck to catch his gaze.

"I know. It's just that I need you to understand that I will *always* have your best interest at heart. No matter what decision I'm faced with, it will be to protect you." Logan's eyes darkened as he spoke.

"Riiight?" I asked confused.

He bit his lip and his body shifted away from me slightly.

"I feel the same way," I began.

"But you shouldn't. That's the problem. You need to worry about protecting yourself. You need to think about the bigger picture, especially if everything we're finding out is true."

"That's ridiculous. My life isn't worth any more than anyone else's, especially yours, and we don't even know what the bigger picture is yet," I protested.

"That's not what I was trying to say," his voice softened.

"I love you. How can I not want to protect you? I want you safe."

He took a sip of his coffee and put the drink down on the bench.

"I'm worried you're going to let this whole Trevor thing distract you from the real issues," he began.

"That is a real issue. As real as any of them," I whispered.

"Yes and no. If there's nothing we can do to stop it, then it's a distraction and your father gets away with whatever it is that he has planned."

"It's not a distraction because I have a plan. Several of them. And one of them *will* work eventually. Getting my mom and your mom back is the most important thing. I understand that, but I'm not going to allow my destiny to be tweaked by some ridiculous turn of events," I couldn't hide my anger. "You of all people should understand that. I *will* get what I want."

He sighed, "Just remember that I will do what I have to do to ensure your safety."

I stared at him for a moment before I spoke.

"Right back at ya."

Logan sighed and brought me close to him. Hopefully the quality he found endearing wouldn't eventually drive him away.

A scream broke our embrace, and I turned my head to watch a scene of terror unfold.

A crowd gathered at the base of the church where only the night before Logan and I had been. Many were pointing toward the steeple, but there was another group of people as well and they were calmer.

"What is going on?" I whispered.

He shook his head as it became apparent we couldn't see whatever it was everyone was pointing at.

We moved down the sidewalk a few feet to see a woman wrapped around the very tip of the steeple. She was using her free arm to flap in the wind. This was the same woman as the night before. She wasn't drunk. She was possessed.

"Oh, no," I whispered to Logan.

He wrapped his arm around my waist as we both stood helpless. This had my father written all over it.

"Check that out." I pointed at one of the spectators who had a bright yellow flyer sticking out his back pocket. He was one of the instigators cheering this poor woman on — exactly like last night when she was on the Land Rover.

"I will see the light," she hollered before letting go of the steeple. Her body fell to the ground with a thud.

Chapter 13

"Have you ever seen evil like this?" I asked.

"Only when your father's involved." Logan grabbed my hand and pulled me across the street to where the very distinct crowds congregated. The EMTs had already taken the woman away, but the horror her act left behind was still in the air.

"Hey!" Logan yelled, coming up behind the guy with the bright yellow evidence of my father sticking out his pocket.

Logan let go of my hand and pushed the guy to get his attention.

"What's up, man?" The guy asked, spinning around. I was stunned to see how young he was, probably our age. From where we had been standing he looked much older. He was dressed in a striped polo and jeans. It looked like he was in someone else's clothes because his haircut looked anything but conservative. His straw-colored hair stood in the form of a mini-mohawk, and he had several rings weaving through his ear. He was pretty spindly, but I'm sure that was on purpose.

"Interested in what you've got going on," Logan spoke very quietly.

"How so?" The stranger replied coolly.

"I think you know," Logan snarled as his fist landed deep into the guy's gut.

A gust of air escaped before he doubled over from Logan's fury.

Logan grabbed him and propped him up, making it look like the guy was ill from the scene in front of us. Not like he just got punched in the stomach. The crowd was so blind from what happened earlier to the woman they didn't even seem to notice this little spectacle. It was amazing how very unobservant the general public could be.

"Can you bring the car right over there?" Logan asked, pointing to the street below.

I nodded, but I didn't want to miss a thing. Watching Logan in action did something to me I didn't expect. It was like a magnet pulling me to him. Seeing his grave expression mix with his apparent strength was hard not to admire, but I closed my eyes and nodded not wanting to slow down whatever Logan had planned — if he even had a plan.

I walked quickly to the car and pulled it around. Logan had such a strong grip on the guy that he didn't dare move in any direction but the one Logan intended.

Logan opened the car door and shoved the guy in the backseat and then plopped himself in the front.

"It wasn't my fault," the guy groaned, still in agony from Logan's punch.

"Where to?" I asked, completely perplexed.

Logan turned around to face our kidnap victim and raised his eyebrows. "You'll tell us where we need to go, or I'll have to force it out of you."

The guy nodded.

"What's your name?" I asked, turning out to the main road.

"Preston."

"How long have you been involved?" I questioned him.

"What's it to you?"

Logan's jaw clenched, "Don't disrespect her."

An internal smile radiated deep within my soul. I liked this support. There was no denying it.

Preston moved slowly in the seat, grasping at his stomach, grimacing.

"A few weeks," he replied. "Take a left up ahead."

I nodded, following his direction and wondered how much he might actually know.

"What got you involved with the activities?" Logan asked, his voice a little softer than before.

"They're trying to do really good things at the camp. Working on fears that we have or whatever we feel is keeping us down," Preston responded.

"Did that woman have a fear of flying?" I asked perturbed.

He nodded, "That and heights."

"So now she's dead or close to it. How's that helpful?" I asked, unable to hide my anger.

Preston didn't respond, and Logan didn't take his eyes off of him. The mountain road we drove on seemed to go on forever. With every turn of the road, the homes were less visible and the wilderness more present. It wasn't a place I wanted to break down.

"What are you trying to work on, Preston?" I asked.

"Acceptance." His voice sounded desperate.

"You want to be accepted or you want to be able to accept others?" Logan turned in his seat so he could get a better view of Preston.

"I want to be accepted," he mumbled.

"Who's teaching everything?" I asked.

"His name is Nicholas Stephen. We only meet with him one on one in the beginning, but then we're divided into groups he thinks will work out best based on our particular needs."

It was hard not to pull over the car and shake this kid. How could he not see what this really was?

"Do you stay on the property?" Logan asked, glancing at me quickly.

Preston nodded, "Mostly. It's a pretty incredible experience. You might want to try it. With your anger issues and all."

Logan's lips tightened, and I did my best not to drive us off the road as I hid my laughter. If only he knew.

"Yeah, we're thinking about it," I replied.

"The meeting sessions along with the supplements he provides makes things much clearer," Preston continued.

"Supplements?" Logan and I asked in unison.

"Many kinds, depending on our issues. All of us receive the Boletus mixture. It's like a shake and tastes great. Kind of earthy."

"Sounds delightful." I rolled my eyes for only Logan to see.

"Up ahead is a clearing. This is where the Great Camp starts. Isn't it gorgeous?" he asked.

I pulled the car off the road.

"How do you get there? There's no road?"

"Not to get to the house. You have to take one of the canoes that are always left right up there." He pointed ahead and began shifting uncomfortably in the seat.

"You've been quite helpful," I said. " We both hope you find what you're looking for. But it comes from inside, Preston. No one can provide that except you. I only hope you figure that out before it's too late."

Logan shook his head as if to tell me it was already too late to save him.

"Does this Nicholas have a partner of some sort?"

"There's a woman who accompanies him to lots of things, but she doesn't provide guidance or anything. Someone told me that Nicholas considers her a hard case. Yet to completely see the light he allows her to accompany him to most everything so she can see for herself the good he can produce."

"I see," I murmured, nodding my head.

"I hope you two find what you're hoping to, Preston replied. "My guess is that it's inside the camp. You'd be surprised how at peace you can become."

The rage was building inside of me, and I closed my eyes not allowing my heart to hear anymore. Listening to what this guy had to say was frightening, but it allowed me to glimpse how my father was handling things. I needed to know more, and there was only one way to find out. I pushed that thought aside as Logan's voice brought me back to reality.

"You can get out now," Logan said to Preston.

We both heard a grunt as he got out of the car.

"You did a number on him," I whispered.

Logan smiled as we both watched him trundle off in the direction of the lake. I turned the car around and got back on the road.

"What do you make of it?" I asked, rolling down the window for some fresh air. The car felt very constricting as I tried to process everything Preston had told us.

"I think your father's feeding them something pretty awful," he replied.

"Mentally or physically?" I asked.

"Both," he replied grimly.

"Do you smell that?" I asked, rolling the windows back up.

"Yeah, I do. Pull over," Logan pointed to a turnoff up ahead.

We got out of the car, and I realized I smelled something earthy.

"Mushrooms," I replied.

Logan let out a sigh.

"That's what my father's using. That poor woman on the steeple was probably on some hallucinogenic mushroom."

"They probably all are... of some sort or another. He must be growing them around here. I really think —"

"Mushrooms like that are nearly impossible to propagate."

"Not happening," Logan interrupted, getting back in the car.

Following his lead, I climbed in the driver's seat to take us back to our place.

"I think it's the only way," I attempted again.

He shook his head, but I knew I would do what I needed to whether I had his approval or not.

Many minutes of silence passed between us. I glanced quickly at him and his face was devoid of expression.

"I'm worried that you're going to grow to hate me," I announced, tightening my grip on the steering wheel.

"Where did that come from?" he questioned, turning to face me.

I took a deep breath in.

"If it's true my father kill—"

"Triss, you've got to quit acting like everything is your fault or that you have any control over others' actions. If your father was responsible for my father's death, it has nothing to do with you. I don't understand why you'd even go there."

"I don't want to be a constant reminder of everything bad that's happened to you," I whispered. "I've seen your expression change over the last couple of days, since I told you about what I saw."

"You don't think it could be for a variety of other reasons?" he questioned. "It's not like the last few days have been all that pleasant. We're dealing with a very evil man and every day we find out even more than the previous day. Am I angry about my father's death? Beyond. Do I hope for payback? Absolutely."

"I feel like your change happened after I told you. I mean I'd understand completely. What are you thinking?"

He sighed. "I know you've decided to do something that I can't stop. I don't want you to explore that side of things — ever. Justified or not. The one thing that is protecting for you from the creatures your father sends is the one boundary I'm afraid you want to cross."

"Somebody's got to stop him," I murmured.

"It doesn't need to be you."

***

We had printed all of the pages I had managed to scan from my family's spell books and spread them over every surface in the house.

"How did my mom ever get hooked up with my dad? She's the exact opposite of him. Her entire family fought against this kind of evil. And why would Aunt Vieta just get up and turn? It doesn't make sense.

"Check this out. I've barely scratched the surface, but here are some of the connections I've been able to make between my father's family and witch hunts beginning in Europe." I said finishing up my last one. "Not surprisingly, when they moved to America so did the hunting."

He came over from the dining table he'd been canvasing.

"Check it out." I shoved the notebook in front of Logan with my list.

1587 – Germany (Trier peak)

1590 – Scotland (North Berwick)

1603 -1606 Germany (Fulda)

1626 – 1631 Germany (Würzburg and
Bamberg Witch Trials)

1648 – NH (Portsmouth)

1656 – 1680 NH (Hampton)

"Whoa," Logan looked up with a mixture of reverence and dread. "These are different than the ones I put together."

"That's not comforting," I sighed, feeling a pounding headache at the base of my skull waiting for its moment to take over completely. Do we have any coffee?"

Massaging my neck, I contemplated what this really told us beyond the obvious. What had my father's family been trying to incite for hundreds of years? Trying to steal property from other witches? Creating distrust in witch communities? What was it exactly that they hoped to achieve?

"I'll grab some. You okay?" he asked. "It's a lot to take in."

"Yeah, I'm just exhausted."

"I don't think we should wait any longer. The only way we'll know is if I go in there." I glanced at him still in the kitchen.

"If I go into the compound," I repeated, a bit louder.

"I knew what you meant the first time," he snapped. Logan spun around, forgoing the coffee, and arrived by my side.

"No, you're not going in there," he said softly, calmly this time.

"It's not up for discussion. He's my father. My mother's been captured. Your mother's been captured. I'm the one who can find things out. You burned your bridges. I haven't."

"Please, Triss. Don't do this. We don't need to know his motives to get our mothers back." He sounded desperate. I knew he didn't even believe what he was saying.

"You can't protect me from everything," I started.

"Well, not if you're going to be ridiculous," he argued. "There's no guaranteeing you'd come out."

"Do we really believe that I'll be safe going forward with him out in the world? If I don't attempt something this constant pursuit will never end because we won't know the basis for his actions."

His glare was cold and distant. He moved across the room, it seemed, as far away from me as he could get.

"Why don't you understand? Your mom's in

there too," I accused more than questioned.

"I'm afraid he'll convince you of things you'd never do if you were out of the confines of his walls. I want my mom to be okay. I want her to be with me this very moment. And believe me knowing he had something to do with my father's death boosts my hatred into an entirely new category," he replied, pausing for a moment. "But we've both lost almost everyone we've loved to him. Why would I rush to give him the last person I have left?"

Opening my mind to what his words implied made me realize how selfish I was being. Would I want him to go in there, leaving me on the outside? Absolutely not, but something was driving me or pulling me to face my father. I wanted to expose his hidden demons. The pull on my heart was becoming too strong to ignore. I could no longer neglect my responsibility in this mess, and I needed Logan to acknowledge that.

"You're right. I wouldn't want you to go in there either. You're all I've got as well," I whispered.

"The problem is that you'll have your entire family in there coaxing you. It's beyond risky," his voice softened, as he realized I was listening to him.

I understood.

When he looked over at me, his gaze fell to the floor. He knew I had made my decision, and there was nothing he could do to stop me even though I understood his concerns.

"I never should've told you how much I

admired your stubbornness." He attempted a grin.

I went to the couch he was sitting on and laid my head down on his lap. His fingers slowly traced my cheekbone.

"Promise you'll help me," I said, looking into blue eyes that were filled with an acceptance now.

"Always, my love," he whispered.

"Kiss me please," I pleaded. The pull of desire running through my body couldn't be contained as our emotions cascaded from love down to heartache reaching back to betrayal all within seconds. The twisted emotions mingling between us created an intimacy — a rawness — that I hadn't experienced before.

He stood up leaving me on the couch, and I immediately began panicking.

"Remember our choices seal our destiny," he breathed.

My confidence began cowering in the corner of my mind as I realize that I might have lost him, over my father. I closed my eyes and pulled in a deep breath as I thought about what I was doing.

Not hearing any footsteps leave, I opened my eyes to see him watching me, smiling with a bemused expression. My skin flushed as he bent down, merely hovering over me. His closeness created an unstoppable electricity between us.

"Will you do me the favor of allowing for a dry-run and coming up with a solid plan before you enter his camp?"

I nodded in desperation.

He began kissing me with a passion that was beyond exhilarating. I wanted more. I wanted to be held. When I reached my hands to his face, he backed away.

"What are you doing?" I murmured confused.

"Letting my absence sink in," he smirked.

I gasped.

He grabbed my hand and led me outside to one of the paths.

"Where are you taking me?" I asked.

"I had a little something planned for us," he paused, "before everything took a sudden turn."

My heart started beating faster as we approached an area that had candles circling a blanket.

"How?" I asked. "Candles out here?"

"LEDs, actually," he laughed. "Out of all of this, that's what you pick up on?"

Embarrassed I tried again.

"It's very sweet," I returned a nervous laugh.

"After you." He held out his hand, leading the way to the center of the blankets.

I sat down on the blankets he had piled high for us, and my nerves began to get the better of me. I was hoping for something that I wasn't sure would happen. I looked up at him through my lashes and saw that he was staring at me intently.

"I hope our discussion didn't ruin whatever your intentions were out here," I said.

"Is that so?" His eyes were hypnotic. "And what do you think my intentions were?"

The heat began running through my body

with that simple question or maybe it was more like an accusation. That's what it felt like. Oh, how could he do this to me with one look or by uttering a few words?

"I, uh —" I said, my mouth dry with anticipation.

"Yes?" he toyed with me.

I could only nod.

"My Triss, finally rendered speechless?" he smiled, his eyes dancing with a mischievousness I wanted to explore.

My Triss. Oh, how I needed to hear that right now.

He sat next to me, and my excitement couldn't be contained.

He began by placing a tender kiss behind my ear, sending chills of an entirely different sort through me.

A moan escaped from my lips, and a fire that matched my embarrassment developed.

"Was that too much?" he whispered, his breath lingering on my flesh.

"No."

His lips glided across my neck, and I felt the beating of my heart would give away my desire in the quietness of the night. His kisses stopped, but his fingers gently traced my jawline.

"I want more." Looking into his eyes, his breathing changed with my statement.

"Is that what you think I had planned?" he breathed, his lips lingering near mine.

I nodded.

Shaking his head, he smiled. He gently cupped

my face in his hands as his kisses began again, and I closed my eyes enjoying the softness of his touch.

But he stopped.

"We should probably get going," he whispered. "Tonight's a clear night to go scout your father's place."

Was I even hearing things right?

"What are you talking about?" I argued.

"I want to ensure that I'm leaving you with something you'll want more of," he growled, his lips touching the lobe of my ear. "Anticipation is everything, babe."

"Is that so?" I rolled over, pinning him to the ground allowing my lips to follow the path I desired.

CHAPTER 14

A bit later we found a good access point down to the lake and parked out of sight from the main road. Logan unbuckled the straps from the canoe that was secured on top of our car, being careful to not make much noise. We needed to make every movement as if someone was right behind us. The wilderness surrounding the lake belonged to my father and that alone was warning enough. There were no other homes belonging to anyone else for miles.

The darkness was unsettling as I followed Logan down the path to the water. He held the canoe above his head providing yet another opportunity for me to be amazed by his strength. When we reached the lake, he bent down and maneuvered the canoe into the water.

Holding the canoe steady, Logan helped me onto the bench so I didn't fall overboard.

"Logan, I'm frightened," I whispered, situating myself in the canoe. I was gripping the sides of the boat so hard that my fingertips felt raw.

"It's only going to be worse once you go in there," he replied grimly. "I wish you'd understand that."

The lapping of the water alongside the canoe was the only sound that we were trespassing. Staring down at the lake water was like looking into a black hole with ripples. It was not a place I wanted to be. I don't know what I was expecting from this expedition. Our goal was surveillance, but on some level I hoped I'd see my mom. Not in the state she was currently in, but the one when she was loving and selfless — normal.

"I've got to see my mom," I replied. "We're so close to getting her back."

"We're close, but she's not ready. We can't just grab her. This is purely to survey everything, okay? We can't risk it."

I sighed, nodding my head.

"Triss, you've got to promise me that no matter what you see tonight you won't go after her. You have to promise me that or I'll put this canoe back on the roof and drive away."

"I get it. I..."

"It's not safe. Even just staking out his home is risky," Logan whispered.

The unsteadiness of the canoe as Logan stepped inside created a wave of nausea. It would figure my father's camp would only be reachable by water, the one element of the planet that made me ill without fail.

As Logan shifted in the canoe grabbing the paddles, I caught a glimpse of dull black metal tucked in his belt, and it put everything into perspective. I couldn't let my emotions get in the way of doing what was smart.

"If we're caught, we won't be okay, will we? Even though I'm his daughter?" I asked, catching Logan off guard.

"We aren't going to get caught," Logan's gaze tore deeply at my soul as he sat facing me.

"Then why do you have a knife?" I asked, my mouth completely parched. "Isn't a wand enough?"

"I'm not taking any chances." Logan's eyes locked on mine with only the light from the moon making them glow.

"I'm sorry for dragging you into this mess," I whispered.

"You didn't drag me into anything. I've got some unfinished business with your father as well." And with that we began making our way across the lake to his encampment; a camp that had been in his family since 1869. We had no way of knowing what it looked like in the present day. All we'd found were old historical clippings, but with those I could tell the main home sprawled in many different directions. If everything had survived through the years, there looked to be several other buildings on the property as well.

Finding out so much about my father's family and place in this town did nothing to calm my fears. Apparently, the appearance of money buys silence around here — maybe everywhere. Great camps have been a tradition of the Adirondacks since the last half of the nineteenth century.

Often where the wealthy were allowed to hide out.

Logan paddled across the lake to where my father's main house stood. The lake was an S shape, and his camp was around one of the many bends. There was nothing lighting our way except the moon and a spray of stars. The darkness of the area was quite intimidating even with Logan by my side.

"Lay down," Logan whispered. "We've got to be getting close to your father's home."

Nodding my head, I wiggled my way down in the canoe while Logan kept paddling us closer and closer.

The gentle swoosh of the paddle pushing and pulling the water stopped as he brought it inside the canoe. We glided up to the lake's edge. Logan lowered himself next to me, and grabbed twigs and branches with his right hand to pull us to our final destination. We weren't taking any chances that might bring attention our way.

Brightness began competing with the night's sky on the bank that curved along the lake. The orange hue hinted at flames, but I knew we'd soon find out. A deep vibration began wrapping itself around me as the bass of drums echoed through the air. The low rhythm was a haunting contrast to the silence of the night.

Logan's left hand slid into mine as our canoe floated into a perfect angle to view the ceremony.

I closed my eyes unsure that I actually wanted to see anything. I never wanted to think of my mom in any other way than the caring, loving being she'd always been to me growing up. I was frightened to see what she might have been turned into.

Logan gently squeezed my hand, and I concentrated on the sound of the drums beating, allowing myself to fill with the courage needed to witness the night's activities. I hadn't come this far to keep my eyes shut.

The bass became lower and slower. I turned my head toward Logan and opened my eyes to see the horror of the events reflect in his eyes.

The activity along my father's property seemed festive. There were people in every direction, and I almost didn't know where to focus until I saw her— my mother — in the middle of dancing men and women.

She was in the center of the circle. With a flowing white dress and gold necklaces dripping off of her, she looked like royalty. Her body twisted and swayed to the beat of the drums. Her long, brown hair swirled with the movements her body made to the rhythm of the drums. It was like I was seeing someone who was possessed, but by what I didn't know. My mother began pointing at each of the followers. One by one they bowed down in worship with her cruel laughter echoing through the air. What was her purpose here? Did she enjoy this power?

My instinct was to run. To get out of these waters as fast as we could. But there was something else pulling me to stay. Maybe it was a morbid curiosity. What would be next? This was quite a show to put on for the regulars. Did this happen every night? It was close to a freak show. Nothing like the magical nights I grew up with, celebrating life and love.

The anger brewing up inside of me was impossible to ignore, but I forced myself to look beyond my mother. We were here to map the place, and I needed to survey everything. Looking behind her, I saw what I assumed was my father's home. Except I wouldn't call it a home, more like a stone castle.

I felt Logan's gaze on me and quickly looked at him.

"Are you okay?" he whispered. "It feels like you're about to do something."

"I'm fine. I won't do anything."

The property bustled with activity in every direction. Near the flames, where my mother was dancing, sorcerers were dressed in long robes of different colors ranging from purple, to red, and black. They all held something in their hands, but I couldn't see what the objects were.

The thick smell of smoke and lake water was heavy in the air, and my eyes began watering as the breeze shifted our way. I looked over at Logan who was scanning all of the figures, undoubtedly searching for his mom.

The robed sorcerers began lining up. Some were fidgeting. Others stood deathly still. The drumming slowed and my mother lowered her arms. The circle around her disbanded, and she slowly walked into the darkness. My eyes lingered on my mom's shadow in hopes it would bring her back. It didn't.

A large man came from the direction near my mom, not dressed in anything particularly ceremonial, and walked over to the flames. He reached his arms to the sky as the sorcerers followed behind him. He began speaking to the flames, chanting, but I was too far away to hear what he was saying.

The drumming stopped at the same time as the flames began to swirl and move to the man's commands.

This man was my father.

I wanted to flee.

The crowd grew larger around my father. Where were they all coming from and where was my mom?

My father sliced the flames in the dark air, allowing them to multiply and sizzle anything in their way. Chairs and leaves disintegrated instantly, and I hoped he wouldn't turn his fire toward the witches around him. Bursts of yellow and orange streaks burned every intended target my father directed them toward. His smile widened with every push and pull of his palm, and I knew at last that his energy was coming from the underworld. An endless supply of negativity and destruction at his disposal was a terrifying thought, but one we'd have to account for.

I winced at the last thought and watched his movements carefully as he controlled the fire with a slight point of his finger or blink of an eye.

This was what we were up against. The fear

was becoming very real.

"Is there any stopping him?" I whispered.

Logan's jaw clenched, as he stared straight forward, leaving me to answer my own question.

The flames grew larger with every thrust of his fist and twist of his wrist. The air wasn't silent. Instead it was filled with the roaring of flames and the murmurs of the crowd. His ability felt unstoppable, and yet I still didn't understand what he really wanted to accomplish. I needed to get on the inside. It was the only way.

"Are you seeing this?" Logan whispered.

"Of course I am," I replied puzzled.

"Are you *really* seeing this?" he repeated.

Taking my gaze off of my father I finally realized what Logan meant. People were collapsing in every direction I looked. The larger the flames my father created, the more energy he needed to gather. And it wasn't only from the underworld like I thought.

"These people? He's draining them of—"

"Life," Logan finished.

For a split second I was in awe, and Logan caught it.

"Impressive isn't it?" he asked.

Nodding, I stared in complete disbelief. I wondered if Preston was in that crowd but pushed the thought aside.

"The ones he's sucking the life from aren't even witches are they?" I asked.

"Probably not. Guessing they're the poor souls who grabbed the phone number dangling on the community board at Starbucks. Lots of Prestons in that group."

"We've got to stop my father."

My mother reappeared hand in hand with someone who I least expected, Aunt Vieta. They made their way close to where my father stood. My aunt smiled and laughed as she spoke with my mother. They didn't seem all that impressed with what my father was doing. In fact they didn't even seem to notice the atrocities that he was committing.

As my father tired of playing with the flames, he extinguished them as fast as he had created them. The sorcerers surrounding my father placed the objects that they had been holding up to their faces. Terror ran through my veins, and all I wanted was to leave this lake.

The sorcerers appeared to become something from another world as their movements became ghostlike; sweeping away the bodies my father had turned into limp forms.

"Close your eyes," Logan ordered.

"What are those?" I whispered, unable to obey him.

"Plague masks," Logan replied bitterly.

"What for?" I asked.

"It's superstition, but it's so the sorcerers souls don't get taken along with the humans as they dispose of them."

I felt broken, like the blood on my father's hands was now on mine for witnessing these events. After all, one can't view something like this and remain innocent. This wasn't about my mother any longer. My father had to be finished before any more innocents were taken.

He left the ceremony as his dirty work was completed for him. Everyone was clearing out pretty quickly, leaving a querulous energy behind. As if some of these people wanted more.

"Let's get out of here," I whispered to Logan. "Everyone's leaving, I think now's our chance."

Logan nodded and quietly grabbed the paddle as he dipped it gently into the water, wiggling it softly enough to get the canoe moving. I looked one more time in the direction of my aunt and mother, only to be horrified as my eyes locked with my aunt's and she gave a quick nod.

"We've got to hurry," I pleaded. "I think my aunt saw us."

Our canoe floated behind the thicket of brush, enabling Logan to sit up and paddle quicker to our entry point.

"There's no way," he finally replied in a hushed voice.

"I really think she did," I protested.

"Let's hope not."

Several sets of flickering silver eyes met us along the bank. I glanced at Logan who wore a dubious expression as he steadied the canoe. I was frozen in the canoe with absolutely no intention of leaving the safety of the lake, which had quickly become my new favorite place.

My solution quickly became challenged as the silver flecks began moving toward the canoe. Did these things not need land?

"What's going on?" I muttered, afraid to look away.

"Remember those creatures you said you didn't believe in back at the cottage?"

Wracking my brain for what he was possibly referring to, I watched as these brilliant little creatures completely circled our canoe. I didn't know how I could be afraid of something so tiny, but they carried such a life force.

"Faeries," I whispered in disbelief. "I had no idea."

"Tried to tell ya," Logan whispered.

"Are they on our side or not?"

"No idea," Logan replied, as he steadied the boat. "Time to tap into those other life forces, babe."

The arrowhead pendant I'd worn since I found it in our attic began to warm against my skin. My fingers grasped tightly around the metal as I let the energy run through me. The darkness of the night held nothing but whispers coming at me from every direction.

"Do you hear that?" I asked Logan.

"Nothing at all," he replied.

I reached for Logan's hand as the fairies lit the entire area with a luminescence that would've blinded most and forced Logan to close his eyes, leaving only me to see the tiny creatures all around us, hovering.

The fairies were no bigger than my palm. They were lanky in form but with a delicateness that was otherworldy and inviting. Their wide eyes held a brilliant curiosity as they took me in as much as I took them in. Their tiny mouths were not moving even though I heard their whispers. I needed to understand their cries — their language. I wanted to reach out but was afraid I would frighten them. One of the more capricious of the fairies, slowly extended its miniature hand toward me, and in turn I felt compelled to return the gesture.

Upon lengthening my arm, the fairy swarm stopped their whispers. Blackness replaced the silver of their eyes as they opened their mouths to display jagged, ivory teeth. My father was no longer our most immediate threat.

Bowing my head in an apology, I awaited their decision. If my mom's stories had any validity, we were at their mercy.

CHAPTER 15

The pencil thin lips of the hovering beings were pressed together as the fairies communicated with each other without ever saying a word. Their eyes slowly drifted back to the bright silver that greeted us earlier.

Logan sat down next to me on the canoe bench and held my hand. We were completely at their mercy. These tiny creatures held a power that most humans couldn't dream of — if the stories I grew up with were true.

I reached up to my pendant, which began getting warm once more, in hopes that I would hear their words.

The whispers were now more distinguishable and far more spirited in tone. An excitement buzzed around the group that I hadn't picked up on before. Although none of the fairies were asking me anything directly, they were asking one another questions about me.

"Is she really the one?"

"Does she have the pendant?"

"Does she know about us?"

"Where do we take her?"

"Can the male with her be trusted?"

I squeezed Logan's hand as apprehension began spreading through me. *Oh, no. I think they have me confused with someone else and once they realize it, what will they do with us?* My hand left the pendant and their voices were silenced. I looked at Logan who only nodded at me. Placing my hand back on the pendant I waited, for what I wasn't sure.

After listening to the fairies get their line of questioning sorted, the fairy I'd attempted my failed gesture of peace with, began speaking.

"Do you know your place in the world?" The male fairy asked, flying to only a few feet from me, taking me by surprise.

Anxiety filled my body. It felt like our lives depended on these answers, and I had nothing more to give than the truth and the truth wasn't much.

"It seems to be coming to me in pieces. I want to stop my father from whatever havoc he's trying to cause in whatever world he's trying to cause it in. I want my mother back, but other than that I don't know," I replied, looking into the glimmering eyes of the questioner. "That's why I was here at the lake. I wanted to see my mother."

"We know, dear," A female fairy moved forward. She had a maternal quality about her — something I craved. "My name is Bakula. Pardon our manners. We aren't used to having to explain ourselves. His name is Dace."

"Nice to meet you both," I bowed once more,

but my voice gave me away. I was terrified. "This is Logan. His mother's been captured too."

Dace ignored my niceties and fluttered about, directing the other fairies to create a way for us to leave the water.

The fear lifted slightly at his gesture, but when I attempted to stand up in the canoe all of them rushed toward me. Glancing quickly at Logan he was smirking. *Why was he so at ease?* And before I knew what was happening, the fairies lifted me up and carried me to the bank.

"We didn't want you to get wet. We've got a long night ahead of us and don't have time to waste with human problems," Dace said pointedly.

I looked over at Logan who was being treated to the same transportation mode. His smile was pleasant and without any of the fear that certainly traced my lips.

The fairies grabbed the canoe out of the water and quickly flew to our car where they strapped it on top and created a foliage camouflage that was undetectable no matter how hard I stared.

"Come, Triss," Dace replied in a husky voice that didn't match his diminutive size.

I reached my hand out to Logan, and we followed the army of fairies deep into the woods with their brilliance lighting the way. Maybe the conversation my mom wanted to have with me was about this, and if it wasn't, I'd say it should've been because I was completely lost.

Seeing the woods through the fairies' perspective was brilliant. Their glow managed to bounce off the foliage, soil, and trees creating a lustrous appearance everywhere I glanced.

"It's quite spectacular," Logan whispered, his eyes sparkling, too, from the fairies' presence. "Guess you should have believed me about the fairies."

I rolled my eyes and hid my smile as we followed them deeper into the forest, unsure of where we were headed, but with every step toward the unknown, my fear diminished. Could this be the answer we were looking for?

"Look at the vines," I said in awe, pointing up high. "I never knew there were vines on some of these trees."

An earthy smell began to replace the woodsy smell as the trees became farther apart and we reached a clearing of sorts.

"Mushrooms," I whispered in awe, watching fairies spring to life from the field in front of us. Hundreds of them — maybe more — offered their dazzling welcome.

"These are our homes in the summer," Bakula said.

The field was covered in a sparkling blanket, and the harder I pressed my fingers against the pendant, the more I heard their pleas.

"Come, dear. We have a lot to cover." Bakula took off in the direction that Dace had gone.

Looking down at my feet, which suddenly felt like gigantic bulldozers threatening the homes of all the fairies, I carefully stayed on the edge of the field. Logan was behind me doing the same with each footstep, as we watched Dace and

Bakula head to where the forests began once more.

"What do you think of all of this?" I whispered to Logan.

"I think they'll do a much better job explaining your purpose in this world than I ever could," he replied mysteriously. "I tried to tell you back when we were on Alki Beach. Remember?" he laughed. "Don't forget *that* or us insignificant people on your climb up."

"What are you talking about?" I giggled.

"You'll see soon enough."

Dace and Bakula were waiting patiently, well one was patient – the other not so much. Dace had his arms crossed and looked aggravated, so we both stepped up our pace. For such a teeny creature, he could really throw his weight around. He was nothing to be messed with.

The other fairies had disbanded from our group, probably going to their homes in the field. There was a comfort in that, knowing these beings had families.

"Sorry," I apologized, meeting their stare. "You're much quicker than we are."

"That we are," Bakula hummed in a beautiful voice. "This way."

We followed Dace and Bakula back into the woods, but this time we were immediately met with a miniature village. I stopped dead in my tracks for fear that I would step on something that was of importance to them.

"Over there," Dace said, pointing to the side of the village where two human-sized handcrafted log seats were waiting for us.

If I didn't know better, it almost looked like they were placed at the head of the village.

Careful to step on only flat surfaces, Logan and I made our way to these beautiful masterpieces.

Before sitting, my hand traced the vines and petals that were carved deep into the wood, layered with lighter carvings of animals and birds.

"Triss," Logan whispered, pointing.

I followed his finger to see my name etched into the wooden surface, and my throat went dry. It was hard for me to swallow. I looked at the other chair, but there was no name engraved.

"Please sit." Bakula motioned.

We both took our seats and I scanned the village that seemed set for nobility. Their buildings were carved with as much care as the chair that I was sitting in. Little chimneys carried smoke out of the homes, and steps led to bridges that were secured to the pines surrounding us. It was quite elaborate.

Dace and Bakula moved smaller versions of our chairs in front of us, readying for a discussion that offered possibilities I never imagined. I raised my hand to the pendant and took a deep breath in.

"The night on the beach," Dace began, and my blood froze. "Was a horrible night for fairies around the globe. We had been waiting patiently for you to turn eighteen."

My hands began getting clammy, and I

glanced at Logan for support. What all did this species know about me and why?

"Not only did you lose your mother, we thought we might have lost our only chance for continued survival," Dace sighed.

"But all hope is not lost," Bakula had a glimmer in her eyes. "You're the chosen one and here you are."

Logan reached his hand over and placed it on my knee, gently squeezing it with anticipation. No one spoke, but I needed words because that was the most unclear statement I had ever heard.

When I realized they had no intention of continuing I leaned forward and smiled, placing my hand out, not even sure why.

Bakula took this to mean something and hopped on my hand.

"Chosen for what?" I whispered, afraid the forests would hear my ignorance.

"To save us. To save the forests of the world, the animals of the world and your brothers and sisters for they are the most lost of all."

"Humans? What do they need saving from?"

Dace laughed and so did Logan, which kind of perturbed me since I wasn't privy to the joke.

"From themselves," Bakula responded, smiling.

"That's kind of a big responsibility for one person," I said, completely bewildered.

"Well, the movement is supported by many participants. We were waiting for the right leader, and that is you, Triss," Bakula said.

"How do you know it's me and not someone

else who should be helping?"

"Your lineage primed you to be the most understanding witch to have come to our world ever—"

"I don't *feel* very understanding. I'm certainly not understanding when it comes to my father's actions," I interrupted Dace.

"That brings us to another problem," Dace began again, not even bothering to answer my complaint. "Your father has been destroying our communities for a certain ingredient found in those mushrooms you saw. It's nothing new. The family has followed us from place to place continually disrupting the purpose of these mushrooms. We cultivated them because they provide us protection. Unfortunately your father, and his family before him realized the hallucinogenic properties. They can manipulate human desires, thoughts, and abilities. Frankly they've found the perfect brainwashing brew."

"So it's not just black magic?" I asked. "It requires *this* substance found in your mushrooms."

"Oh yes, dear. No human, witch or otherwise, could ever have *that* type of power over another human, at least to that extreme. It takes help."

I felt Logan's gaze on me and turned to face him. His deep, blue eyes were filled with compassion. The burden that was being thrust upon me was nothing I thought I could handle.

"With these chemicals, it can become very easy to persuade someone to choose a path they might not normally go down," Dace followed up.

"What do you think I can do to help?" I asked. "I had planned to go into the compound, but that was purely to get our mothers back and find out what my father's plans are."

"We can tell you a little bit of what your father's plans are," Dace replied quietly. "But it would still be quite beneficial to have you go into the compound."

"If you already know what her father's plan is, why should we put her in harm's way? Isn't there a way to get our mothers back without her going in there?" Logan interrupted.

"You love her," Dace said softly.

"More than anything," Logan nodded.

"She can cause a weakness in her father that no one else could provide," Bakula replied.

"He hasn't seen me for eighteen years. I doubt he holds a soft spot for me," I argued. The mere mention of my father got my blood pumping.

"It may seem that way, but we can give you tools to accomplish it," Dace continued.

"Like?" Logan asked on my behalf.

Dace turned to me, and Bakula hopped off of my hand to sit back down in her chair.

"We offer you our gift of foresight," Dace replied.

"You can see the future?" I asked.

"Of sorts." Bakula looked over at Logan and then back at me. "We can see every option available and based on certain actions, we can see where it all might lead."

I thought quickly to the chair Logan was sitting in and the absence of his name engraved on it. Yet, I'm sure they knew he was coming.

Bakula nodded at me. She knew what I was thinking.

"We always have a choice," I whispered.

"Always," Dace agreed. "Your father had a choice eighteen years ago. Logan had a choice as well."

The warmth spread through my body as the realization of what Dace's words meant. I caught Logan looking at me, gauging my reaction. Dace and Bakula's lesson was an intimate expression of our own fears and paranoia leading to a possible conclusion, and we had the power to change it.

"You have a stoic mind, Triss," Bakula said. "That will only work in our favor."

"Some of us might call it stubbornness," Logan smiled, and I couldn't help but smile despite the very serious moment in time.

"I will help however I can," I replied. "I hope it's enough."

"It will be. Your decision ensures it already." Dace said, fluttering about with activity.

"Now let's have the engravers carve the correct name in your partner's chair," Bakula said, who was an apparent romantic at heart.

"Thank you, Bakula," I whispered, giving her my pinky to shake, "and you, too, Dace." Who was already busy waking up the artisan who would finish the chair next to mine.

"No, thank you. Your choice has given us all hope once more, but we need to start planning now. Time isn't on our side," Bakula said, her voice solemn.

"But kids," Bakula added, making me feel like my mother was in front of me, "remember that nothing can tear you two apart except for your own fears and paranoia."

I nodded, and stole a glance at Logan who was wearing one of the most confident smiles I had seen on his lips in quite some time.

"Thanks Bakula," I whispered, grateful for this tiny woman full of knowledge I never would be able to replicate.

"Now, let's shoot for getting you in there in three days," Dace was back with a blue print of my father's property that was ten times as large as he was.

Logan's eyes darkened, and I knew we were in for a long night ahead of us.

CHAPTER 16

"**D**o you think it can be done?" I asked.

Logan nodded. "I do. I'm not that hot on the idea of you going in there alone, but maybe they're right. Maybe it is the only way."

We didn't get back to the house until early morning from our meeting with the fairies. Instead of allowing myself to feel overwhelmed, I forced myself to fall asleep and start over again with a fresh outlook. I glanced over at Logan who looked worn out and like he didn't follow the same plan. We had curled up together on the couch, but I had woken up alone.

"Did you sleep at all?" I questioned.

"Meh, enough."

"I don't even know what time it is," I said, reaching for my phone and noticing a message. "Did you already fill in Jenny?"

"I managed to get in touch with everyone Dace mentioned," he replied softly.

So he hadn't slept at all.

I gave him a grateful smile and thought about

how much our lives had changed in such a short time. Logan's lips quirked in an almost-smile as if he knew what I was thinking, and the thought of leaving him made me wonder about my choice. Maybe we could just run away together.

"You always have this way about you," I started.

"Yeah?" he prompted, smiling as he looked up from a page he was reading.

"It's pretty incredible, actually."

"How's that?" he asked, completely bewildered.

"You're so in control, so strong. I feel so protected around you even when I don't need protecting." I replied with mild embarrassment. "I'm going to miss that when I go inside the compound. I *know* I'm strong enough. It's not that."

"What is it then?" his voice softer, and his eyes taking in everything about me.

"It's that! Right there... that look," I whispered. "You make me feel like everything I have to say is important — valued. I'm not going to have anyone to bounce ideas or my wacky assumptions off of."

He looked down at the table quickly and moved the papers he was looking at to the side.

Oh, no! Did I completely freak him out?

"Wanna sit down over here?" his words were burdened with something I didn't understand.

"Sure," I replied as cheerfully as possible. I had no clue what was going on.

I plopped down in the chair next to him and

yanked on his seat to angle him toward me more.

"There. That's better," I teased. "If I'm in for something heavy, I need a full on frontal view of you."

"Is that so?" His grin was wide.

"Yep. That way if I get really mad, I can just look at you, and it'll remind me of why I put up with you."

"Wow. That's the only reason, huh?" His eyes had softened, and my worry began to fade slightly.

"That and your mammoth house back in Illinois," I teased.

He smiled and touched my cheek, creating a flurry inside.

Did he find something out when he was calling everyone to fill them in on our plans? That might be it. Maybe there's more infiltration on my father's side than we accounted for. His voice cut into my thoughts with something I didn't expect.

"Remember when you tried on that old dress from the attic?"

"Yeah I do." It seemed so long ago but it wasn't that far in the past at all. Dancing in his embrace felt magical, like anything was possible. How had things gotten so complicated?

"I felt like the luckiest man in the world getting to hold you, yet I was so worried that you would push me away."

"I'm sorry I ever made you feel that way," I whispered. "I never meant to, but it was like," I paused for a second, "too good to be true."

"I guess it was in a way, and it was short-lived." His laughter lingered.

"Wasn't it though?" My mind quickly thought back to the Trevor situation.

"You believe what Bakula said about spells of the heart, right?" he asked.

"Yes, and might I add... I-told-you-so," I said grinning. "I knew that side-effect was bogus."

"Well, it's only bogus because you're so bullheaded," he shot back with an adorable smirk.

"If you believe in me and I believe in you, we'll be set," I said. "Which I always knew."

"Right, that's exactly how I remember it," he replied coyly, but then his eyes began shielding something.

He frowned and looked over at the sheet of paper, bringing it toward him again.

"I want to show you something," he said, pointing at the piece of paper.

"What's up?" I asked perplexed, only seeing a drawing.

"It's," he hesitated. "It's a method for us to share things and —"

"Yeah?"

"I know we're young, and I don't want to pressure you." The confidence that Logan usually exuded was completely absent. Instead, he wore a shy grin.

"Would you spit it out?" I teased him.

"You know that tattoo I have that links me to your father?" Logan asked.

"Kind of hard to forget." I rolled my eyes.

"That's not the only type of tattoo that can link beings. There are ones that are far more intimate, and I thought maybe we could share — " His eyes held onto mine, waiting for my response before he continued.

My heart skipped a beat, and all I could do was blink at him.

"Too much?" he asked softly.

Not realizing I was giving him the wrong impression I began shaking my head quickly, thinking about what to say, but words seemed inadequate.

"I...I would be honored," I whispered.

His blue eyes burned into mine, as a look of wonder spread across his face.

"Really?" his voice was hoarse. "You would do this for me?"

I shook my head and reached over to his hand.

"I would do this for me," I smiled.

"You have a glorious smile," he grinned.

"Do I?" I began getting lightheaded as excitement ran through me. I had no idea what to expect, but I was looking forward to finding out.

"Maybe this one can replace the spider spell?" I teased.

"Pretty sure the *nectunt* will replace it," he murmured, his eyes penetrating my soul. "Do you want me to give you some details?"

"Yes, please explain the *nectunt*," I replied, scooting closer, trying to shake my sudden dazed feeling. "Quite a name."

"It's going to hurt—"

"You should've started with that," I

191

interrupted.

"No way. And ruin my odds? I even made sure I was wearing the jeans you love." He looked at me with hidden amusement.

"I can see that," I said, laughing. "And it worked."

"I'm thankful that this will cover all bases with the whole love-spell free-will thing." He winked at me.

"Whatever. I'm telling you, all those little things that we kept being paranoid about with the Trevor connection were probably me just being my worrywart self. We were so freaked out that we jumped to the worst possible conclusion every time thinking it was the side effect. It was almost like we were going to ensure some tormented destiny would arrive at our door whether we wanted it or not," I laughed. "I'm serious. I knew I never had anything for him. You better believe me next time."

"I hope there's not a next time," he said sternly.

I swatted at him and waited for him to continue.

"We will use this," he said, moving the drawing directly in front of me. "But where this part is empty, we can place an addition inside that means something to both of us."

"I'd say daisies, but I won't do that to you," I teased. "Butterflies are probably out too."

"For you I'd do it." His eyes were sparkling, and I felt so lucky to be sharing this experience with him.

"You know what they say about couples who get matching tattoos, right? That kind of signals the end," I said, laughing nervously. "People always break up after they get matching tattoos."

He started laughing, and I loved watching him. It was a split second where we were more like ourselves than ever.

"Well it's good that ours aren't exactly the same then. Besides these aren't *those* kind. These are deeper."

I smiled, wondering what he meant.

"So there's no getting out of it? We're really linked?" The excitement was building.

He nodded. "Pretty much, but you heard what Bakula said, matters of the heart and all."

I sat there thinking of images from what we'd experienced together and images that might work the best. The snake seemed fitting, but no matter how grateful I was to Logan for producing that weapon for me, I don't think I'd want an image of it on my body.

"What about the arrowhead?"

"I think that's perfect." He nodded, unable to hide his smile.

"It is, isn't it?"

"So how does it work?"

"We'll be signaling to our ancestors, along with the world we live in, our commitment to one another."

"Wow."

"We won't be sharing a replica of the same tattoo. The image will be split between us," he continued.

"Like a locket?" I asked.

"Yeah, I guess it's kind of like that. We each have half of the image and our energy is able to go between the two. We'll be able to share abilities between each other as time goes by. Right away, however, we can communicate through this." He pointed to the upper part of the stencil drawing. "I was thinking we might do the ritual before everything begins."

"Before I go to meet my father?" I asked, my mouth dry.

He nodded. "If you don't want to, I understand."

"No, I totally want to do it before then. What all is involved with the actual spell?"

"It isn't that complicated, but it can be exhausting depending how far we take it." His mouth twisted upright and his expression was completely irresistible.

"What does that mean?" I questioned playfully, hoping it meant what I wanted.

"It's a really intimate experience in the Wiccan world and if we add the human—"

"We are definitely adding the human component," I interrupted, playfully scowling.

"Whatever you say, babe" he replied amused.

"Should we start?" I asked.

Logan began laughing at the same time that I realized exactly how eager I must have sounded.

Logan slid the chair back and pulled me into his arms. His gaze held an intensity that excited me.

"You are my everything and more, Triss," he

whispered, pulling my hair back from my face.

"And you are mine."

Scooping me up, he took me toward the stairs and my breath caught.

"Are you ready?" he asked softly.

I nodded causing his lips to curl into a smile as he began carrying me up the stairs. The door to the bedroom was open, lit with candles in every corner, and daisies in every direction.

Choking back my happiness, it felt like my world was spinning.

"It's beautiful," I gushed.

"Not as beautiful as you," he murmured, gently lowering me onto the bed.

"You've already got the girl, Mr. Greene," I reply coyly.

He leaned over me with his lips barely touching my skin as he traced his mouth down my arm, sending shivers through my system.

"Are you cold?" he asked quietly.

Catching his gaze, I shook my head no. No words would come out.

"No matter what we face, I'll always be there for you."

I looked into his eyes and felt the desire take hold. I wanted to be with this man forever and leave everything behind.

"Turn on your side," he whispered, allowing his lips to trace the curves of my arm.

"I can't move if you're going to continue. You're lips are more than a little paralyzing."

A salacious grin covered his mouth, as he backed away, trading his lips for his fingers.

I turned on my side like he requested, unsure of what he had planned. I glanced at the box he grabbed and then back at him.

"What's inside?" I asked, narrowing my eyes at him suspiciously.

"I'm not going to tell you because you'll only laugh," he smiled.

"Well now you've *got* to tell me."

He grabbed the tiniest of the bottles and opened the cap, placing it near my nose.

"Go ahead," he offered.

I smelled light vanilla.

"That smells really nice."

"It's a calming oil, once our spell is finished between us, we'll dab it on our skin."

"Now you're the healer?" I teased.

He sat next to me, and placed my hand in his. I felt the heat from his body, his desire. I stared into his smoldering gaze, and I couldn't stop the anticipation from building. My eyes fell to his lips. They were so full and waiting to be kissed.

"So is this like a normal tattoo?" I murmured.

He shook his head not taking his eyes off mine. "Once I begin the spell the image we chose will place itself into our flesh."

"Into our flesh. Not onto our flesh?"

He nodded and bit his lip.

I couldn't take it any longer.

Maybe we can save that until last," I whispered, pulling him toward me.

"I don't see why not," he smiled, hovering over me.

Logan's lips slowly caressed mine sending an

electrical current through me, but he didn't let his lips land in any one place. Instead, he teased me by gliding his lips along my neck and then down to my collarbone before quickly stopping. He nuzzled my neck, and I could take no more. A small moan escaped from my lips as he traced his teeth along my flesh.

"Too much?" he asked, pulling away. His blue eyes pierced mine with an intensity that frightened me, but in a way that I longed for.

"Not at all," I breathed. "But you seem so—"

He shook his head, pressing his finger softly against my lips. "I've thought about being with you for years, and I'm going to make it as memorable as possible."

A smile spread across his lips, and his eyes danced over my fully clothed body. *I would have to change that.*

"Well, it's working," I whispered, bringing him back down to me.

"You're the only woman I've ever wanted," he breathed, as he pressed his body into mine. My hands slid along his back until I found the end of his shirt. I pulled it up and began kissing his chest with a desperation I'd never felt before.

"I love you," I moaned.

Logan cupped my face and brought it to his. The longing in his eyes only grew with every second that passed between us. He ran his fingers through my hair as my mind turned to mush.

My fingers traced along his shoulders, and I gently pushed him back. He sat up removing his shirt, with his jeans hanging just low enough to make my heart flutter. His legs straddled me as I lay on the bed, and I admired how absolutely divine he was. I didn't ever want this moment to end.

His hands hovered over my body, and the aching inside became almost unbearable. I closed my eyes and took a deep breath in. I slowly let it out and opened my eyes to see his lips quirk into a slight smile.

"Yeah?" he asked, grinning.

"I don't think I can take much more," I whispered, my breathing ragged.

His eyes danced along my body before he scooped me into his arms, allowing me to roll on top of him.

I placed my hand under his neck, bringing his lips to mine knowing that our souls would soon become one.

CHAPTER 17

"We're meeting everyone on Whiteface Mountain. Plenty of space to roam and finalize plans," Logan replied, as he backed our car out of the driveway.

I nodded, still in a daze from the night before. I never wanted this feeling to end. I didn't really have much sleep and was probably running on empty, but it certainly didn't feel like it.

"You look absolutely radiant," he murmured, glancing at me.

"I wonder why that is?" I asked, chuckling.

He flashed a crooked smile, and I felt flushed.

"You certainly have a way." I reached over and placed my hand on his knee, he picked it up and placed a quick kiss on my knuckles, igniting my senses once more.

"If only," I started.

He looked at me and nodded, "If only."

We drove in silence for a little while as I thought about the possibilities of how everything could end. The fairies said everything is about choices. In every circumstance, I'll see the options available for the chooser and will have to use my intuition to see what path they might choose.

"There's a part of me that wants to run away from

everything, except that it would only find me again."

"It would only find *us* again," Logan interjected. "You're not going anywhere without me."

"Except tomorrow," I frowned.

Logan's eyes darkened, acknowledging my words and panic began spreading through me.

"I'm worried I'm not going to be able to handle everything," I said, looking out the window as the trees whipped by the window.

"At any time we can come get you. Remember that. Don't try to be a hero, ever," he scolded. "No matter what."

"I wouldn't." I pursed my lips together and leaned my head back on the headrest.

He turned the car off the main road, onto the gravel leading us to the park entrance.

"Do you think I'll always be able to see as much into the future as they implied?"

He nodded. "I think you'll be able to see events that *may* happen based on people's choices. They could always choose differently though."

I bit my lip and looked out the window.

"Just trust your gut, and use the gift they gave you as a supplement. Don't rely on it, rely on yourself."

I turned to face him. "Thank you."

His presence was intoxicating. Everything was magnified since last night. I needed to get outside.

He flashed a lopsided grin and hopped out of the car.

We climbed up the hill until I heard lots of voices and then saw a large group.

Jenny stepped out from the crowd, and I let out a squeal. I knew she was supposed to be here but having her in front of me was a different story.

"Thank you for coming. You have no idea how much I appreciate it."

We're all here for you and for your mom. And Ellsy." Her eyes darted to Logan.

"Thank you, Jenny," Logan replied, walking to the crowd that I'd pulled Jenny from.

"My parents are here too, and they brought some friends. We're gonna make things right."

"You have no idea how much I needed to hear that right now," I murmured, attempting to smile.

"I can only imagine." She turned back toward the group, waving at her parents who walked over to us.

"Oh, Triss. I'm so sorry. We've gathered as many as we could. Only the people we trust. We're certainly second guessing everything and everyone now," Jenny's mom, Tamara, replied.

"I understand," I replied, nodding. I caught Logan's glance as he listened intently to someone I didn't recognize.

"All right everyone. We don't have much time. Triss will be going in tomorrow afternoon," Logan's voice boomed. "There's more to his ability to persuade than only his personality. It appears he's been using hallucinogenic compounds to help the process along. Because of this, no matter what, we can't eat or drink anything on or surrounding his property. As such, we've got plans to keep Triss going in there as well."

Everyone hushed and turned their attention to him. He stood on a boulder speaking to the crowd as if he'd given directives a million-times before. I was in awe.

"You guys have really grown up fast," Jenny whispered.

I nodded and a smile spread across my lips. I wasn't sure if that was a good thing or not, but that was what had happened. Watching him speak to the crowd was mesmerizing. This setting really suited him, but the reason was unfortunate.

"Triss will be in there for a short time. If there's any problem we'll have to go in immediately and get her out of there. I've got a schematic that each of you will have in case that happens."

Leading people was his calling. The crowd was responding well, cheering him on. I suddenly felt like I was the wrong person chosen.

Logan's eyes locked on mine.

"Break into groups and we'll wander around and give you more specifics for your teams. We must stop him from hurting any others," he finished.

The group cheered and applauded as the gravity of his words surrounded me.

He draped his arm over my shoulder, and I felt wholly protected. I didn't want to leave this feeling, but I knew I'd have to soon. We drifted over to one of the larger groups.

I gasped when I saw Jenna, who was one of the elders from the Witch Avenue Coven, standing in the middle of the group Logan was leading me to.

"It's okay," Logan whispered. "She's on our side."

"Triss," Jenna replied, holding out her hand. "I'm so sorry about everything. You're having to face things I don't even understand. None of us do."

Her long, white hair was piled on top of her head with a clip. She wore a black dress, with a red shawl. There was something different about her. She looked exhausted, older than when I saw her at the ceremony.

"Everything okay?" I asked.

"The coven is in turmoil. The priestess is at her wits' end. I'd say thirty percent of our coven has split off to join the Praedivinus order. I've never seen a divide like this in our world."

With everything Logan and I had been dealing

with, we'd managed to stay sheltered from the crises at the covens across the country. Hopefully, the damage was reversible.

"Enough about that. We can figure out all the politics of everything later," she replied, frowning. "Logan thought it would be the best if I taught you how to perform the Soul Traveler spell."

I looked at Logan and he nodded. "She's said to be the best in the country."

"The most accurate," Jenna interrupted.

"So I'll be able to see if my mother has any of her own soul left?"

"It's kind of like that, yes."

"How will I know when to perform it?"

"It's best done at night when she's sleeping."

"I'm going to leave you two while I check with the others," Logan muttered, kissing my cheek.

I nodded and turned to face Jenna.

"If this doesn't give you the answers you're hoping for," Jenna began, "I'll be there for you however I can when you return. I know that's not much, but it's the best I can offer."

"I appreciate that. I do. Seeing a glimpse of my mother didn't give me much hope," I whispered, forcing the sadness back.

"You saw her?"

"From a distance."

She pursed her lips together and grabbed my hands.

"If this doesn't tell you what we hope, you must not get distracted. You'll need to detach your soul from hers and end the spell immediately. You can't try to change anything about her either. You'll have to let go."

"I understand."

"Let's go over there where we can concentrate,"

she replied.

I followed Jenna to a clearing and sat down, my eyes still tracking where Logan was standing. His expression was somber as he listened intently.

"Normally this is a spell that we wouldn't try on another without practicing a time or two, but given the circumstances we have no choice," she said, bringing me back to the task at hand.

"Could you get hurt?" I asked, adding another to my ever-growing list of things to worry about.

"Not hurt as much as incapacitated for awhile." She forced a smile.

"Oh."

"You'll be fine," she said, reaching for my hand.

"It's not me I'm worried about."

She smiled, unwrapped her scarf and placed it on the ground where she lay down.

"The goal of this spell is to understand whether or not you can sense your mother's soul. When the time comes, you will close your eyes and think of her as your mother, not the woman she appears to be now. Remember her story, her history and when you feel the energy of her past repeat '*Anima Viator*' slowly until you feel above your self."

"What do you mean above my self? Like literally?"

"You know that feeling when you've started dreaming and you lose all sensory engagement to the physical world. You might catch yourself twitching, but there's nothing you can do to control it?"

I nodded.

"That's the sensation we're going for. That moment that you've left your own body, your soul will be traveling to your target."

"Whoa."

"Are you ready?"

"Yes." It didn't matter if I was or wasn't. I had to

master this.

I felt Logan's gaze on me. But I didn't look over. I needed to concentrate. I lay next to Jenna and thought about everything she said. Thinking of her over the years as I grew up in the coven, I tried to tap into her energy. My body relaxed slightly as I focused my attention on Jenna's spirit.

"Anima Viator. Anima Viator. Anima Viator."

Hovering over my own body, I saw my lips move repeating the phrase as instructed. I panicked and wanted to slip right back into where I came from. *I was out of my body!* I didn't want to be outside of my body looking in. I didn't like this feeling at all. I looked over at Jenna and saw her body still, and her breathing slowed.

I had to do it. Waves of Jenna's spirit washed over me as I turned my attention to her. I could see her dreams, thoughts, and desires. Brilliant blues, purples and reds spiraled around me as I shared space with her soul. Fear began racing through my body. I didn't belong here. If I had a body to shake, I would have. Instead I attempted to dive into my own shell, and woke up with a sense of vacancy.

I opened my eyes to have Logan holding me.

"Is she okay?" I asked.

"Jenna's fine," he whispered. "I'm more worried about you. How are you feeling?

"Tired and depressed, but it worked," I said, giving him a crooked grin.

"Of course it did." He shook his head. "Because you did it."

I wanted to see her, but she was no longer where I last left her.

"Where's Jenna?"

"She's over there letting everyone know it worked."

"But why doesn't she feel as horrible as I do?"

"You were out for about thirty minutes or so. She woke up as soon as your soul left hers, but the soul traveler has far more recovery to go through than the recipient. That's why your mom will never know anything happened, according to Jenna.

"Wow. Things never stop getting interesting do they?"

The wind kept blowing strands of hair in my face, aggravating me incredibly. Now was probably not the time to try to grow out my bangs. Logan gently lifted my head, and pulled my hair to the side, tucking it behind my ear.

"That's better," he whispered.

"I'm scared there's not going to be a soul to feel in my mother. Or at least not hers."

"I know, baby. But one step at a time."

He bent down to place a kiss on my cheek, but a loud clap startled us both.

"What was that?" I asked, sitting up.

Logan looked toward the sky and over to the crowd who were all wondering the same thing.

"Thunder maybe? I'm not sure. Let's get you up."

"Do you feel that?" I asked, uncertain if it was my latest experience or if the ground really was moving.

Logan grabbed my hand as we ran to the others.

"Everyone, get out of here now," he hollered. "We've got visitors. They're coming from behind us. We can't let them see us all together."

My head was pounding and the idea of successfully running down the hill didn't seem promising. The group quickly disbanded, scattering in every possible direction.

Logan's fingers were woven between mine, but he wasn't running as fast as the others. Instead he was slowing until he stopped. Everyone had managed to get off the hillside. Why were we stopping?

"There's no point in running," he whispered.

"What do you mean? Who's coming?"

He turned to look behind me, his gaze steady. I took a deep breath in and spun around to see the entire hillside covered with a sea of cloak-wearing witches. Cowards sent by my father.

"What do you want?" Logan growled.

"We've come in peace. We heard we had some out-of-town guests so we only wanted to welcome you."

"I doubt that," Logan replied, moving me next to him.

"No. It's true. Nicholas wanted to warmly welcome you to the Adirondacks. In fact, he'd love it if his daughter would come for a visit."

"Do you have your wand?" Logan's words popped into my mind, but his lips weren't moving. That tattoo was working!

Afraid I'd botch something up, I simply nodded.

"Don't use it unless they strike at you first," he continued.

"So what will it be? Can we expect your company soon? We know you're aware of where we live, since dumping poor Preston off," the leader said.

"I have no interest in coming alone," I replied.

"Your father only wants to see you. He's dealt with your boyfriend enough to know he has no need for him."

The anger was bubbling inside of me waiting to explode.

"Then I guess my father will be waiting for quite some time," I yelled over the wind that was picking up.

"You have until sunset tomorrow to arrive at the Great Camp or we will take you forcefully and destroy everyone you love in doing so," the leader said.

My heart was racing. How dare my father threaten me. I reached for my wand and readied my stance.

"Don't do it, babe," Logan whispered. "It's not worth it."

"Thank you for the message," I hollered over the howling wind. "Tell him I'll think about it."

The group members bowed their heads and retreated.

"To have this many people interested in us, we must be doing something right," Logan replied.

I smiled at him as he brought me into his embrace.

"I've got a really important tip," he murmured.

"Yeah?" I asked.

"Always wait until someone else strikes first. But once you begin, fight until you can no longer fight."

CHAPTER 18

"Are you ready?" Logan asked.

We were in our bedroom, and I could hear the bustling of everyone downstairs as the nervous energy soared.

Shaking my head *no*, I replied a simple, "Yes."

"You're gonna be okay, baby." He brought me into his embrace, and I wanted to stay in his arms, but I knew there was no turning back. Everyone and everything had mobilized and were waiting for my part in this whole thing — my pretend capture.

"The sooner we get going, the sooner you'll be back in my arms." He was doing a good job of staying strong. His voice was resolute, hiding any sign of uncertainty that I felt.

Logan wasn't rushing me, always the gentleman. He waited until I released my arms and took a step back, readying myself for the encounter of a lifetime.

"Everyone know what's expected of them?" I asked.

He nodded.

"All right, let's go." I shakily grabbed my bag and wondered if there were any cracks in our plan. It seemed solid, especially since Dace and Bakula became involved, but a tiny seed of doubt wanted to sprout, and I had to push it down continuously. If nothing else, I had to act strong. I couldn't meet my father with a wobbly handshake or a trembling hug.

"So we've got the vials that I prepared?" I asked, making myself go into warrior mode. We were headed down the stairs.

"We've got the vials, bottles, and several sets of dried bouquets in case you need something else we didn't account for. That was Jenny's idea," Logan replied. "I thought it made sense."

"And the snake?" I asked.

"The snake has been boxed up and will be released on the outside of the walls," Logan replied. "And the pendant will be at the end of the wall, near the lake. We've got food drops prepared for you too."

I felt the ache in the tattoo that Logan and I shared. Even though he was doing an incredible acting job, our shared bond told another story. And it was comforting to know his heart hurt as much as mine.

"If you need anything from Dace or Bakula —" Logan began.

"I know... I'll contact you," I interrupted, giving him a little smile. A slight grin spread on his lips.

"At least you're not losing your fire in all of this," he teased. His eyes were hauntingly beautiful even though they held the sorrow of the moment.

The longer I stayed in the house the worse it was going to be to leave him.

I nodded at him, and he opened the front door. I felt the crisp fall air hit my skin. The beginning of evening started to creep into this part of the world, and I realized we'd better hurry so I could get in to see my father before sunset.

Jenny had been in the garden, and came running up to me, and gave me a hug.

"I love you, Triss. Your mother *will* be proud of you. You'll get her back, and she'll see what you've accomplished," Jenny said, holding back the tears.

"Love you too, and thank you for coming. Please thank your parents for me," I replied.

A lump in the back of my throat formed as the words sunk in because this trip was no longer solely to get my mom back. I hoped with everything inside that I would be able to turn her back to her old self — the beautiful, selfless woman she was before she became an Altered Soul — but there was no guarantee.

I was going into the compound determined to stop a legacy of my father's making. I no longer wanted his history to create anyone else's future. That was my goal.

Logan placed his hand on my shoulder, and I let go of Jenny only to see hundreds of people, many who I didn't recognize, standing around us.

"*Protegat Animosique Unum,*" They began

singing, sending chills up my spine. *"Tueri Divina. Protegat Animosique Unum. Tueri Divina."*

"Thank you," I replied to them all, as I climbed into the car.

"Spirited one, huh?" I asked when Logan got into the driver's side.

"You caught that?" His eyes twinkled. "I can't think of a better adjective for you."

I looked down quickly uncertain of my place in all of this. Was it only because I was my father's daughter? Would my mother's ancestors answer our calls like the fairies hoped?

"Protect the spirited one. Protect the divine. It couldn't be more true," he whispered, grabbing my hand as we drove out of town, and I was left to wonder if any of it was true.

The closer we drove to my father's Great Camp, the more my tattoo throbbed. My skin felt like it was on fire and when it wasn't burning, it was pulling and twisting — only it wasn't.

"You're feeling that too," I stated as I saw the grimace spread across his face.

"It will be nice when what we share is joy and goodness. I doubt it will be quite this painful," he laughed, and I committed the beautiful melody to memory.

"Tell me about it." I squeezed his hand, seeing that we were only a minute away from where I was going to be dropped off.

"I wish you'd let me walk you to the lake," he said. His voice was almost hoarse.

"We can't," I replied softly, shaking my head.

Logan turned the car onto the shoulder of the

road as we arrived at my drop-off point and turned off the engine.

I closed my eyes and took a deep breath in. This was it.

"Triss, you are my world," he whispered. "If *anything* goes wrong, you've got to tell me. We can come get you out."

His arms wrapped around me and I buried my head in his shoulder. He lifted his hands and caressed my hair, my face. He didn't want to let me go.

"I will do anything to protect you," he whispered with his mouth pressed against my hair. "You know that, right?"

I shook my head and began to push away, but his lips caught mine in one last effort to make his point. The desperation in our kiss relayed everything that we couldn't say out loud. The tears threatened to fall as my mind wondered if this would be the last time I was in his arms. I admonished myself for thinking such thoughts and as if to prove my point, began backing away faster.

"I should probably get going." The atmosphere between us shifted as he released me into the uncertainty that lay ahead.

The painful expression he wore stabbed at my soul.

I hesitated a moment, placing my hand on his chest. His eyes were wide and solemn, shaking his head as if to reassure himself.

"I love you, Logan," I replied, feeling the back of my throat begin to constrict. I couldn't cry.

There was no way I'd be able to show up to see my father with tear-stained cheeks. "And remember that I'd do anything to protect you too." I winked at him, hoping to lighten the mood, and was relieved to see a smile break on his lips.

"Always a competition," he teased, but the sadness in his eyes couldn't be hidden this time.

I got out of the car, grabbed my pseudo-surveillance bag, and looked back at him one last time.

My stomach twisted into knots as I turned around and walked along the trail to the lake entrance. Relief spread when I saw the canoes floating. The first task of me getting to my father's camp was working out.

I threw my bag in the canoe closest to me and realized how much easier it was to get in a wobbly boat of any kind when there was someone else to hold it steady. *I refuse to fail right out the gate!* Pulling the canoe closer, I decided that it might be safer if I walked along the edge leading the canoe to an area where I could manipulate my surroundings.

Tugging on the canoe's rope, and tripping my way over to a mass of tangled grass and brush, I stood on the mound while I attempted to half crawl-step into the unstable fiberglass death trap.

My heart was already racing, and I hadn't even started paddling toward my father. Giving myself one last heave, my body toppled into the canoe. *I made it!*

Not allowing myself to get overly confident, I looked around the vacant water and pushed off with the paddle.

With every stroke bringing me closer to my father's clutches, my stomach twisted in knots. I needed to be seen, and the rest would fall into place.

I smelled smoke in the air and wondered if there was yet another ceremony I might be intruding on. That would make the process go quicker... more chances to be seen. Rounding the corner, I saw a bustle of activity. It was a nice evening, and it looked like everyone at my father's camp must have been taking advantage of it. I stopped paddling and let the canoe glide slowly to the shore hoping my presence would become known.

The realization that I was truly alone hit me. I was floating in the middle of a lake waiting to be found by a father I didn't know, a mother who seemed to have forgotten me, and an aunt who possibly had a hand in planning the events that got me here. Never feeling this amount of isolation before I stared straight ahead at my father's property, attempting to turn the loneliness I was feeling into anger. That would be far more productive.

My tattoo continued to burn, and I wanted to tell Logan I was about to enter the grounds, but I couldn't. I didn't want anything to give away the secret of what we shared between us.

"Trespasser," a woman's voice hollered.

My heart started racing. This was it. This was

what I was waiting for, and I didn't have to wait long. A group of people began running toward the bank. I scanned the crowd for anyone I might recognize and found no one.

I began quickly paddling in the opposite direction in an attempt to look like I didn't want to be captured.

"That's no trespasser. She's my daughter," my father's voice boomed. "Now go pull her in and help her to safety."

Hearing those words prickled my spine as I watched ten or so of his followers run toward the water, toward me.

"Oh, my Triss," my father spoke, "I knew our paths would cross. Welcome home."

He walked a couple feet down the bank. I slowed my paddling, squinting at him.

"Don't be frightened. I'm your father. I wouldn't do anything to hurt you."

My eyes darted to the ten or so witches who had come to stand by his side.

"Bring her in," he commanded.

I brought my paddle inside the canoe and grabbed my bag.

"Don't do whatever you're thinking," my father warned. "Put the bag down."

I nodded and placed it near my feet, puzzled that he thinks I'd be foolish enough to try something from where I was.

The group had gotten to my canoe and began pulling me in. More people had gathered along the bank's edge, but still I still recognized no one. As the canoe slid onto the mud, I started to get out of the canoe.

"Help her out. Don't let her fall," my father snapped. "She's blood. Start treating her with the respect she deserves."

I attempted to swallow, but my throat refused to make that movement and the nausea began rising. I avoided my father's stare and glanced at the group of men who had just gotten admonished by someone who was close to their own age. I didn't understand how they could let someone treat them like this, chemicals or not.

The gray haired man, who upon closer inspection, was probably older than my father grabbed my bag. There was nothing in it other than what we wanted them to find so I was fine.

"I've got it," I said, standing up in the canoe with a strength and stability I certainly didn't have on the other side of the lake.

"No, Miss. We must help you," one of the men whispered.

These poor souls.

I extended my arm out, and he bowed under it, picking me up unexpectedly. I wanted out of his arms so badly. He walked me up the bank toward my father and set me down.

"You look frightened, Triss," my father said.

Here he was. My father. I wanted to look away, but I couldn't. His features were strong, and if I didn't know what he was lacking internally, he might be considered handsome.

He extended his broad, thick-fingered hand toward me, and I fought the impulse to jump back. I didn't want to touch him. I didn't know what to do.

"Did you come to spy or is this your way of accepting my invitation?" He sounded amused.

I shrugged my shoulders.

"Beatrice, are you alone?" he asked. *Beatrice!* He was the one who sent that being in after me at the cottage, but why didn't it finish its job? Could Logan be right about the purity thing?

"I'll take that as a no," he replied, pointing at the men behind me. "Canvas the lake and bring me the others."

Finally finding my voice I spoke.

"There are no others. I'm the only one," I said, looking up into my father's eyes. They were as clear as mine. I wondered what my mom's would be like after being here so long.

"Go anyway," my father ordered. "The person you're looking for is Logan, a former student of mine. I'm sure he's out there somewhere."

I knew he was nowhere near the lake, but my heart still constricted when I heard my father mention Logan's name.

"Where's my mother?" I asked, staring directly into my father's gaze.

"Napping. She does that a lot. You'll have to excuse her."

"Not coming to meet me is the least of the things she has to be sorry for," I snarled, unable to hide my anger.

"Don't be cross at her. She loves you, as do I."

It took everything I had not to scream at him that this wasn't love. This was hate, deceit, narcissism, evil, so many things, but love wasn't one of them.

"What were you hoping to find out on your little mission, my dear?" he asked, touching my chin. The revulsion shot through my body, and I was unable to hide it. He slowly shook his head and pursed his lips. "We'll have to change your ideas about me. Did you get my note? You could have come anytime to see her."

His ability to distort reality was impressive, and it also explained why he could cause so much damage without the help of magic or mind altering chemicals. I had to find out if he truly believed the words he was speaking.

"Triss." I heard Ellsy's muffled voice echo through the air. My eyes shot in the direction of her yell. It came from one of the buildings to my left, but which one? There were so many.

"Run, Triss. Get out of here," she cried.

"Let me see Ellsy," I said to my father.

"Can't let you do that," he replied.

A woman's arm waved from the farthest building out a tiny, barred window. I turned my attention quickly to my father.

"Well, what *will* you let me do?"

He wrapped his arm around my shoulder and began walking us toward the main house.

"First things first, I've got a room prepared for you. It's been ready for months. Trevor's room is down the hall from yours. He told me of your bond. I think it was a wonderful choice. Couldn't have worked out better if I had planned it."

An internal smile spread through my system at my father's snide remarks. Love was a powerful tool, and I guess I'd have to demonstrate how important it really was.

My father led me to the side entrance of the main house. I felt like I was suddenly transported back to medieval times. It really did look like a castle with the stonework and turrets. Even the side door was monstrous.

He swung open the door, and there I saw Trevor and Aunt Vieta standing in the kitchen talking.

"Hello, Aunt Vieta,"

My aunt looked over, a horrified expression spread across her face as our eyes locked. The glass she was holding slipped from her fingers, crashing to the ground while a smile spread across my lips.

"Surprised?" I asked sarcastically.

CHAPTER 19

The burgundy and gold brocade tapestries that hung around the four-poster bed made me feel like I was in another era, one that certainly matched the circumstances. I was sitting on the mattress, which required a step stool for me to get on, contemplating what I needed to do next. The longer I stayed in this environment the more chance for error. Everything was so secluded from the real world at this Great Camp, I could see how easy it could be to slip under my father's control.

I slid my hand down to my side, and quickly let my fingers feel the warmth of the tattoo. Even though it was in my head, it made me feel that much closer to him, and I needed that right now.

The room my father put me in gave me a view of the lake out a corner window and the other window pointed at the heart of the compound. I tried to see where Ellsy was being held, but I couldn't see the building from my room. I wanted to tell Logan about her, but I couldn't risk it yet. I needed to wait until I was in bed. Probably even touching my tattoo was a bad idea, but I couldn't help it.

I scanned the room again, trying to think of next steps. I was certain he put me in this oversized room for extra effect, to remind me how small and insignificant I was in the whole scheme of things. Everything in this room was mammoth. The dresser, the chests, even the chairs were enormous. I now knew what Alice felt like in Wonderland.

I was beginning to get really thirsty, but I refused to drink any liquid from this house. I had two bottled waters in my bag, which never left my sight, and I was debating whether I should dip into one of them yet. The first drop-offs should already have occurred, so it was up to me to figure out how to get to them without being noticed.

"Triss?" Trevor's voice shocked me.

I turned toward the door, which he had already opened, and stared at him.

"Yeah?" I asked.

"Dinner's going to be ready soon. Your father has something special planned since you arrived ahead of schedule."

"Do you enjoy being his puppet?" I snapped.

"Is that what your precious Logan calls me?"

"No, it's my own term, and I think I'd say it's pretty accurate."

I raised my knees to my chin, hugging them to me. I felt violated merely being around Trevor. This was not the person I knew, and he certainly wasn't someone I loved.

"I take it he healed up after our last encounter?" Trevor smiled.

Refusing to give any clues about Logan, I turned away. The images of almost losing Logan quickly flashed into my mind, but I forced them out.

"What happened to you, Trevor? I don't get it."

He sighed. "Nothing *happened* to me. I found my calling. I'm good at it."

I shook my head.

"But you're not. Don't you see? My father's been helping you along this entire time. Maybe my aunt has too, but it's not you. You're not that good."

He couldn't hide his anger.

"I don't know what Logan's been telling you, but I've been practicing the dark arts longer than he has."

"Only because he quit. He started before you, and I'm sure he was quite good. He masters everything he practices."

Logan's blue eyes flashed in my mind, and I felt like he was briefly here with me.

"You said it, Triss. He quit."

I smiled and let go of my knees. I scooted over to the edge of the bed and let my legs dangle, thinking about what to say next.

"Do you know why he quit?" I asked.

"I do." Trevor took a few steps into my bedroom. "But I doubt you know the *real* reason."

"Enlighten me then." I stared into Trevor's eyes and felt nothing.

"Logan's not a good guy, Triss. He did things your father couldn't even explain away." Trevor folded his arms and narrowed his eyes waiting for a response that wouldn't come. "Your father's not as bad as you're making him out to be. Logan quit because no Dark Arts Sorcerer would even touch him."

The fury was burning through me. I wanted to end this charade now — end Trevor. The anger was building every second I stared at him, but I couldn't look away. I wouldn't look away. I didn't want to give him that power. I remained silent so my tongue wouldn't betray me.

"I know you don't believe me, but it's the truth." He shrugged his shoulders and left my room, closing the door behind him.

The tears began streaming down my face, and I buried my head into the half-dozen pillows on the bed to muffle my sobs. The loneliness was indescribably painful, but the sadness overrode all of my emotions. How was I going to make it through this?

"Don't cry, honey." My mother's calm voice sailed to me as she placed her hand upon my back. "You'll be okay. We're together now."

I slowly turned, afraid for what, not who, I might find looking back at me. It felt like a serpent was slowing entwining itself around my soul.

"Mom?" I whimpered, seeing her beautiful auburn hair cascading down her shoulders. I was afraid to look into her eyes.

"I love you," she whispered, holding out her

arms.

I allowed myself one moment of pretend as I felt her embrace around me. One moment where I imagined that this was the same woman who I had loved for eighteen years, but it couldn't be. That woman would never have left me.

Backing out of our embrace, I brought my eyes to hers and saw the emptiness that I feared staring right back at me. *How did he do this and why?*

"It's good to see you, mother." My shield was back up.

"Oh, Triss. You too. I've been waiting so long for you to come live here with us."

Was she even in this world?

"I'm sorry it took me as much time as it did. I had a lot to take care of first."

She grabbed my hand and pulled me off the bed.

"Let's get you in one of these outfits." Her voice was filled with excitement as I became the project that Ellsy never was. "Have you looked in your closet yet?"

I shook my head, staring at the floor while I tried to regain my composure. There were so many emotions fighting with one another, I didn't know what to do. Was this how it started? No. I was here by choice. I had a mission to complete.

"You have such a sullen look on your face," my mother chirped, touching my chin briefly like she had done so many times before.

I looked up horrified, catching her vacant

stare. Oh, how I longed for Logan. This was a mistake — a very bad mistake.

"Voila," she said, swinging the doors of the closet open. "What should we put you in? Something fit for a princess, I'd say."

Her actions revealed a walk-in closet that had more clothes stuffed in it than I had ever had in my lifetime.

"Who did all of this?" I asked, trying to gauge the timing of everything.

"Oh, your father had many things in this room before I even got here. Now some weren't anything you'd ever want to wear, so I fixed that." She laughed at the memory, as I cringed at the shallowness.

"How about this?" She pulled a black satin dress out of the closet, and I shook my head. Placing it back in the closet she seemed bothered.

"What about this one?" This time a silvery sequined disaster was in front of me.

"I..I wouldn't be comfortable in that," I replied, attempting to smile. "Not yet, anyway."

"We've got to get your confidence up."

"My confidence is fine. I just don't want to wear something that elaborate. I'd like something simple."

"I think your father has something special planned for tonight," she said annoyed.

"I heard."

"From who?"

"Trevor."

"Oh, he's such a wonderful boy."

She was completely distracted from her moment's earlier annoyance.

"This might be fitting. You can wear it once before summer is completely over."

She held up a white linen skirt and a pale, turquoise oversized sweater. It felt like every second I was here, my mind dulled that much more.

I nodded and pretended to care, but I had to ask one question.

"Where is Ellsy, mom?"

"She hasn't been feeling well since she arrived, so your father's been taking care of her."

"She's at the house?" Already knowing the answer.

"No, dear." My mother shook her head. "I didn't want to tell you this, but Logan has gotten into some trouble. She's not dealing with it well and your father is so wonderful he's got special staff taking care of her until she gets well again."

This web of lies was so elaborate, I didn't know if I'd be able to see things as clearly as I should.

"I see."

"You remember Logan don't you?" she asked. "He's the one who kept sending letters long after you stopped reading them?"

Her words stabbed my heart. Did she know what she was doing? Aunt Vieta had to have filled them in on everything. What was my mother trying to accomplish?

"I'll curl your hair. How does that sound?" she asked.

Absolutely horrible.

"Sounds nice, thank you."

She placed the clothes on the bed, and went over to the vanity and plugged in the curling iron.

"This will give us plenty of time to catch up before you get whisked away to tonight's events."

She patted the bench that she pulled out and waved her hand at me.

Plenty of time to catch up? Thirty minutes was enough time to catch up. Wow.

I sat down and stared into the mirror, watching my mother's reflection as she parted my hair. Was she really only an Altered Soul? What I saw staring back at me seemed more like a Vacant Soul. It was as if her soul was gone. She was gone.

"Tell me, how did your Witch Avenue Coven ceremony go?"

How did my ceremony go? The anger was soaring through my system. *How did it go?*

"Just peachy," I replied through gritted teeth.

Trying to calm myself down, I closed my eyes. This was not her fault.

"It seemed like it went well."

My eyes flashed open to see her looking back at me.

"What do you mean?"

"I was there," she replied, smiling. "You don't think I'd miss my little girl's big day do you?"

"What do you mean you were there?" I tried again. "You were missing. The coven declared you dead."

I couldn't keep it in any longer.

"While you were off gallivanting and playing let's pretend, I was back at home trying to figure out what happened to you — if you were dead or alive. And you were there?"

"Your father didn't want me to be. I begged him to let me go, and I had to promise him I would remain hidden."

"He *let* you go? Since when did you need permission?"

"Oh, it's not like that."

It was pointless to talk to her like she was rational. Rather than continue to become infuriated with each new development, I smiled at her and laughed it off. All I could do was hope the soul traveling I performed would tell me if she was even worth trying to save. I swallowed hard at that last thought and forced the sadness away.

"So what do you do here most days?" I changed the subject.

"I greet visitors who are interested in your father's teachings. I spend a lot of time out collecting herbs and things. He's got an amazing collection in these woods."

"I bet he does."

"There are so many beautiful gardens. You'll be in heaven. They'd be a perfect place to get married. Although, a winter wedding would be absolutely lovely too."

"What are you talking about?"

"To Trevor," she replied, placing the last curl

in place.

"Right."

"How's Aunt Vieta?" I asked.

"She's doing pretty well. Trevor and her have become pretty close. It's nice to see, since his family seems to have detached themselves from him."

"Really."

"I'm excited for you to be introduced to everyone. It's grown to be such a nice, big family. We're really lucky."

"What about the non-believers that visit? What happens to them?"

"They usually see the light." She smiled.

"Do you miss Seattle?"

She paused for a moment before speaking as if I might have actually struck a nerve.

"To be honest, I don't remember much about it. I think I enjoyed it, but I knew you needed saving and coming here would do that. And the funny part is, I don't even remember what I thought you needed saving from." She shook her head, and smiled. "Funny getting old."

"You're only in your forties. That's not old."

"Regardless, I came here with one intention in mind and that was to keep you safe. And here you are, safe as can be."

Her joyous melody reached deep into my soul as I wondered if this was what was going to happen to me. Coming here thinking I could save the people I loved only to be the one needing saving.

I was in over my head.

CHAPTER 20

"It's so wonderful to meet you." I shook the hand of yet another stranger pronounced to be my new family, as I scanned the room for my father or mother. I hadn't seen them since I arrived down here, which wasn't necessarily a bad thing.

Servers wandered through the crowd offering tiny hors d'oeuvres and drinks all of which I let go right by me. The dining room was more like a banquet room and was packed with people. They couldn't all be staying here. Could they? Organ music began filling the room, and everyone quieted. I didn't even see an organ. Turning my head in the direction of Chopin, I saw the curtains open to reveal an organ player.

This was absolutely surreal. Everyone turned their attention to the front of the room, and I forced myself to do the same even though I was sure it was only to watch my father and mother strut their stuff as they entered.

The organist switched to a dramatic piece, signaling my parents' arrival like we were at a wedding ceremony or something. Shaking my head in disbelief, one of the followers mistook my intention and whispered to me, "Incredible isn't it?"

"That's one word for it," I whispered.

As the music was softened, everyone began finding a seat around the table that stretched the entire length of the room. In fact, I wasn't even sure one continuous table could be built that large.

"Triss," Trevor's voice called.

Drats!

His hand crawled up my shoulder, and it was everything I could do to not throw it off of me, but instead I spun around and smiled.

"Feeling better?" he asked.

"Immensely."

"Your father wants you sitting with us at the head of the table."

No more being snide or ambivalent. From this moment forward I had to put forth my best performance to date. I had to convince everyone that I wanted to be here no matter how much that blurred the line between reality and this...

As I followed Trevor, I felt the entire room's eyes on me. If I actually cared what these people thought, I'd be completely embarrassed by this reverence. Lucky for me, I didn't care one iota.

"Triss, you look lovely," my father said. "Doesn't she look lovely everyone?"

His hand waved toward me and the entire room broke out in compliments and applause. It was hard for me to wrap my head around what my father was getting out of this.

Smiling I nodded to the crowd and took my seat.

"Thank you," I replied.

Trevor sat next to me, and both my mother and father were at the head of the table. I wished that I was skilled enough to let loose a spell in here. It would be sensational. If only—

"It's nice to see your spirits have lifted so much," my father began. "I thought seeing your mother would put things in perspective."

"It certainly did," I nodded in agreement.

Someone from behind placed a salad plate in front of me, and I froze. This was going to be my first test. How could I do this with so many eyes on me? I picked up my fork and began moving the lettuce around, hoping someone would begin speaking again. Nobody did, but why would they when they're on the verge of becoming catatonic.

"So what do you have planned for us tomorrow?" I asked my father, who was taken aback by my eagerness to talk.

"Oh, well. I think your mom wanted to show you some of the grounds, the gardens in particular. Isn't that right, my dear?"

"I thought that would be fun. That way we'll be out of the way with everything going on tomorrow."

"What's everything?" I asked.

My father scowled at my mother who dropped her gaze to the table. She never would have done that. It killed me inside and made me so angry I wanted to scream at the top of my lungs, but I couldn't. I had to maintain control. I felt Trevor's gaze on me, and I wondered what he was thinking.

"We've got some people stopping by who are interested in using our facility," my father replied.

"Well, that sounds fantastic," I muttered, waiting to catch my mom's empty eyes.

The room was full of laughter and discussion when it struck me that my father was attempting to build his own version of a family. He left us, but he created a world where there were people everywhere he went. He created a community where he was a vital part, and where he felt needed. This had been his family for eighteen years. I guess it's not completely true about not being able to choose your family.

"Would you mind if I went with Triss and her mom tomorrow?" Trevor asked.

"*Evanesco*," I whispered, watching a part of my salad disappear.

"That would be a fantastic idea, son," my father replied.

I glanced at Trevor and grinned.

"That would be nice," I whispered. "And I'm sorry for earlier."

He nodded and placed his hand on my knee under the table.

Feeling completely uneasy and frightened, I turned my head to him and flashed a smile.

"Maybe you could come meet us later in the day?" I asked, looking at my father to distract me.

"I'll see if I can get away, but I doubt I'll be

able to."

"I understand," I replied.

"Are you done with your salad, Miss?" The man was behind me again, waiting to trade out my salad plate for the entrée.

Nodding, I watched as my salad plate was taken away. No one seemed to notice that I didn't actually eat any of it.

Stroganoff was placed in front of me.

"Isn't that one of your favorites?" My father beamed as if this was a huge accomplishment. I felt my eyes darken, but I blinked it away.

"It is. Thank you."

Trevor removed his hand from my knee as his dinner was served, and I felt like I could breathe again.

The conversation became lively as my father greeted a nonstop parade of visitors, giving me ample opportunity to practice several more disappearing spells as my plate became emptier without anyone being aware.

"Triss, this is Marco. One of my right hand men," my father said, surprising me. He'd been pretty much excluding me all night.

"Nice to meet you," I replied.

"Pleasure is mine." He bowed his head, and I caught Trevor glowering at the man.

The evening went on for what seemed like hours. The special dinner my father had in my honor was nothing more than serving a meal that I liked. There were no announcements, for which I was grateful, and no mention of me at all on a large scale. The entire event was focused on him, and I knew that's how it had to be. A true manipulator could never allow a power shift away from them — ever.

"Can I walk you to your room?" Trevor asked.

I shot a glance at my mom who was eagerly awaiting my response.

"Sure. Good night, mom."

I looked around to find my father, but he was busy with one of the many groups waiting to get his attention.

Trevor slid his arm around my shoulder, and we walked down the long arched hallway. With every step away from the crowd, I felt more alone.

"I know you've been fighting the spell's effects, but there'll come a time when you can't," he whispered.

His body hovered over me as did his words. The weight of his arm made me claustrophobic, and all I wanted was to get to my room.

"Would you like to see the library? He's got an amazing section on herbs and ointments."

Shaking my head, I turned to look at him.

"I'm so tired. This day hasn't turned out how I expected, and quite honestly, I'm exhausted."

"I understand."

We walked up the stairs to my room and rather than allow me to walk into my bedroom, he stood with his arm still draped over my shoulder.

"Would you allow me one kiss?"

Lowering myself out of his grasp, I turned to him and touched his face.

"I would want it to mean something, Trevor, and I'm not there yet," I whispered.

The kindness I relayed in my message stole the last amount of energy my body had left to give. I reached for the doorway for support, and Trevor nodded. An all-knowing smile covered his lips as he took my words as a mini-victory for a someday that I knew would never exist.

"Can I ask a question?"

"Anything," he nodded.

"Do you like me for me or because of who my father is?"

His smile faded and he narrowed his eyes.

"You should ask Logan that," he snapped and turned down the hall.

"I'm sorry," I hollered, offering a feeble attempt at an apology.

At last, I could be alone.

Closing the door quickly, I locked it and began stripping out of my clothes. I pulled open the dresser drawer and grabbed the first thing on top. I slipped the oversized satin nightshirt over my head and dove under the covers. This was the safest I'd felt since I arrived. If only I could stay here the entire time.

I knew locking the door did little in a house where my father had a key to every door, but it would hopefully buy me enough time if I heard someone coming.

I closed my eyes and thought of Logan. I missed him so much. His smile and the way he teased me; the loving way he'd touch my chin, and his kind and gentle soul. My mind thought back to the many times tonight where people felt it was their duty to correct my idea of Logan. I knew I wasn't the one who needed correcting.

"Goodnight," my mother whispered through the door.

Could I be this lucky?

"Goodnight, mother," I replied. "I hope you have a wonderful night's sleep."

"You too."

I listened intently as my mother walked back down the hall to her bedroom. I waited and waited until I heard the click of her door. Success!

Excitement and fear coursed through my veins so much so that I could no longer stay in bed. Throwing the covers off me, I got up and paced the floor. Noticing brightness outside, I went to the window and saw a few people starting a bonfire. I scanned the small group and didn't see my father included. I grabbed the curtain and slid it closed. I walked over to the mirror and flipped on the vanity light. I looked horrible. My in-between-bangs wouldn't stay put. I had bags under my eyes, and I was pale. I turned the light off and crawled back into bed.

I couldn't wait any longer. I needed to know if my mom could ever be my mom again. I wondered what would happen if I tried to do this and she wasn't asleep?

Closing my eyes, I forced myself to leave the worry behind. Instead, I began thinking of my mother. I could see her smile as we sat together in the floral shop, chatting endlessly, and preparing the following day's orders. My mind then flashed to Christmas and our traditional walks along the shorefront.

Feeling connected with her spirit, I took a deep breath in. This was it. Soon I'd know...

"Anima Viator. Anima Viator."

Looking down at my resting body, I took flight. It wasn't like with Jenna. I didn't immediately merge with my mother's soul. It was quiet. Silence whirled around me and nothing else. The bright colors didn't flash in front of me. Did this mean my mother was gone? Not understanding how I was hovering over my mother, I began to turn back until I heard her voice, faint as it was. Locking onto it, I allowed myself to merge with her thoughts. There was hope for her. My father hadn't gotten to her subconscious yet. Not wanting to press my luck, I began disassociating.

Unaware of how long I had been out, I opened my eyes to darkness. I walked over to the window and saw that the bonfire had already died out. I must have been out for quite awhile. My muscles ached and my stomach hurt, but I wasn't sure if that was because I was hungry or the process I endured.

I could tell Logan the good news about my mom. I just wasn't sure how to tell him about his mother.

I crawled back into bed and pulled the sheets up to my chin.

"Vocatio ad Dilectione Mea," I whispered, touching the warmth of my tattoo.

Closing my eyes I waited for his reply, feeling the wetness begin to edge my lids. Would this be enough?

"Hey, baby," his voice echoed through my mind.

"Oh Logan! It works."

"Are you okay?" The gentleness of his words floated through my body.

"I am." I found my physical self, shaking my head no. "But I miss you."

"I miss you more than you could know," he whispered.

Was this communication making things better or worse?

"I'm going to try to see your mom tomorrow. I think she's the only one here that hasn't been altered. I performed the spell on my mom. She's there somewhat, but I don't even know —"

"We can't think that way."

"I know. I can't believe the change in her though. When I performed the spell on Jenna I got a strong sense of who she was. When I did it on my mom tonight, I barely could sense her. Time is running out."

"I'm so sorry, but be careful."

"I will. This whole place is frightening. I know he's using the chemicals from mushrooms and who knows what else, but I have to say his mind control techniques are like no other. The people around here idolize him. It's beyond scary."

"I can't even imagine. It kills me that you're in a place like that for a cause we don't even know we can win."

"If I didn't believe we could win it, I wouldn't be here."

I felt his smile. I wished I could feel his embrace, the strength in his arms as he wrapped himself around me, but I couldn't.

"Did you eat?"

"I'm not hungry, but I've had water. I should be able to get what I need tomorrow. I'm walking the grounds with my mother, and she's pretty out of it so it shouldn't be difficult."

"Dace thinks they have enough antidote for everyone now. But, Triss, if the bond is too deep it might not work on your mom."

I was silent for a moment, quieting my mind.

"All we can do is hope. When will it be dropped off?"

"Tomorrow night."

It was quiet between us once more until he asked the question I dreaded.

"Have you seen Trevor?" The words made me ill. I didn't want to lie, but I didn't want Logan to worry. I chose truth.

"I did."

"And?" his internal voice pained.

"There's nothing to worry about. I love you. There's no danger, but I promise to tell you if anything crosses the line on his end."

I could sense the relief spread through his body.

"I've got something planned tomorrow. You may see it or you may not, but I didn't want you to be alarmed."

"That's vague. Tell me what you're doing."

"I can't."

Then I realized that Logan wasn't certain that I could remain unaltered.

"Oh. You think I might get turned?"

"I think it's better this way. Stick to the original plan and everything will go fine. This is to protect you."

My bossy self wanted to argue with him, but I knew he was right.

"In a world of lies, know the love I share with you is real. We can count on it and each other. We're going to have to depend on that more than anything," he continued.

"I love you, Logan. We should probably stop in case the party lets out downstairs and someone actually decides to care about me."

I could feel his laughter. He understood me in a world where no one else ever would.

"Goodnight, my love."

"Goodnight," I whispered out loud and internally.

"Goodnight," my father's voice echoed from my bedroom door that he opened. "I'm surprised you knew I was here."

"Like father like daughter," I whispered, trying to hide my fear.

Was there anything else I said out loud? Did he know?

"Have a wonderful night. It's nice having you home," he replied closing the door.

CHAPTER 21

Being within the walls of the Great Camp churned a loneliness that I hadn't prepared for. It didn't help knowing that this was part of a plan. In the here and now, I was alone. I tamped down the fear that wanted to paralyze me, and the paranoia that made me second-guess every thought and movement I made. There was no one here, besides Ellsy, who knew of my father's evilness. I had to get to her.

My father's camp was filled with people who seemed oblivious to his master plan. I watched them wander along on their way to complete some inconsequential task my father or his circle thought up. It was quite sad.

Walking toward the building that housed Ellsy, my mind strayed back to Logan. How much it must hurt him knowing his mom was here being held against her will. I remembered the pain I felt when I first thought about my mother's disappearance. Now I wasn't sure what I felt.

I didn't have to meet my mom or Trevor for

another hour or so, which should give me enough time to see Ellsy. I didn't know what to expect. My hand turned the doorknob with an ease that concerned me. It was unlocked. I pushed it open only far enough to allow myself to slide through.

The room was completely empty. There was the familiar grey, stone for the walls and flooring, but there was no furniture. It felt damp, even though we were in the early part of fall. The building reminded me of a storage shed that was emptied quickly.

There was a spiral metal staircase in the corner that I walked to.

"Who's there?" Ellsy's voice called out as my feet hit the metal steps.

"Are you alone?" I asked, not sure what I would do if the answer was no.

"Yes," she cried. "Triss, you shouldn't be here."

I ran up the steps and found her sitting in the corner, shackled. Hay was spread out for bedding on one side of the floor. Her hair was a tangled mess, and she looked deathly thin but still managed to smile.

I ran to her and hugged her not wanting to let go. She felt like bones. Tears streamed down her face, and I couldn't hold mine in either.

"I'm so sorry," I mumbled.

"Triss, this isn't your fault," she said, releasing me.

"Here," I said, reaching into my pockets. "I have some granola bars. I know it's not much, but I've got more stuff waiting on the side of the wall. I'm going to get you out of here."

She shook her head. "No, Triss. You need to only be concerned with getting yourself out of here."

Not wanting to divulge any details, I only shook my head.

"What made them put you here?"

"The moment I arrived I created a problem and —" she stopped. "You need to get out of here. They're going to be back."

"How many?" I asked, standing up to leave.

"Usually two," she whispered. "Triss, how's Logan?"

"He's good, amazingly so," I paused. "You've raised the most incredible man I've ever met."

She smiled. "Thank you."

A brightness quickly flashed in her eyes.

"No, Thank you." I held her hand.

"Be careful."

"I'm meeting my mother and Trevor today, but I will be back. In the meantime, make sure you eat these. You'll need your strength, but this place is coming to an end. I'm not leaving you, so you need to stay as strong as possible."

I bent down and gave her a quick hug, I peeked down the stairwell opening to make sure no one had come in since I arrived, and it was all clear.

I opened the front door slowly and made my escape back to the main house where Trevor and my mother were waiting.

"Where to first? I asked, trying to calm down from my encounter with Ellsy.

"I thought the gardens of the gods would be a great introduction," my mother replied.

"Sounds incredible," I lied.

Trevor reached for my hand, and my gut twisted in a violent response that my lips couldn't repeat. Letting him grasp it, I looked at him and smiled.

"Thanks," he replied softly as we went outside.

He had the ability to be decent if he let himself. My mother carried a basket similar to the one we used to carry at home in Seattle for our gathering purposes. I wondered if she was content. For someone so oblivious would I be doing her a disservice getting her to come back to reality?

"It's really nice having you here," Trevor said, interrupting my thoughts.

"Thank you."

"It really is," my mom seconded.

We were following along behind her on a path that was edged in periwinkle.

"Have you been to wherever we're going?" I asked Trevor.

"Selfishly, that's also why I wanted to come along. It wasn't only to spend time with you." He smiled. I've been so busy planning and helping your father there's a lot of this property I haven't seen."

"What have you been helping him with?" I asked.

"He's been waiting for this meeting for quite sometime."

"Who is it with?"

My mother turned around and gave Trevor a warning stare. *Oh, now she comes to life?*

"I'll tell you later," Trevor whispered.

The earthy scent began emerging the longer we stayed on this path. Were we headed to more mushroom fields?

"Almost there," my mother hummed.

Rounding the corner my eyes met rows and rows of beautiful gardens. As far as my eyes could see, there were flowers in every direction. There were ornamental gardens, herb gardens, vegetable gardens, anything I could imagine was right in front of me. I also noticed many workers tending to the plants.

"Wow, those red sunflowers are huge and so gorgeous," I replied, understanding the army of workers it would take to keep this going.

"What's beyond the gardens?" I asked, as Trevor and I wandered through the flowers. My mother had roamed off in another direction, and surprisingly I was relieved to be with Trevor. I wondered if he knew anything about the mushrooms.

"I really haven't been to this area, but I know your dad's propagating all types of things everywhere he can find room."

A woman was deadheading all of the flowers, and we walked by silencing our discussion until we were farther away.

"Who's my dad meeting?"

"There's an elder of the Praedivinus Order who only comes to the states every decade or so.

I guess your father has only seen him two other times," Trevor whispered, as if there were recording devices in the fields.

"I thought my father was the head of that?" I asked.

"You know about it?" he asked, narrowing his eyes.

"Only what I saw on the flyer at Starbucks." I divulged.

"Well, he's next in line, but he's the head of it in the states."

"What is the goal, do you know?"

"Transcendence of the soul."

"Wow. That's kind of a lofty statement," I blurted out.

Trevor stopped walking and glared at me.

"Are you making fun of it?"

"Not at all. I think that's a pretty hard thing to accomplish on a wide-spread scale."

"You haven't seen him in action. Your father can work wonders."

"Is it all magic or does he have any help?"

"What do you mean?"

"Like potions you guys drink or —"

"Everything is done by searching deep within one's own soul." Trevor interrupted.

He has no idea, but why isn't he as far gone as my mother?

"Kids?" My mother's voice rang through the air. I suddenly felt like I was ten again.

I bent down and ripped some lavender to smell. Bringing it to my face I froze as I recognized the earthy scent that was definitely not lavender. Dropping the herb, I ran to the nearest worker.

"Do you guys fertilize everything out here?" I asked, startling the worker.

"Of course. You can't get gardens like this without fertilizer. It's all organic though. Nicholas wouldn't have it any other way."

"Everything's beautiful," I muttered.

"What's your deal?" Trevor asked, coming up behind me.

"Nothing," I said, wiping my hands on my clothes.

"You look like you saw a ghost."

I started laughing trying to throw him off.

"Come on, let's go get some lunch. This is just me with low blood sugar."

We met up with my mom and walked back to the main house. Stopping in the kitchen, I grabbed some fruit that I never intended to eat and watched Trevor carefully. He seemed to get more nervous on our way back, and now that we were in the kitchen, he seemed almost terrified.

"What's up?" I asked. It pained me to continue this playacting. Did I really care?

My mother came up behind me and rested her palm on my shoulder.

"Is that all you're going to eat?" she asked.

"For now. I think the dinner from last night is still with me. I was actually going to go take a nap." I looked at her and realized I was treating her as a stranger, but I was only following her lead.

"I know the feeling. I gotta go finish some stuff

for your dad," Trevor replied, waving as he left the kitchen.

"I was thinking about doing that too," My mother replied, leaving me standing in the kitchen by myself. Looking around the space, I was completely stumped at how easy it was to rid myself of everyone. I plopped the fruit back in the bowl and took off back outside.

I walked by the building that Ellsy was being held in. There were now two people chatting downstairs exactly as she described. I nodded at them as they watched me with curiosity as I continued toward the woods.

As I neared the forest, I heard a large knocking. Looking up quickly, I saw a woodpecker, pecking away at a dying tree. It was such a large creature and quite beautiful. It seemed fitting as the dead wood crumbled from the sky. Lately it felt like the sky was falling.

Walking into the darkened woodland, the chirping and warbling from the many birds sounded wonderful. It brought me as close to peace as I would find for the moment.

I found the stone wall that was only as high as my hip, and I followed it along the property, attempting to get my bearings. I was getting thirsty and looked for one of the markers that indicated I was getting close to one of the drop-off points. If I could get a few nutrition bars and a couple bottled waters, I'd be set. My eye spotted the grey piece of fabric tucked in a branch and relief flooded my system.

I leaned over the wall and found the bag

immediately. I quickly stuffed the bars in all my pockets, and twisted the cap off of one of the waters, drinking it as fast as I could. I placed the empty bottle back in the bag and grabbed two more. I tucked the bottles in my socks and secured each around my ankle with a ribbon that was provided. This brought new meaning to the word bootlegging as I pulled the cuff of my jeans back down over my hidden goods. Tossing the bag back where I found it, I decided that I might as well grab the pendant at the end of the wall since I was out here.

I wanted to believe that Logan was watching me. Like he and the others were only hiding in the woods, waiting for me to come search everything out, but I knew that wasn't the case. I was alone.

Reaching the corner of the wall, I slid my hand along the wall, until I found the coldness of the metal. I quickly fastened the chain around my neck and hid the pendant under my shirt. Rather than make my way back along the way I came, I decided to weave my way through the woods. Calmness met me out here amongst the trees and the birds chirping. It centered me. I could see the buildings from where I was, and I didn't want to go back yet.

I sat down and leaned against the tree, wondering if I'd be able to find out what I needed from my father and if that would even prove anything. It seemed like the only way to stop the traditions from my father's past was to stop him and ensure that I didn't pick up any bad habits along the way.

A bank swallow landed on the ground in front of me and began singing her song. I thought back to when Logan and I were at the beach and somehow I compared myself to a crazy cat lady. Even though it seemed like the weight of the world was on our shoulders, and I narrowly avoided being attacked, I'd felt loved and comforted. Like the possibilities all led to a good place. I didn't believe that any longer. Instead, it felt like any choice I made was going to be the wrong one.

The bank swallow flew away, and I closed my eyes letting the sounds of the forest wrap around me. The cheerfulness of the songs surrounding me came to an abrupt halt as their silence warned of a predator. I opened my eyes to see my father talking with the elder Trevor had mentioned earlier.

"I don't know what more you want me to do," my father snapped, running his fingers through his hair.

"If we're going to get this to market in time, you must speed up production. This whole thing with your daughter is holding us up. Either get rid of her or I will. She's of no use to us."

"But she holds powers from her mother that I know we can tap into," my father retorted.

"You haven't done well at choosing so far. Think about that Logan kid. That was a waste. He's not still around I hope. I don't have time for your screw-ups. I'm getting older, and I want to see everything the way the masters have planned for centuries."

I could see my father clearly and was sure if he took his eyes off the elder, he would see me too.

"I'll step up production, and my daughter will not cause any disruptions. Let me deal with her." His eyes flickered to mine and I remained frozen.

"Now let's get you back to the house before we head to the production facility." My father placed his hand on the elder's back and directed him toward the house.

I held my breath until I hovered on the verge of passing out. Was my father trying to protect me or did he only believe that I was of some use to him? I knew he saw me, but he probably didn't give my presence away more for his self-preservation than mine.

The birds began their songs again, and all I wanted to do was hop the fence and never come back.

"Triss," a voice whispered.

Was that Logan?

"Triss, over here," Logan commanded.

It wasn't in my head or was it? Without moving my head, my eyes scanned the forest, and I saw no one.

Feeling the warmth from the *nectunt*, I placed my hand over it.

"Are you here?"

"No, Triss. I'm not. Why? What's going on? Did you hear something?"

"Nothing. I'm fine." I returned. *"Just wishful thinking."*

The limbs to my left snapped back, but I saw no one, nothing to cause the motion. My eyes traced the branches, hoping to see a squirrel or bird hopping around, but I found nothing except leaves rustling. I leaned my head back and frowned. Could the mushroom dust from the lavender be causing this?

"What aren't you telling me?" he asked.

"Nothing. I've got to go give some items to your mom. She asked about you. She's proud of you."

I felt the pain as he thought of his mother. I wanted to ease his suffering, but there was nothing I could do until we got her out of here.

"I'll talk to you tonight. Love you."

"I love you too, Triss."

Standing up, I heard the voice directly behind me.

"Why are you fighting your father's wishes?" he commanded.

I looked to see Logan standing by the birch, but it wasn't really Logan. I rubbed my eyes, and tried to refocus on the being. What was going on?

"Who are you?" I yelled.

A pixelled retransformation began as Logan's features began vanishing. I wanted to scream, but no one would care even if they heard me. As I stood motionless watching the imposter transform into his true character, I began doubting everything, but most of all my abilities. I needed to get out of here.

My hand slowly reached around to my back pocket, gripping my wand.

"Don't bother." The impersonator replied as

he stepped toward me. It was the old man my father had been talking to. His face was marked with battle scars, and he looked older than humanly possible. "How'd you know I wasn't Logan?"

"My father will come looking for me," I replied, lying to myself and ignoring his question.

"No he won't. I'm still with him. I have the uncanny ability to be more than one place at a time." His laughter bounced off the trees. "And you know as well as I do he wouldn't come for you anyway."

"Who are you?" I asked, hoping to buy myself time.

"I'm the future." He lowered his voice.

I remained silent.

Licking his lips he began again. "I will not let you disrupt the process."

"I don't think you have a choice." My laughter dripped with rejection as he leapt toward me.

His hand came down on my shoulder, and the anger of eighteen years without a father ran through me. This was the man who turned my father against his family. I turned my head and bit his hand. My teeth entered his flesh and a wave of hatred followed.

"That's what I thought," he snarled. "You're not special. You hate like the rest of us."

He shoved me to the ground, and I wiped my mouth. The sickness began spreading through me. What had I done?

"Who said I didn't?" My eyes flashed to his, then to his bloodied hand.

"Your father," he snarled. "But you do. You do hate."

"You're wrong," I replied, looking away from the man.

"I'm seldom wrong."

"What did you promise my father eighteen years ago?" I asked. "What did you tell him to steal him away from his family."

Remembering Logan's words I kept pushing down the disgust and hostility, trying desperately to disallow hatred to seep back in to my blood. I was not going to prove this person right, whoever he was.

My fingers started tingling with the desire to destroy this old man. I had to stop myself.

"Children are supposed to listen to their parents," he replied, twitching. "I only showed my *son* the possibilities of a world he attempted to abandon."

"You're my grandfather?"

CHAPTER 22

"Eben," he responded. "Grandpa Eben. Hmm. Never heard that before."

He paused and looked down at me. "Not sure I like it."

I glared at him, saying nothing.

"I'll allow you one pardon since you're my granddaughter. Give me your allegiance, and I will forget this ever happened."

"Why do you need my allegiance if I'm like everyone else? Why not destroy me?" I smiled, springing to my feet.

"You're certainly naively determined." His eyes darkened, and I knew I'd struck a chord. I backed up until I felt the tree trunk behind me for support.

"I call the wind to my side. I sing to the creatures above and below," I whispered. The breeze picked up with a certainty that didn't exist before. "Be by my side in this world and the other."

Eben's rage grew with every second that passed. What was he going to do to me?

I heard a snap coming from behind, and Eben

took his eyes off of me long enough for me to start running. My heart raced with fear at the realization that I had nowhere to go, but I kept running.

"Come back here, girl," he hollered.

The first flame whipped by me, lighting the ground on fire. He may have dark magic on his side, but I had youth and speed on mine.

My lungs began feeling heavy as I darted through the trees, fire bouncing in every direction. And then it hit. I'd been struck. Collapsing to the forest floor, I rolled on my back to get the flames extinguished but nothing worked. I heard footsteps coming near me, and I struggled to get up, to run again, but my body collapsed once more. My mind drifted to blackness.

A buzzing and throbbing woke me up, but I was too afraid to open my eyes.

"We have to get you out of here," Trevor whispered, shocking me to my senses.

"No," I shot up. "I can't leave."

"Whatever you think you came here for isn't going to happen," Trevor replied softly. "You need to leave and never come back. Never be connected to the Wiccan world again. It's the only way for your survival."

"Where am I?" I asked, seeing nothing I recognized.

"My room, but it's only a matter of time before they find you."

"Why are you helping me?" I asked.

"Because I love you."

"If you love me, you'll help me get my mom and Logan's mom out of here safely."

"He's too powerful, Triss. It can't be done."

"He's not any more powerful than you or me."

Trevor shook his head, and extended his arm to touch my cheek.

"Get me to Ellsy at least. I need to give her some items."

I saw fear lodged behind Trevor's eyes, and I wasn't sure he could get past it.

"Please."

He shook his head and helped me off the bed.

"I'll take the items for you, but I won't let you go there."

I was getting somewhere. I sat back down on the bed and raised my legs up, lifting my pants up to reveal the bottled waters.

"You're willing to risk your life to give her water?" he asked, narrowing his eyes.

I nodded.

"Why?"

"My father doesn't have power so much as he's been poisoning everyone's mind with the food you eat and the water you drink."

Trevor's jaw dropped open. "That can't be."

"Well it is."

"That meeting my father was having today?"

He nodded.

"I think it was to go over distributing it beyond our community. And that man he was meeting with was my grandfather."

Trevor's expression turned to horror, and his skin paled to a ghostly shade.

"I know. It's pretty horrible." I replied. This was what Trevor used to be like. I could talk to him. He seemed normal before—

"I destroyed him," he muttered.

"Wait. What?"

My world was spinning.

"I didn't know," he replied. "I was trying to save you. He wouldn't listen to reason. He wouldn't stop throwing fire. I heard him begin the chant for the Golem, and I knew I had to stop him. I banished him to the underworld."

"You can do that?" I asked.

"It's a pretty common spell in black sorcery."

My body began to overheat with worry as I remembered my grandfather's words.

"When he met me in the woods, he implied he could be two places at once. That he was also with my father."

"Oh no." Trevor raised his hand to his temple. "Triss, you don't understand what we're dealing with. You have to leave. Your grandfather is very much alive. I've only made him angry."

"What about you?" I asked. I began emptying my pockets of the granola bars and tossed them on the water bottles for Ellsy.

"I'll be fine," his replied solemnly.

"Please make sure she gets these."

"Triss, she's not there anymore," he replied.

My soul felt like a bottomless pit of despair. I was too late. We were too late.

"She went missing." He slid everything under his pillow and grabbed my hand, pulling me to the door.

Missing? She didn't go missing. This was the surprise Logan had told me about, but that meant he had been on the property. Oh no. Please no.

The hallway was deathly silent as we snuck along the wall, hiding in the shadows. My heart was pounding so fast I wasn't sure I'd hear anyone coming.

"We're going to go out the back entrance," he whispered.

I followed him down the stairs and knew this was far too easy. It was only a matter of time. My hands were wet with anticipation, and my mind was impossible to calm, but we made it outside. How could this be?

"This way," Trevor said, pulling me to the land behind the house. The darkness provided cover, but also the realization that I didn't know this part of the property. But I didn't care. All I could think of was Logan.

"Stay here," he whispered, pointing to a very tiny area.

The only way I could fit under the boulder was to curl into a ball.

"Triss, I'm sorry but this is as far as I can take you. Wait a little while and then do your best to run. Run as fast as you can and don't stop until you reach the wall."

I nodded, and he took off in the direction we came from.

I placed my hand on the *nectunt* to reach Logan. I needed to make sure he was all right — that Ellsy was okay — but there was nothing. I felt nothing.

"Logan," I tried pushing the communication through, but it went nowhere. It was an empty word rattling around in my own mind.

I clamped my eyes shut. What did this mean? Where could he be?

I heard a rustling in front of me and opened my eyes to reveal a large shadow towering over me.

"Aw, there you are," my father replied, reaching down he grabbed my neck.

"What have you done with him?" I whimpered.

"Who?" He grinned so wide, his teeth glistened in the night's sky.

"How did you turn so evil?" I asked, as he pushed me in front of him. He knew I wouldn't run. There was nowhere and no one to run to.

"The embarrassment you caused me in front of my father, your grandfather, is unforgiveable. He left angrier than I've ever seen him. He's an old man, Triss. Do you realize I might never see him again? And my ignorant daughter chased him off. I saved you from him," he ranted.

"You're making no sense."

"I saw you in the woods, but I didn't let on that you were there and this is how you repay me?"

I didn't even know how to reply. My father was insane. Dragging me across the property we finally arrived at the destination he intended.

"Do you think I got to this place of power by being foolish?" My father accused, shoving me into the shed that once housed Ellsy.

I clenched my eyes shut as my body slid against the floor, greeting every stone with pain. The anger was doubling inside, but I had to follow the plan. I promised Logan I would no matter what. It wasn't only my life in jeopardy.

My flesh burned and stung as air began to touch the open wounds, but I wouldn't shed a tear, not over this. *Not over my father.*

"Not at all," I replied.

"Then why are you making me punish you like this?" he barked.

Images of my mother from the night before haunted me, and I vowed I wouldn't become like her. I wouldn't become an Altered Soul.

"I'm sorry. I don't know what I'm doing wrong," I said.

Opening my eyes, I stared at the back of the room. I quickly scanned the bottom of the wall and saw the shackle. Would he shackle his own daughter?

"You don't, huh?" He began pacing behind me.

Shaking my head, I kept my mouth shut as I waited for his reply. I didn't want to look at him. I swallowed my anger and steadied my voice. I'd come too far to lose control.

"Do you think I didn't know you and your little boyfriend snuck up the lake to spy on me?" my father boomed. "I *allowed* you to leave unharmed."

My heart quickened. He knew Logan was going to be here tonight. Oh, God. Please no.

"How naïve do you think I am, *daughter*?"

The grotesque recognition of our status began controlling me. I could no longer control myself. Not with Logan out there alone unknowingly planning his own demise.

"Daughter?" I snapped, turning to face the man I wanted to kill. "Don't you dare call me that. You're a sickening sight, pathetic, and I'm *nothing* like you."

My rage was unstoppable. Logan had no idea that this was a trap. We had been in control of nothing this entire time.

"Oh, I don't know about that." He smiled. "By the way, haven't you been worried why you can't get a hold of him? Is your little communication spell not working any longer? The entire point of communicating silently is so you don't utter the words goodbye for a fool like me to hear."

"You're worthless. You couldn't stand on your own if you tried," I yelled.

"At least you're feeling the hate. That will be useful." He turned around, sliding the lock in the door ensuring I went nowhere.

The angry tears began flooding down my face. There was nothing I could do to warn Logan. What was my father going to do to him? Or did he already have him? I slid down the wall slowly as fear began to paralyze me. The blood was trickling down my palms, pooling at the tips of my fingers and I didn't care. I felt like time was leaving me behind.

I rested my head against the wall and stared at the ceiling hoping for some sign, but my lids began getting heavy with anguish.

"Triss."

My eyes blinked open and I attempted to orient the voice when I saw her. Aunt Vieta was staring at me, only a foot away.

"How did you get in here?" I hissed, glaring at her.

She ignored my question and knelt down quickly, placing a note in my hand.

I didn't understand her. I didn't understand her actions, and I probably never would.

"Take care, Triss," she whispered, turning around and exiting the shed without another word.

Quickly unrolling the piece of paper, the confusion began spreading through me once more. Was she helping me or nudging me to make the wrong decision again.

I held in my hand the image that both Logan and I shared, bonding us as one. How would my aunt know about this spell and what was it meant to tell me? My other hand shoved my waistband down an inch allowing me to see the ink on my skin, praying it would tell me something — anything. It did nothing of the sort. It was cold and lifeless. Had my father already hurt Logan?

I dropped the note on the floor and closed my eyes. Curling my legs into me, I braced myself for an outcome I never wanted to imagine.

A breeze from the open window began to pick up, and I tightened my legs into my body, gripping my knees even more. I looked up to see if I could even reach the window to close it, and it didn't look promising. It was up too high. I wondered how many people my father housed in here? My stare dropped back to the floor when I noticed there was something else scrawled on the backside of the note.

It was Logan's handwriting. My hands trembled as I reached for the piece of paper that now seemed like the most important document in the world.

I love you, Triss
I always have and always will
Stick to the plan
I'll be all right
Whether it's in this world or the next
We'll be together
We've got to release these souls
Yours forever,
Logan

My heart began beating so fast, my face turned flush with sorrow. He was writing me a goodbye note. Did he always know this was part of the plan? How could he do this to me — to us? I couldn't stop the panic from spreading throughout me. My breathing was ragged with the anger that began filling me once more.

I couldn't stick to the plan. Not now, not if it involves losing him. I folded the piece of paper as tiny as possible and stuck it under my bra strap as close to my heart as I could place it.

Knowing my father, he was going to make what was coming an example for his followers. Step out of line and you can expect to be punished. If my father's ego could be counted on then there would be an audience for Logan's arrival, and I'm certain my father would want me to be part of it.

I promised Logan I wouldn't resort to black magic in order to stay protected from the spirits from the underworld, but I couldn't stand by and watch him die.

"You'll have to forgive me, baby," I whispered for no one other than myself.

"Triss, stop," Bakula whispered, scaring me to death.

"How'd you know I was in here?" I whispered.

"We were able to see the choice you were about to make," Bakula said, fluttering to the front door. "It led us here."

"Dace, have you unlocked it?" she asked impatient.

"Just about," he replied.

"Logan, he's in harms way." My voice panicked.

"We can't stop decisions that have already been made," Dace whispered apologetically.

The door sprung open, and I ran outside toward the lake with Bakula and Dace flying away. We couldn't afford to have them seen.

The property was deathly quiet, scaring even more as I wondered where everyone was. By the time I got to the lake my heart was pounding.

I heard a group slowly edging up behind me. A murmur of excited voices met me next.

"Would you like to see a little better?" my father's voice boomed.

He threw a flame and another, creating a bonfire, not unlike the one I saw the first night when Logan and I were on the lake. I turned my attention back out to the water, and my heart fractured as I realized Logan was out there in a boat, and he wasn't alone. Trevor was with him.

"Don't take one more step toward him," my father ordered.

I heard whimpering in the direction of the boat and ignoring my father stepped forward to see Ellsy tied up in the bottom of the boat with her mouth taped shut. Her head was propped up on one of the wooden benches, as tears streamed down her face. My heartbeat quickened at the thought of what my father and Trevor planned to do to them. I forced my stare from Ellsy to her son.

"I love you," Logan mouthed, his deep blue eyes calm.

Trevor's blade was digging into Logan's flesh, but Logan refused to wince. He stood strong, keeping his eyes on me, barely blinking. The boat bobbed only slightly in the mostly still lake, making the opportunity too perfect for me to miss.

"Do what he says," Logan echoed.

"No. I'm not taking orders from anyone any longer," I replied, shaking my head. "That includes you."

My stomach constricted as I launched my verbal assault. I loved him too much to speak to him like that, but I had no choice.

Not backing down, I took a few steps closer to

the water and heard the crowd of gasps behind me. Makes sense that my father would want an audience for something so atrocious.

Trevor's eyes narrowed on me as he tightened his grip around Logan's neck.

"Please let him go, Trevor," I stated, feeling my weapon curl its way around my ankle. Apparently he was a better actor than I realized. The element of surprise had been meant for my father, but I wasn't going to chance it. The new intended target was Trevor.

"I don't think so." Trevor's laughter made the boat rock more than he expected causing him to stop abruptly.

The fury in Logan's eyes couldn't be hidden as he realized what I decided to do, but I didn't care. I wasn't going to let two people who I loved die in front of me.

"Don't defy your father, Triss," Logan grimaced as Trevor dug the blade against his neck.

Trevor smirked as he looked beyond me, over my shoulder. I wasn't sure who in particular he was looking at until I heard his voice.

"Ooh, this should be fun," my grandfather replied from the crowd. "Kind of ironic."

"Isn't it though," I replied acidly, as my weapon slowly slid its way up my body and wrapped around each of my fingers. With the darkness of the night, they wouldn't see it coming until it was too late. The adrenaline rushing through my blood was taking on a new form. I looked quickly behind me as the dislike for certain individuals turned to pure rage.

My eyes landed on my mom, whose eyes were now filled with tears. She could no longer stand up and was leaning against the Adirondack chair that held my father. Was she any closer to becoming herself?

The coldness of the arrowhead pendant against my chest reminded me that time was not on my side.

I raised my arms up quickly, allowing the snake to turn to the bow before anyone realized what was happening. Taking aim at Trevor's chest, I released the string; satisfied it would reach its intended target.

"Fragor Sagitta," I uttered, watching the sharp point turn to flames as it burrowed its way into Trevor's body.

Rather than release Logan when Trevor collapsed, the tip of the knife went into Logan's flesh as they both fell into the lake.

Ellsy shot out a mumbled scream as I stood there numb. What had I done? The crowd surrounding my father went still and then erupted with joy. I turned to face them all, letting my bow fall to the ground before turning toward the lake.

"Triss," my mother sobbed. She knew my father was going to end me, and so did I.

My father's laughter rattled through the air as I dove into the dark waters searching for Logan. The water stung my fresh scrapes with every stroke, while old downed trees and aquatic life harassed me. I couldn't find him.

Coming back up for air quickly, I swam back under the area of the small boat searching as fast as I could. He had to be around here. My heart shattered bit by bit with every second that I was unable to locate him. The slipperiness of the lake grass teased my senses with every grasp. Thinking I landed on Logan's wrist time and time again, only to be let down by the swaying of the underwater weeds ushering me to another place in the darkened waters.

Shooting my head up for air, the crowd had now converged closer to the lake. Thoughts of Ellsy flickered into my mind, but thoughts of Logan drowning forced her out. Diving back under, I kicked to a new unexplored area when a hand grabbed my arm, tugging me farther under the surface.

CHAPTER 23

I woke up to my body being dragged along the bank, but it was so dark I couldn't tell by who.

"Logan?" I whispered.

"It's not Logan," a female whispered.

"Jenny?" I asked startled. "What's going on?"

"I'm getting you to safety."

"No. Stop right now. I've got to get Logan."

She stopped moving me, and I stood up freezing, wet, and muddy. But I didn't care.

"Where is he?"

I heard rustling behind her and my body stiffened.

"Who's behind you?"

"Everyone's here and ready. He still wants us to follow the plan."

"Where is he? Is he okay?" I was completely agitated.

"He'll be fine."

"He'll *be* fine or he *is* fine?"

Jenny ignored my question and refused to look at me. She turned around and walked to the wooded area, and I followed behind.

"What about Ellsy?"

"Logan flipped the boat and got her to safety while you were underwater."

"Where is he?"

Silence.

"Well?"

"He went back."

"What?" I screamed as quietly as possible.

I reached up to my pendant and felt its warmth but heard silence.

We were still on my father's property and there was no doubt he knew we were here — that many us were here. We had peppered our presence on the outskirts of the property, each group containing about thirty members, and I needed to ensure everyone still mobilized on our signal. What was he doing?

"Do you have a lantern?" I asked.

Jenny began cranking the one tied onto her belt until a dim light displayed the many faces staring back at me. I didn't see Logan's mom.

"Where's Ellsy?" I asked.

"I had to sedate her," My aunt's voice came from behind.

My heart began beating so rapidly I became lightheaded. I glanced at Jenny who didn't seem concerned and neither did anyone else.

"What are you doing here?" I snapped.

Aunt Vieta's expression was solemn as she reached out for my hand, but I wouldn't extend mine.

She pressed her lips together and looked to

the ground.

"I don't have time for this. I've gotta check on the antidote, and then I'm going in after Logan and my mother."

"Triss, I came here for your mother's sake. I wanted to keep after her as best I could. I tried to leave you clues."

"Save it." I said, knowing nothing was going to get figured out in this moment.

There were supposed to be fairies mingled with each group of witches, but I didn't see any. They were the ones who were supposed to have the antidote we needed to administer.

I reached up to my pendant, hoping to hear the voices of the fairies, and excused myself to a less inhabited part of the woods.

"Dace, Bakula," I whispered, holding onto the arrowhead.

Silence.

Something was wrong.

I ran over to Jenny.

"Do you know what's going on with the antidote?" I asked.

"There was a hiccup, but they are going to be ready with it as soon as we launch the boats," Jenny replied.

"And Logan went in without everything in place? Did he stick to the original plan?"

She nodded.

"Alright, I'm going in. When you see the fires, bring the boats. We'll hope that the antidote arrives in time."

"Triss, Logan told me to keep you away," she

whispered.

My mind flashed to the letter he wrote, and I refused to choose that as my destiny. I refused to live with a ghost of a person. I needed the real thing.

"If he told you to stick to the original plan, I'm part of it," I said, shaking her hand off mine.

"Wait for the signal. There's going to be a lot of souls that need saving tonight."

Turning around, I walked back to the water where boats of all kinds were bobbing, waiting for their purpose. I chose the smallest one and hopped in without even thinking.

The anger inside me was threatening my ability to see clearly. What was this martyr thing Logan had going on? He couldn't do this alone. His mother was safe. Mine wasn't. It wasn't his job to save her.

I grabbed the oars and began rowing. The breeze off the water combined with my wet clothes was downright icy. That would give me something other than Logan's actions to worry about.

"Triss," a male's voice whispered.

The chill of my skin quickly turned to a raw heat of fear. That was not Logan's whisper.

I looked behind me, and I was only about twenty feet from the shore. I didn't see anyone except Jenny.

"Over here," he whispered again, this time rattling the tall grass as he spoke.

My mouth became dry as I saw the eyes looking at me. It was Trevor, but that was impossible.

"Please, I can help," Trevor continued.

I stopped rowing and sat in the boat unable to do anything but stare at him.

I shot him. I saw the arrow go into his chest. This was a trick. I had to get to the compound. I turned my attention back to the oars and began rowing again.

"You know how your grandfather was in two places at once?" he was on the verge of yelling.

I began trembling, but I didn't know if it was because of the chill from being drenched or my complete inability to understand what was occurring.

"This was part of Logan's plan," he continued. "The one he shielded you from."

Why would Logan trust Trevor? Why would I trust Trevor? My mind was spinning with possibilities all of which seemed infeasible.

"Prove it to me," I replied, staring at his shadow.

"You share a *nectunt* together." He replied, his voice shaking. "You are forever linked as one. I accept it and respect it."

"That's not proof."

"He told me to tell you that he would have chosen daisies, whatever that means." The sorrow in his voice bounced off the lake waters right into my heart. Every word he said killed him.

I rowed quickly to the lake's edge. I didn't understand what was going on, but I didn't have any more time to waste.

Trevor smiled as I neared and bent over to reach for the boat. It wasn't a sneer or a smirk that was plastered on his face. No show of victory. I made the right decision.

"I'll row," he whispered, climbing into the boat. "We don't have much time."

"Why did Logan change the plan?" I asked, shivering as the speed of his rowing swept us through the lake.

"He was worried you'd become an Altered Soul. He didn't want to give you all the details in case your father was able to—"

"How long have you been involved with his plan?" I interrupted, as we glided into the last stretch of water.

"Only since you arrived," he began. "Something clicked when we were discussing the dark arts and Logan's reason for leaving your father's teachings. The last several days, before you arrived, I saw your father use his powers of manipulation to distort people's realities...witches and otherwise. I watched him deplete others of their history and in turn he altered their futures. As you and I were talking, I realized he had been doing the same thing to me, and I hadn't even realized it. And I was attempting to do it to you."

I remembered that both Trevor and my mother planted that same idea about Logan. That's how my father does it. He starts planting small seeds of doubt, twisting memories of past occurrences until the actual events can't be identified any longer, and then he creates new ones.

"I *knew* the truth. I knew why Logan left and no one could have told me otherwise." I replied, thinking of him.

He nodded. "I know. I saw that truth reflected in your eyes as I spoke to you in your bedroom. You were quiet. You didn't feel the need to argue with me. That response started changing things for me. I saw how your mom was responding to you during dinner. It was as if she had an altered version of her reality toward you. You guys had been so close, and she acted like you were a plaything." He paused. "I also realized you weren't ever mine."

I shoved away the anger as the reality of his statement hit me, but rather than concentrate on my mom I spoke to the other half of his words. "I was never an object to be claimed."

"I know that now." He maneuvered the boat onto the mud, and I jumped out. My feet splashed in the water. It didn't matter. I was already soaked.

"When I sent word to Logan that I'd help him get his mother released that's when the plan changed to what you saw."

"When was that?" I asked.

"The first night you were here, after dinner, I contacted him."

So that was the surprise Logan told me about.

"Thank you, Trevor," I replied.

He hauled the boat out of the water as I felt for my pendant once more.

Still nothing.

"Are you ready?" he asked.

"Is there such a thing?"

"Logan's on the other side of the property, readying the signals."

"So he's still sticking to that part of the plan?"

He nodded. "The plan from this point forward is how it was, but he's not going to be thrilled to see you."

I scowled at him not understanding why.

"He has some unfinished business with your father, and he didn't want you to witness it."

"Well, so do I," I replied, taking off in the direction of Logan.

We crept along the property's edge, but I could see that the main home was bustling with activity. All the lights were on. I wondered what my mother might be doing. My father's followers were scattering like ants, preparing for us.

"At least my father thinks you're dead," I whispered, trying to lighten the mood. I must have learned it from Logan. "That's gotta count for something."

"The element of surprise."

"Let's hope," I replied.

A branch fell in front of me, and my pulse quickened. I stopped and looked up into the tree it fell from. There in the shadows was a familiar gray figure.

"Trevor," I hissed. "Run!"

"What are you talking about?"

"Get to Logan. Tell him the Golem are back."

"I'm not leaving you."

"I'm not helpless. I've handled them before.

Get out of here." I yelled.

Trevor took off running, and I began slowly backing away from the tree that housed the creature.

Was I still protected like Logan presumed? I did try to kill Trevor. But it wasn't *really* Trevor so maybe it wouldn't count. Whatever the case, I couldn't depend on being untouchable.

My stomach clenched at the sight before me. I was surrounded. The Golem crawled in every direction, up the trees, on the limbs, on the ground before me. The darkness couldn't even diminish their grotesque appearance. They were most definitely Golem, but there was something slightly different than the ones I'd encountered in Illinois. These creatures contained marginally more human qualities, but I couldn't put my finger on how.

Barely covered with stretched, grey skin the stringy muscles of the beasts contracted with anticipation. They were waiting for a command, my father's command.

Every direction I looked, the limbs were coming to life as the trees around me housed these creatures. I felt trapped between the tall pine and spruce trees watching as they transformed before me.

"Unguibus pugionibus," I whispered. Sharpness began replacing the flesh of my fingertips.

I was electrified with a mixture of fear and anticipation. What were these beings sent to do?

Walking through the woods, I let my claws

scratch the bark of the trees, as I waited and wondered, but never letting my gaze fall from the Golem as they stalked me. Their silence became a weapon, and it was unnerving. The beings had been sent for me. They didn't follow after Trevor and that was something I needed to know. Now I had to wait.

Reaching up to my pendant, hoping for something other than quiet, I heard them — the voices of the fairies.

"Bacula," I whispered. "Are we ready?"

"Yes, all the fairies are in their places and the antidote is ready to be administered. We're waiting for the flames."

"Thank you. Something's come up. I might be a little delayed, but we'll get the crowds moving."

"I know, dear," she replied. "You're stronger than all of them combined if you choose to understand their existence."

I released the pendant, scratching my neck in the process. *Geez that hurt.* I felt the stickiness of my own blood and wiped it away as I thought about what Bakula meant. These Golem were different but how?

A low hum began in the creature closest to me followed by the others joining in his song. They moved closer to me. It was going to happen.

The Golem in the tree nearest to me, fell to the ground, readying his stance for an attack. I didn't move, I only watched. There was a familiarity about his movements, his mannerisms. I was inhaling ghosts from my past.

"Who are you?" I whispered, staring into the

darkened holes where the eyes should've been.

"What's it to you?" the being squealed into the night's air, unleashing shrieks from the others.

It was Preston.

My head began spinning with the realization that the souls my father stole to feed his flames, ego, and greed were captured and stored for his use at any time. Who knew how many he had at his disposal?

My fingers began to tingle as I watched the Golem begin their descent, dropping like bombs from the night's sky.

"As I've told you before, don't disrespect her, Preston," Logan yelled in our direction.

My pulse quickened as I watched Trevor and Logan approach the infested woods. Logan stared directly at the Golem. Logan's broad shoulders caught the shadows of the night, creating an omniscient presence. His expression dripped with venom as he took his stance, I waited to catch my breath. I was in awe of Logan's power.

"They were sent for me," I muttered.

"If they attack one of us, they attack all of us," Logan replied, his eyes holding the darkness I'd come to understand.

"Preston," I began, looking at the Golem in front of me.

The creature tweaked its skull.

"I'm sorry my father did this to you, but we will make it right. If you'll let us."

Preston swiped at me causing me to fall backward, landing on the woodland floor.

Instantly the other Golem surrounded me. Hostility dripped from their mouths as they circled me.

Bold with a desire to destroy these creatures, I sprang to my feet, slicing and pawing in every direction. As I felt my fingertips piercing through their fragile skin, an inhuman arm wrapped its cold strength around my waist, whisking me up the pine tree behind us.

Logan and Trevor had already begun their assault. Magic wasn't needed. We were running on pure adrenaline and contempt. As blades and fists found their targets, chunks of clay-like flesh were thrown into the air turning into nothingness.

Preston tightened his grip around my waist causing me to struggle for air.

I looked down and watched as Trevor and Logan, once enemies, now worked for the same cause, to destroy my father.

I kicked and swiped, unsteadying Preston from the tree enough to feel his grasp loosen.

It was my time.

Spinning around, I forced my palm through the shell of his chest. He gasped for air as I continued my onslaught of blows, striking him as hard as my fury would allow. Pieces of him sailed to the ground until he no longer existed beyond a pile of dust on the forest ground.

A Golem wrapped its arm around Trevor's neck and with every move Trevor made the Golem tightened his grip. Trevor gasped for air. I fell onto the back of the Golem, allowing my claws to scratch down the path of its gray flesh until I threw my fist into the Golem's head, leaving it to shatter into thin air.

"Thank you," Trevor whispered, grasping his throat.

I turned to see Logan ramming a stick through the last Golem. It staggered and fell to the ground. And to think this was only the beginning.

Trevor began walking through the woods, and I was grateful for the quick reprieve.

Logan glanced at me, his eyes softening as he smiled

I felt the *nectunt* begin to warm once more.

I ran over to him, feeling his arms wrap around me.

"You did it, baby," he whispered.

"We did it," I whispered into his ear.

"What happened to you? Why couldn't we communicate?" I hid my sobs of joy, sadness, and disbelief as he hugged me.

"It was too dangerous. Once I realized Eben was your grandfather, I knew I had to stay quiet. If anyone could've tapped into us, it would've been him. I didn't even know the guy was still alive.

"Alive and active. I think he's the cause of it."

I felt his arms slide down my back, but I didn't want his touch to end.

I kissed him quickly, but he let his lips linger long enough to make me return for more.

I wanted this night to be over, so we could start our life together.

Letting go of me, his expression changed as I

saw the fires behind him.

"The time has come," he whispered.

CHAPTER 24

There was fire in every direction I looked. The beauty of what the flames represented couldn't even be described. The building that housed Ellsy and I had already been destroyed. The stone was the only remaining element. I was sure Logan put extra gasoline around it. I would have to thank him for that.

Followers' screams echoed through the air with the realization they were alone. Their fearless leader was nowhere to be found: my father – the coward. We needed to get these people to the lake as far away from him as possible.

The lake was filled with small boats of every kind, waiting to be filled with unsuspecting patients. The silver glimmer surrounding each boat was the occupant's admission. One dose of the antidote from the fairy, willing or not, and their soul would be on the way to being released. Dace and Bakula instructed the fairies waiting at each boat that no one was to get across the lake without the antidote.

My eyes searched the crowd for my father. I saw many of the people who were at the dinner, the farmers, the guards but not my father. Complete chaos was ensuing. People were running around attempting to stop the fires but there was no stopping these flames.

Someone had to step up to corral these poor souls.

A line of our people began forming from the lake, up the bank, toward the property in order to usher the crazed followers in the right direction. The chants of peace and calm began harmonizing through song in the night's smoky air. But more was needed.

I grabbed the first lost soul wandering in front of me and led her to the line of people waiting.

"Get her to the boat. Start the process. I'll get more," I replied to the first person in line.

I spotted Marco, one of my father's right hand men, wandering off toward the woods.

"Oh, no you don't," I whispered, running toward the defector, reaching for my wand. I sprinted passed Logan as he was ushering a group toward the lake, and he hollered after me.

"I've gotta create a perimeter," I yelled.

My voice startled Marco who stopped and turned to face me.

"Where do you think you're going?" I panted, standing only feet away.

"Non Impetus," I hollered, before he could respond, purposefully leaving off *Temporarium,* as his body stiffened into a frozen state.

Logan came running up behind me.

"Nice work. Who was that?" he asked.

"Marco. He was one of my father's favorites. I've gotta get the perimeter secured. Think coyotes will keep everyone on the inside?"

"Absolutely," Logan smiled, reaching for his wand.

"*Coyotes Oppugnare*," I whispered, closing my eyes and repeating it several times.

A purpose driven growl came from behind, and I turned to see my spell in action.

"Nothing like a snarling pack of coyotes to keep people in line," he whispered, unable to hide the pride he felt for me.

Feeling secure with the perimeter, we ran back to the center of the action.

Trevor was arguing with someone I didn't recognize, but I didn't have time to worry about it.

Aunt Vieta was directing someone toward the lake.

"Have you seen my mom?" I asked her.

She shook her head no, and I turned toward the main building.

"Everyone! My father has a line of boats waiting for you. Please head to the lake," I screamed as hard as my throat would handle. "He doesn't want you worrying about saving anything but yourselves."

God, I hated lying to make him sound better than he was.

A shift in the energy began to take hold. The shrieking began to be replaced with muttering of self-preservation.

"Where is she?" I muttered.

"I don't know, but we'll find her," Logan replied.

"Do you hear that?"

A deep drumming began reverberating through the air.

"Oh no," he replied. "We've got to get these people to the boats. Forget the orderly chaos just get them off this property."

I ran to our people and spotted Jenna.

"My father's starting a ceremony. We've got to get these followers off the grounds. Get them in the boats and worry about the antidote in the center of the lake. If they don't have it before they get in, that's going to have to be fine."

She nodded and began spreading the word to everyone. Understanding the urgency, they began grabbing and pulling anyone they could toward the water.

I saw Logan near the woods. He turned to look at me and held out his hand to stop me. My father must be there. I shook my head and began running toward him. He held out his arms to grab me, but I wouldn't let him.

My mother was standing in the middle of the sorcerers, with her flowing, peach dress blowing in the wind as the followers bowed down to her.

"This could have been you," my father yelled over the drums, looking at me. "You could've found your full potential."

"Is that a threat or a misguided promise?" I hollered, struggling to get out of Logan's embrace.

"Baby, I love you. Please don't. Let me handle it," Logan whispered.

"I've got this," I replied.

Looking at each of the sorcerers who were dressed in their plague masks and ivory robes, I shook my head and landed my gaze back on my father. They were preparing to take more souls.

"Well?" I shouted.

"Whatever you want it to be," he said with a sneer in his voice.

"I'm not going to allow your actions, or that of our families, to remain invisible to the witches of the world. Your false history will no longer be viewed as reality."

His jaw clenched and so did his fist. I knew he wanted to hit me or worse but that didn't stop me from continuing.

"The time has come for our family's legacy to be stopped."

"What do you know? You're just a girl."

My father knew what his presence did to people, especially people who provided some sort of opening, but I wouldn't allow an opening to exist. His jabs only made me stronger, but that was the difference. His words infuriated me but brought comfort to others depending on what he tapped into.

"Just a girl?" I laughed. "I've heard worse."

His anger was bubbling over. He was used to his words having an effect, and they had none on me. Whether someone was experiencing loss, guilt, or shame my father deciphered it quickly and played on those emotions, providing a promise of tranquility to the individual who was suffering. Unfortunately, it looked like the tranquility was brainwashing, but often the people were so desperate for peace they fell for it. I still didn't believe that my mom could be put in any of those buckets though, and that's what wouldn't stop bothering me.. She seemed so happy at home with me. There had to be more.

"So how much of the hallucinogenic do you stuff at the end of their plague masks?"

"I don't know what you're talking about. I purely use my power of persuasion."

"You're not that powerful. Otherwise you would've gotten me," I taunted.

"Triss, be careful," Logan whispered, his hand slipping into mine.

I looked over at my mom whose eyes caught mine before she crumpled to the ground and began crying. What was she sensing? She covered her face with her hands as my father went to her side.

Aunt Vieta came running up behind us, gasping at the sight of her sister.

Looking behind my father and mother, I spotted another group of sorcerers hastily planning something. They were also wearing ivory robes, but they weren't looking this way. What more did my father have going on?

"It's not about us any more, my love," my father spoke to my mother, touching her cheek. "The time has come. It's time to destroy the ones who don't share our vision."

My father's eyes flashed into a violent rage that was more beast than witch as he raised his arms to a fiery blaze of terror.

"Help me get her," I screamed, pointing at my mother, worried she'd get swallowed by the flames. My father ran in the direction of the other sorcerers, leaving my mother in a heap.

True love.

Sweat poured off of me instantly from the heat as I ran toward her. Logan was right behind me, but we couldn't get to her in time as the life exited her body.

My father's laughter wrapped its way around my soul bringing me to understand the power of hatred.

I cried my silent tears for my mother, and prayed I would meet her again someday, but first I had to free those that remained. I had to stop him.

Aunt Vieta grabbed my mother, whose body was completely lifeless, and hauled her away from the woods toward the lake.

"I'm going after my father. I love you, Logan," I whispered as I took off following my father.

Logan yelled after me, but not wanting to hear his words I ran faster. I made it to where the sorcerers last were, but my father was nowhere in sight. The smoke was thick in every direction, and I wasn't sure I'd even be able to catch his shadow.

The buildings that housed many of the operations that I'd never even seen were completely ravaged with flames. There was no place for my father to go but into the backwoods. Not exactly what I had planned.

I heard coughing and spun around to see Trevor behind me, watching me.

"Do you know where he went?" I asked, unsure of the look in Trevor's eyes.

"Haven't seen him," he replied, coughing into his shirt. There was blood when he dropped his arm.

"Triss," Logan yelled, but I couldn't see him. The smoke was clouding everything.

"Stay where you are," I yelled at Trevor. "Logan, follow my voice. Trevor's coughing up blood."

I began walking toward Trevor who had now fallen to his knees.

"Logan, are you near?" I asked, feeling his touch from behind.

Logan grabbed Trevor and tossed him over his shoulder with ease.

"Let's get him to the lake," Logan said.

I shook my head, but he couldn't see it.

"My father went into the woods. I've got to find him."

"Don't let the hatred drive you," Logan replied.

I knew he was right, but it felt like it was something I could no longer control.

"Find out what's wrong with him."

"We have more people to help. People are lost; their souls need to be released."

"*We* needed to release the souls. *I* need to stop my father."

"Triss, please don't do this," Logan pleaded with me.

And like that I made my choice. It was no longer about my survival it was about destroying my father and everything he stood for. Logan didn't fill me in on all of his plans, and I didn't fill him in on mine.

With every step closer to the forest, my lungs brought in smokeless air that kept the energy pulsing through me. It felt like a new world was before me. I had a purpose.

My legs hopped over the downed trees with ease and my body glided through the limbs as if I was a ghost. The adrenaline pulsing through me brought a new clarity.

This man, my father, was more than a dark sorcerer, he was a killer — a killer of souls, spirits, and witches alike. Not even realizing how long I had been running, I stopped to catch my breath and get my bearings when I saw him.

He was no longer dressed in jeans and a button-down. He was wearing a black cloak, standing with a presence far larger than his actual size. He had his hands pressed together as if waiting for something.

Or someone.

I'd fallen into his trap.

The anger fueled me to run to the middle of an empty forest to face a man who had magical abilities that far exceeded mine. What had I done? Would my plan still work?

The group of dark sorcerers surrounded me.

"Are you afraid?"

I shook my head.

"You should be."

"When will it ever be enough?" I asked, staring into the face of a cold-blooded killer.

"There's no such thing," he replied coolly. "That's what separates *us* from others. Our family's drive is never ending, allowing us to achieve more than most could ever dream of. We have willpower and strength deep within our soul. We're not weak-minded."

"Don't lump me in with you."

"There's nothing wrong with it."

I shrugged, looking down at the forest floor, refusing to look into his eyes until I was ready to see what my mother's ancestors could provide.

"I'm surprised," I began.

"At what?" my father asked, dropping his arms. I stared directly into his gaze, feeling the wickedness down to his core.

"That you would call yourself strong-willed, but you'd let an old man tell you what to do. Your father no less. I'd never let that happen." I dropped my eyes and felt the smile spread across my lips.

"How dare you," my father's voice roared.

"Do you disagree?" I shot my father a warning glance.

"You will die by my hands."

"It's only one of many ways to die, father." I smiled and felt the familiar slither wrap around my ankle.

"Don't reach for your bow," my father commanded.

"I wouldn't think of it. The element of surprise is no longer there. You saw what I did to Trevor."

I laughed and didn't stop laughing. I started caressing the spruce's limbs.

He squinted his eyes at me, and the sorcerers narrowed their presence around me.

I reached up quickly to my pendant.

"Now," I whispered.

"On our way," Dace replied.

"What are you doing?" my father laughed. "Playing pretend? You still have that pendant from your coven ceremony? You do know that's a replica right?"

"Yeah, I know. It reminded me of my mother and the good her side stood for," I lied. "Until she met you."

I started singing under my breath until he began again.

"I was the best thing that happened to her."

"Yeah it appears that way," I replied sarcastically.

Anger completely stole the tears that I wanted to shed in the name of my mother, but that's how it had to be.

"Do you hear that?" I asked unable to hide my grin.

My father shook his head and glanced at the sorcerers surrounding me.

"You can't emancipate yourself from blood," my father hollered.

"Oh, yes I can." I smiled. "And it's about to happen. Wanna see?"

My father began getting nervous not because I

offered more strength or magical prowess but because he thought he was dealing with crazy. And crazy could never be predicted.

"Mmm, now do you hear it?" I asked.

Snarls and yips were getting closer by the second. I looked at the trees around me and surmised which might be the best to climb in case of an emergency.

"What have you done?" my father asked, slowly backing away from me.

"I called a few forest friends to help me. It seems I got in a little over my head."

A symphony of growls and biting snaps appeared behind me. The sorcerers began disbanding much to my father's dismay.

"You should've stuffed more drugs in their masks," I laughed nervously as the coyotes began getting closer.

Watching my father's gaze shift to behind me, I turned quickly to see the brilliant light rolling through the forest. My friends had arrived.

I saw my father reach for his wand, but as the wave of fairies and witches encroached he thought better of it. One of the dark sorcerers next to me was foolish enough to charge me with his wand, casting a spell that I managed to deflect, but it announced that the time had come for self-defense.

The bow fell into my hand as I took aim at my first victim. I'd seen enough fire for the night, letting my fingers release the string. I watched the arrow sail into the first predator, and he dropped.

The coyotes paced back and forth as if waiting for a command that I couldn't give them, not yet anyway. For once in his life, I wanted my father to fear. Taste what it felt like to be thrown a future that wasn't certain. His eyes held the same vacant stare that I had seen many times before from his followers.

The fairies began making a perimeter around us as the little creatures showed their mighty fangs in anticipation for what might lay ahead. They could never enter our world without an invitation, and I had given them that.

"Fairies hate our kind," my father seethed. "You just called them in for your own death."

"They hate *your* kind." I laughed.

The cowardliness inside of my father took hold as the witches marched side-by-side, chanting cries to the wilderness, unleashing a disturbance that rocked everything in its presence.

The wind began whipping through the trees as the coyotes continued their howls, and I stood looking at my father waiting for his response.

"Where's your father now?" I asked quietly.

He continued giving me a cold stare.

"We're ready when you are," Jenny whispered, standing a few feet behind me.

"Yes, we are," Aunt Vieta and Jenna replied in unison.

I nodded and waited. It would only be a matter of time before my father's anger got the best of him.

Regardless of what darkness he could tap into,

my father knew he was outnumbered. His desperation would make him behave violently, and then I could act. I might not be the strongest witch *yet*, but I certainly had friends in high places.

"*Cogita Confluebant ad Defensionem Creatura Mundi Vincere Malum,*" I whispered.

Watching the moonlight slowly vanish as the flocks of birds began making their descent created a powerful stir deep inside for the power the wilderness had to offer. I had so much to learn in our world.

"Triss what have you done?" my father snarled.

"I'm finding my full potential. Have you heard of this thing called gray magic?"

His face paled. "There's no such thing."

"There very much is, and I'm starting to learn about it. It's fascinating."

I felt movement behind me. My father's eyes bounced to our newest arrivals, as disdain spread across his face.

"I'm right behind you, babe," Logan said.

"Why don't you come right beside me," I stated.

"Absolutely." His voice was low, almost seductive.

"*Descendit cum Caelum,*" my father hollered, pointing his wand in my direction. The rain dumped from the skies, pushing the birds in every direction.

That's all it took. I was free to protect myself.

"Down with the sky," Logan hollered back,

laughing. "That's it? I raise you! *Descendit cum Arboribus.*"

The trees around my father began crashing down all around him.

I heard my aunt calling to the skies to stop the rain as I watched my father dodge trees and limbs.

The fairies moved closer to my father as he pointed his wand directly at Logan. Trevor stepped from behind me, and targeted my father with his wand.

"Feeling better?" I asked Trevor.

"Immensely."

"Good," I replied, not taking my gaze off of my father.

Logan leaned into me, quickly pushing back my hair.

"She's alive," he whispered.

Two words I never expected to hear.

"Let me do something else for you," he said softly.

"*Inhabilitare Indefinite*," Logan hollered as his wand flashed a blaze of electricity to my father.

My father was frozen in time. I reached up to hold my pendant and heard the fairies' voices full of glee.

"What did you do?" I asked bewildered.

"I incapacitated him indefinitely. Or until we say so." He smirked.

"My god, I love you," I whispered, wrapping my arms around his neck.

"Gray magic, huh?" he asked bemused.

"I think that was the whole point of the spell

book from the cottage. It contained spells that were both white and black... who's to say which is what?"

"And when and why?" he finished my sentence.

"Exactly. Makes perfect sense doesn't it?"

"Perfect," he laughed.

Aunt Vieta was standing over my father's paralyzed body cursing him out, performing her own sort of therapy as the coyotes continued circling. It was an odd scene, but one that I welcomed.

"Can you take me to see my mom?" I asked.

Logan nodded.

"Has she had the antidote? Were we too late?"

He slid his arm around my waist and took me through the crowd of witches, many who I didn't know, but all who I would spend the rest of my life thanking, as he thought about what to say.

"She's been through a lot. They all have. It's going to be up to us to truly release their souls."

Nodding, I placed my hand on his, anxious to see my mom.

"Triss?" a girl who I didn't recognize came bounding up to us.

"Yes?" I asked, smiling. "What's your name?"

"Bennie," she replied, licking her lips.

I froze.

"Pardon me?" I questioned.

"I was wrong. *You* will be our future," she licked her lips again. "Your father might have been right. You don't hate like the rest of us. There will be a use for you in my plan."

She licked her lips again and twitched.

"Eben," I whispered. My mouth went completely dry.

"Who?" Logan asked, turning to me.

"That was my grandfather." I said, staring at the spot the girl once was.

"That was him?"

I nodded. "It's not over. In fact, I think it's only begun."

Coming soon:

RELEASED SOULS
(WITCH AVENUE SERIES #3)

ABOUT THE AUTHOR

Karice Bolton lives in the Pacific Northwest with her husband and two English Bulldogs. She loves the snow and gravitates towards the stuff as often as possible! She enjoys skiing and tries really hard to snowboard, but often makes a nice little area to sit while everyone zips by on their board. She enjoys writing, and she also loves to read just about anything with print.

16576051R00165

Made in the USA
Charleston, SC
29 December 2012